The Time Travels of Kate Levy

By

Roger Himmel

Introspect ☯ Publishing LLC
Raleigh, North Carolina

[1]The sentence, "Make room for the old man who is now entering!" can be found in volume 7, page 254, in an article about Rabbi Joseph ben Abba in The Jewish Encyclopedia printed in 1906.

[2]M.S. Morris and K.S. Thorne, "Wormholes in spacetime and their use for interstellar travel: A tool for teaching general relativity," Amer. J. Phys. 56, pp. 395-412 (1988)

[3]English translation of the French National Anthem is found in the Appendix.

ISBN: 979-8-9988174-0-3 - (Paperback)
ISBN: 979-8-9988174-1-0 - (E-Book)

Library of Congress Control Number: 2025909077

For personal appearances or interviews, please Email:
SpeakersBureau@RogerHimmel.com
Visit the website www.rogerhimmel.com to ask questions, get answers, and learn more.

WWW.IntrospectPublishing.com

Cover design and text formatting by Silicon Book Publishers, Oakbrook, Illinois.

Dedication

To my gracious and indomitable sister Carole, who, when I was
three, taught me the names of the colors, the letters of the alphabet,
how to print my name, and so much more.
Thank you dear sister.

And

I am especially grateful to my wife Liliane,
for her encouragement, critical editing, and numerous readings.
Where she is orderly and technical, I am the opposite.
Somehow we make it work.

Preface

Other than jumping out of a plane, turning points in our lives occur when we least expect them. They are just as impactful. For me, a paradigm shift in my belief system happened in 1977, when I attended a week-long Gateway Voyage at the Monroe Institute and met Robert Monroe. The experience changed my life by expanding my consciousness. Although I began having out-of-body experiences when I was four or five, the ones I had in a private room in Faber, Virginia, were life-altering. I returned to the institute two more times, and also attended weekend Gateway sessions in California. This novel is based on some of my experiences.

Although authoring a novel is a solitary occupation, no one finishes writing a novel alone. There are a number of friends who were early readers of this novel in its various forms. My dear late friend, Dale Franklin, encouraged me to pick it up and continue writing when I had given up. David Gardiner, my high school English teacher at Cheshire Academy, who has been a wonderful friend and mentor throughout my life, read an early draft and made valuable suggestions. Charles Rosenberg, a fabulous writer of six mystery novels, gave me excellent comments with my final drafts, many of which I implemented. And my focus group of Chris, Patty, and Arielle thank you for your ideas and support.

I also deeply appreciate another soul on her own journey through this physical reality in which we all exist, Karen Malik. I first met Karen over 45 years ago through the Monroe Institute, when she was Director of the Western Division. Her easy manner and thoughtful insights and suggestions helped many thousands of people like me, who are all searchers of the infinite. Lastly, thank you to the soul of Robert Monroe for developing Hemi-Sync® and establishing a special place, The Monroe Institute.

Roger Himmel, Raleigh, North Carolina

On Children

By Kahlil Gibran

(1883 Bsharri, Lebanon – 1931 New York City, NY)

And a woman who held a babe against her bosom said, Speak
to us of Children.
And he said:
Your children are not your children.
They are the sons and daughters of Life's longing for itself.
They come through you but not from you,
And though they are with you yet they belong not to you.

You may give them your love but not your thoughts,
For they have their own thoughts.
You may house their bodies but not their souls,
For their souls dwell in the house of tomorrow, which you
cannot visit, not even in your dreams.
You may strive to be like them, but seek not to make them like
you.
For life goes not backward nor tarries with yesterday.
You are the bows from which your children as living arrows are
sent forth.
The archer sees the mark upon the path of the infinite, and He
bends you with His might that His arrows may go swift and far.
Let your bending in the archer's hand be for gladness;
For even as He loves the arrow that flies, so He loves also the
bow that is stable.

From *The Prophet* (Knopf, 1923). This poem is in the public
domain.

Chapter 1
Greenwich Village, New York, October 2076

After a tough night's sleep, Kate Levy awoke way too early Saturday morning, dreading the day her father had planned for her. Like most teenagers, she groaned, turned over, pulled down hard on the soft knit hat she wore nightly, hoping it would force her unruly dark curls to straighten, and went back to sleep. She wasn't ready to face the embarrassment of buying a bra at Bloomingdale's with her dad hanging around.

At the exact moment his daughter turned over, Joe Levy was squinting with one eye at the vintage analog table clock he found at a Soho flea market. He saw that the green-glowing radium dial showed it was not even six. Joe was dreading the day ahead, taking his daughter shopping at Bloomingdale's. It was something his late wife Lauren would have loved to do, but it was not to be. He was now both mom and dad to their beautiful daughter, Kate. As much as he savored every minute he had with his daughter, being a substitute mom and grieving father was tough. Lauren's tragic death made him bitterly angry. He loved his wife so much that losing her left him feeling deflated. They were a team. If thoughts could kill, the drunk who caused the accident would be dead meat. Speeding in circles around Washington Square after taking his car off AI Drive, it hit the curb, flew over the sidewalk, and crashed into his wife. "*No,*" he thought to himself, "*I've got to stop thinking like this or I'll go to a very dark place. Bodies will start piling up all over Greenwich Village. I'm no killer. I'm an accountant. Better talk with my online shrink for some anger management therapy.*" Joe pulled the covers around himself for warmth, and to shield himself from sadness. He didn't have an easy time returning to sleep.

Pacing back and forth in their ultra-modern white, black, and chrome living room while waiting for his always late, '*Be right there*,' daughter, he thought about all the beautiful things Lauren had given him. First and foremost, their daughter Katie, who he loved more than life itself, even though she drove him crazy. Being married to Lauren and raising a child together, Joe realized that it is our relationships that make life worth living; and that time is the greatest gift of all. He had never thought of time as a gift. It wasn't until Katie was born that Joe finally understood how overpowering his love was. He owed so much to Lauren.

Turning on his vintage sound system, he yelled, "Come on, Katie. If you take any longer, the robotic mops will be cleaning the floors!" He cranked up the volume on his prized McIntosh amp, which powered his rebuilt Carver speakers, and sang along with Ray Charles.

"You are one weird father," Joe's daughter shouted as she entered their living room. "I mean, like, come on. You're into turntables with needle pick-ups, amps with vacuum tubes, and vinyl records in paper sleeves. Records? In an age when everything's been digitized online, and you can get thousands of perfect tunes, did I say PERFECT with not one scratch..."

"... It's my hobby, sweetie. Anyway, it reminds me of your mom," Joe mumbled as he turned off the sound system.

"I know, Dad, I miss her too," she said, running over to hug him.

"We loved singing together when we moved into this co-op a few years before you were born. We put our meager savings together to fix up this fixer-upper. Your mom had just gotten a huge commission check for a photo shoot and told me that I had to either poop or get off the pot and put a ring on her finger."

"Dad!"

"Well, that's what she said." He looked around the sunny, light-filled room at the large, framed images that Lauren had taken.

Displayed on the walls were her famous photographs from high
mountain tops that captured fluffy white clouds and soaring majestic
eagles; emerald-green leaves of an Amazon rain forest at twilight, the
setting sun just peeking through the canopy after a downpour; and,
of course, the not-so-famous private images of their daughter, Katie,
as an infant putting her tiny toes in her mouth. That one was Joe's
favorite. He sighed long and said, "So, are we ready yet?" He
already had on his dark brown corduroy coat with a tan plaid
Burberry scarf draped around his neck. He and Lauren always
loved Manhattan in the fall. He smiled, remembering the times they
took Katie to Washington Square Park in a stroller, all of them
bundled up in wool coats, plaid scarves, and woolen berets.

"Almost. Just gotta find the right hat." She looked at herself in
the mirror near the front door, rejecting first one hat and then
deciding on another. She fixed her hair, messing it up on purpose to
look retro-casual, and nodded with satisfaction at her reflection.
"OK. Ready."

The chilly October afternoon wind swirled multi-colored red
and yellow maple leaves around their shoes as they left home. They
quickly walked to catch what New Yorkers called "The Tube," a
maglev Vactrain that would drop them off at Bloomingdale's
Lexington Street station. It was early Saturday afternoon as they
passed Romano Brothers Market, their favorite grocery. The sun
reflected off the market's glass windows, helping to showcase the
large Honey Crisp apples and brown Bosc pears nestled in woven
wooden baskets near the entrance. A few minutes later, they
stopped at a street vendor's cart to buy a bag of hot roasted honey
nuts before descending the stairs to catch the tube below. The old
MTA subway station, patched for decades, but recently refurbished
to keep its old station look despite the modern Vactrain, still
smelled wet and cold. Going through security and payment
processing, they each placed their thumbs on a plastic security
scanner and looked briefly at a camera that digitized their faces.
Instantly, a software program compared their faces to their digitized
thumbprints. MTA debited Joe's bank account as they walked

through a scanning device that sensed bombs, chemicals, biologicals, and other weapons as they waited for their tube. The crunchy, warm roasted nuts tasted sweet and salty and helped make the security intrusion less offensive. Katie turned away from her dad and whispered into her iCuff to call a friend.

"Will you please stop talking into that thing? It's like another appendage of your body. You'll make me sorry that I bought it for you," Joe had to raise his voice over the incoming tube's swoosh and rumble.

"OK, OK, so talk. I can do more than one thing at a time. It's called *multi-tasking, Dad!*" Kate rolled her eyes, upset with her dad for interrupting her. But deep down it wasn't her dad she was angry with; what she was really hurting about was the pain and emptiness she felt from losing her mom less than two years ago. She and Lauren had been close. They even painted their fingernails and toenails together. When she wasn't traveling, they had long girl talks and loved to go thrifting. She bought the hat she wore today with her mom at a Salvation Army Family store. She adored her famous photojournalist mother, who did assignments for the Getty Photo Archive, National Geographic, and the Library of Congress. The accident that took her mom's life had shaken her to her core. It happened so fast. No warning: here one moment, gone the next. She was never able to say goodbye—no final hugs or kisses. No happy endings like in the movies. What shook her the most and brought tears to her eyes, was knowing that she would never again enjoy her mom's little pixie kisses; or smell the fragrance of her jasmine-scented perfume while Lauren held her close and whispered in Katie's ear, "I will love you always and forever, my sweet princess."

When a baby suddenly let out a loud wail, Kate and Joe quickly awoke from their private reveries. The infant directly across from them had lost its Binky. They watched as the baby's mother slipped the pink "It's My Binky" back into the infant's mouth. The woman smiled at her newborn wrapped snuggly in a pink baby blanket. Both were blissfully unaware of the other passengers around them. Next to the baby, an older man in tattered clothes coughed and wheezed. He had a dirty scarf wrapped around his neck for warmth, and mumbled to himself. They heard snippets of Spanish from two women sitting on the other side, arms intertwined, laughing. The Vactrain stopped numerous times as some passengers left while others boarded. The older man stood up and held onto an overhead bar. He began screaming at someone or something that wasn't there and angrily looked down at Kate, looking up at him. She quickly looked away, put her arm around and through her dad's, and pulled him closer. He squeezed her hand tightly. His look told her everything would be all right. She took a deep breath, remembering that when her mom was alive, they always rode in a self-driving Taxi from their apartment to Bloomingdale's.

As their tube arrived at the 5th Avenue and 59th Street station, Kate and her dad left and walked to the store. "So, what do you want to do first?" Joe said.

"Dad, I need a bra."

"What do you mean?"

"What do you mean, *what do I mean*? Jeez, sometimes you can be so dense. Dad, I'm a girl. I need a new bra. *Huh*?" Both arms flew up as if she couldn't believe what she was hearing. "*Hello*?"

"Oh, OK. OK."

He started to walk with her. "No, papa, I'll get the bra. Uh, why don't you go find a nice new tie or a pair of happy socks or something and meet me back here in fifteen minutes?"

"You have enough money? Here, I'll give you some money," he said, reaching into his pocket to give her some cash.

"No prob, I got a pay app on my iCuff." She showed him her wrist. The last thing Joe Levy wanted to do was make his daughter uncomfortable, so he kissed her on the forehead when she leaned toward him. Kate immediately left to buy a push-up padded bra that she knew would drive all the jocks at school nuts, especially Stanley Schneider.

It was while she was looking through a display rack of brightly colored bras that a sparkle near the base of another display rack grabbed her attention. From where she stood, it looked like a small gold necklace. She walked over and bent down to get a better view and couldn't believe what she saw. The necklace wasn't lying on the tile floor but hovering slightly above it. Spinning from the thin gold chain was a small, elongated hand. When she reached out to touch it, the tiny hand leaned toward her like a magnet to steel.

As she moved her hand towards the object, she heard the swooshing sound of wind. The wind became a low-pitched rumble. She tasted sand in her mouth and smelled dampness, like the musty smell from the girl's locker room at school. The low rumble gradually subsided and became a chorus of voices repeating the same sound, *"Echad, Echad, Echad."* It was then that she saw a man. He was the oldest person she had ever seen. He wore a turban and a white kaftan that reached down to the floor. He had long white hair and a white beard. His eyes were bright blue. But his skin looked like no other skin she had ever seen. Although the man was very old, his skin was as smooth as a baby's. And it glowed. His skin glowed like moonlight. He looked straight at her with his bright blue eyes. She silently thought, "What is he doing in Bloomingdale's Bra Department?"

A woman's slender hand broke the spell as she grabbed the gold necklace. Her fingernails were manicured in a bright blue or green. Kate couldn't tell because the colors seemed to change. She'd have to remember to ask her where she got the polish because it was killer.

"Ah, there it is. Thank goodness you found it. I was worried that I had lost it." The woman tightly gripped the necklace, her arm thrashed back and forth as if the necklace was fighting to escape. She extended her right hand to Kate and said, "Thank you so much. I'm Sara Lazarus, Fashion Jewelry Buyer." To Kate, Sara looked like she could be a fashion model or ballerina: tall and thin, with a light brown complexion, almond-shaped eyes, and long dark hair tied in a dancer's tight bun. She wore a simple black dress with high black boots.

"Uh, you're welcome. I'm Kate. I was just looking at some bras, and I saw something sparkly. It caught my eye, and, the strangest thing, I thought I saw an old man who glowed."

"Well, it sounds to me as if you've been having a daydream. Although I didn't buy these necklaces for Bloomingdale's this year, we may get them next. I hear they will be big in Paris at Galleries Lafayette. Thank you so much for finding it." Sara turned and quickly walked to the row of elevators. Kate followed right behind her.

"You know," Kate said, "I don't understand how necklaces can defy the laws of gravity. Newton's first law of gravity states that any object at rest will stay that way until another force acts on it. And something sure was acting on it." They both entered the elevator.

"I don't know what you mean." The elevator's doors closed behind them.

"You know darn well what I mean. That necklace was floating! I tasted sand, heard the wind, and saw a real old man."

Sara pushed the 9th-floor button and Kate heard a high-pitched sound louder than a screaming tornado. The elevator's lights blinked off and on. It felt like the elevator would go straight through the roof. The walls curved in and then popped back out. And that sound. That strange, screaming, windy sound was all around them. Then, as quickly as it started, it stopped. The lights came on strong, the automatic bell signaled, and the doors parted with a *swoosh*. Kate's ears popped just like they did when an airplane landed. Quickly, Sara stepped out and turned around, blocking Kate from leaving.

"I'm sorry, honey. This is an Employee Only floor," Sara said sadly. She reached around and pushed the button for the second floor. "Thanks again."

"But..." and the elevator's doors closed.

When the elevator's doors opened on the second floor, Kate rushed out looking for her dad. She almost knocked over an elderly couple with their grandchildren. Running through the bra department, the early Christmas tree display, and Godiva Chocolates, Kate dashed onto the escalator to the Men's floor. When she spotted her dad, he was seriously analyzing two pairs of socks: a black one with orange and purple polka dots and another with red, green, and purple stripes. "Hi honey, which do you like best?" he said holding them up.

Kate gave them a quick once-over. "They're both lame. Listen, Dad, you gotta come with me." She pulled him by the arm.

"Hey, wait a minute. You know how long I've agonized over this?"

"What's to agonize over? They suck. Old men in golf shirts and shorts wear them."

"But they're on sale."

Kate stopped and looked at him. "Dad. This is big. Something weird happened to me, and you gotta see it yourself." On the way, she told him what happened. She told him about the floating necklace, the old man with white hair, the screaming, swooshing noise, the woman, Sara Lazarus, and the elevator.

Joe didn't know what to say. "Maybe you ate something? Could it have been the honey-nuts? You know, maybe they gave you an upset stomach. Maybe you got a little light-headed."

"It wasn't the nuts, Dad."

"Well, it sure sounds pretty incredible."

Kate pulled him towards the elevator. When it arrived, some people got off, and they got on. "OK, Katie, calm down. I know you experienced something. Now, what floor did you say it was on?"

"Nine."

Her father looked for the ninth-floor button. "Honey, there is no ninth-floor button. There is no ninth floor."

"What? But I'm sure she pushed the ninth-floor button. It's the Employee Only floor." Kate pounded on the space where the ninth-floor button should have been. Nothing happened. The button was not there. "This is crazy. I saw it. How could it not be here?"

"Excuse me, dears," an elderly woman quietly said, "But uh, I'd like to get out now." She smiled nervously. "Y, yes, I don't know what floor this is, but any floor will do. Yes, yes indeed. Any floor at all." She quickly left the elevator, leaving them alone.

"I have an idea, honey. Why don't we try to find this employee? What did you say her name was?"

"Sara. Sara Lazarus," Kate said, not understanding what was going on.

"And she said she was in what department?"

"Fashion Jewelry. So, you believe me?"

"Don't worry. We'll get to the bottom of it. Let's just find this Sara Lazarus person." He placed his arm around her shoulder, and they took the elevator to the first floor.

It was a busy Saturday at Bloomingdale's. The first floor had cosmetics and jewelry. Some women were getting made-up at the counter displays, while others were trying out the latest new fragrances. Babies cried in their strollers. An old Taylor Swift tune played over the sound system as Kate and her dad walked to the jewelry displays as fast as the crowd would allow. When he got to the jewelry counter, Joe asked to speak to the manager. In a moment, a man dressed in a black suit approached them.

"Hi, I heard you folks wanted to speak with the manager. I'm Chris. How may I help you?"

"On the second floor today, I met the Fashion Jewelry buyer," Kate said.

"Oh, you mean Suzie."

"No. She said her name was Sara Lazarus."

"But we don't have a Sara Lazarus here."

"What?" Kate could not believe what she heard, and turned around smacking both legs.

"I've been working here six years and manage all the Jewelry, and I know for a fact that the Fashion Jewelry buyer is Suzie Yamamoto," Chris said.

"Are you sure?" Joe said.

"But I found a gold necklace on the floor and gave it to her, and she thanked me and said it would be a big seller in Paris at some Gallery or something, and I followed her into the elevator and went to the ninth floor..."

"...Oh, that's impossible. We don't have a ninth floor. And you said you found a gold necklace and gave it to her?"

"Yes."

"Well, I better tell store security. If you'll wait right here, I'll be right back." He quickly walked away.

Joe looked at his daughter. Her eyes were red and filling with tears. Her neck started to blotch a soft pink.

"But Dad. I know what I saw. I know what I heard. I am not lying."

"Honey, let's just relax for a minute. We'll go get something to eat and talk about it..."

"Wait a second. Hold it just a minute. Boy, am I STUPID!" She hit herself on the forehead with the palm of her hand. "I've got Archive App on my iCuff!"

"What's Archive App?"

"It's an App just for the C10s that automatically records the last 12 hours of your day in audio! It hooks up to the Bluetooth bug on my handbag. See?" She held her handbag up to show him a metal clip shaped like a giant snowflake.

"Well, I'll be...and that snowflake records everything?"

"Yeah, it's connected to a special audio circuit in all C10s. Everybody has 'em. Erases automatically every 12 hours. I always have it with me in case I miss something in class. Come on, dad. Let's go. I have an idea." She grabbed his hand and pulled him, running to the elevator.

They rode the elevator up and down until they were the only two people left in the compartment. With her iCuff held high and earbuds in her ears, Kate played back the audio recording just before she heard the high-pitched sound. Quickly, she put the recording on speaker mode. When she did, all hell broke loose. The elevator tilted. Its walls, ceiling, and floor expanded in and out. Joe held tightly onto the inside rail. Kate held onto her dad. Their legs lifted out from under them. This was a different experience than the one Kate had had the first time. Now, she was scared. She felt a vibration that made her feel sick to her stomach. Kate thought that if vibrations were angry, these were becoming big-time angry. She felt as if she were about to hurl. Both were stretched like bubble gum, tossed against the walls, floor, and ceiling, their bodies compressing and expanding and pushing them deeper into a swirling vortex of color that looked like it could go on forever. Just when they thought they were going to pass out, e v e r y t h i n g...b e g a n... to... s l o o o w... d o o o o w n. One moment, they were stretched as long as forever, unable to hear a thing, and the next second slammed back to normal. Their ears popped. The elevator's overhead lights burned out, except one that fizzed, shooting sparks downward. They were on the floor when the doors opened with a swoosh. Intense multi-colored light exploded into the compartment, momentarily blinding them with its brightness. They weren't in Bloomingdale's anymore.

Chapter 2
Timespan 3257 PC

"Let me guess," a voice from above them said. "Lost our way, perhaps? Took the wrong turn, did we? Missed our floor? Ah, I can see that's not it. Wait. Wait. Wait. I know. I know. Don't tell me. You wanted to boldly go where no one has gone before, right?"

Kate tried to see who was speaking but couldn't because the light was so bright. Squinting through almost closed eyes, she managed to squeak out, "It's, really, to boldly go where no man has gone before, but murph..." Joe quickly put his hands over her mouth before she could say another word. He shielded his eyes from the glare until his eyesight returned to normal.

Towering over them was a machine, a person, or a combination of both. It stood about seven feet tall with broad shoulders. Its surface was reflective like a mirror. The surface area, like sunglasses some people wear, could darken or become lighter. When it was lighter, it blended into everything around itself; when it was darker, it had a human silhouette. "Forgive me, but I digress. My programmer programmed me to digress. She finds it amusing. But where are my manners? I am, naturally, Jorge, Juan Pablo, Jose, Javier, Joaquin, Al-Kazar, but you can call me Jorge. The "J" is silent.

"Where are we?" Joe asked.

"Where indeed," Jorge intoned. "Perhaps a better way to phrase the question is: *When* are we? Or *when* are you, as the case may be, since I know where I am? Yes, when is certainly more appropriate, given the nature of the Higgs Continuum of space-time as postulated by Peter Higgs in the early twenty-first century. Now, won't you come with me? We need to fix that thing," he glanced around at the broken elevator, "and send it back *properly this time.*" He glared at Kate when he said properly, and she knew she had done something terrible.

Jorge helped them out of the elevator, and they stepped onto a hard, transparent floor of clear glass or plastic, strong enough to support the elevator and them. A continuous wall of the same material as the floor was curved around them. It seemed to Kate as if they were inside a giant clear bubble. Through the walls, she could see hundreds of other bubbles like the one they were in and many people entering and exiting bubble devices. One of those people was walking right towards them. Even though she wasn't dressed in Bloomingdale's black, and her hair wasn't tied in a tight bun, Kate recognized who it was.

"Dad," Kate said, as she pulled him down and whispered in his ear, "It's her. Sara Lazarus. She said she was the Fashion Jewelry Buyer at Bloomingdale's."

"Well, I have a strong feeling that she doesn't buy jewelry for Bloomies," Joe said as he watched the good-looking woman walk toward them.

Sara smiled at them. She wore a white skin-tight jumpsuit made of a seamless piece of material. Around her waist, she wore a bright blue belt with a small purse-like pouch attached to it. When she placed her hand palm down on the transparent bubble, it caused the dome's molecules to loosen their bonds and come apart. They floated harmlessly down before being silently whisked away through microscopic holes in the floor. Sounds that had once been muffled were now distinctly heard.

"Hi, Katie. I think it's best if I keep that iCuff of yours for a little while." She held out her outstretched hand, and Kate reluctantly gave her the iCuff. She put the device, earbuds, and snowflake in her hip pouch and said, "I promise to give them back, but not for at least twelve hours." Then she turned to Kate's dad and held out her hand. "Hello, Joe, welcome to Timespan. As your daughter told you, I'm Sara Lazarus, formerly of Bloomingdale's Lexington and 59th Street store. She smiled. He grinned back.

"Well, I uh, yes, hello to you, too," Joe managed to say with a grin a mile wide. "This is, well, um, unexpected, isn't it, Katie?"

Kate looked up at her father, smiled at his obvious flirtation, and said, "Yes, it sure is unexpected, Daddy."

Overhead, millions upon millions of stars shone brightly through the immense curved ceiling of the Timespan structure. Joe Levy thought the place had to be larger than twenty-five football fields. He saw thousands of people entering and exiting the same type of clear bubble container in which he and his daughter had arrived with their Bloomingdale's elevator. He said aloud to no one in particular, "It feels a lot like Grand Central Station here."

"Ah, yes, the infamous Grand Central Station, what a good metaphor," Jorge said. "The famous New York landmark with sixty-three tracks, forty-five platforms, forty-nine acres, and over seven hundred daily trains. Why..."

"...Yes, that's enough. Thank you, Jorge." Sara cut him off quickly since he could go on forever. We'll have the history lesson at another time. But it is an apt comparison. Timespan is a station of sorts. It's a deep-space time station. Six platforms of this size make up Timespan. It's in deep space because of the artificial gravitational power requirements needed to stabilize and expand the Higgs Boson field.

"And what does that gold necklace with the spinning thing-a-ma-jig that violated the natural laws of gravity have to do with all this?" Kate asked matter-of-factly.

Sara looked down and gave her a half-smile. "Well, young lady, that is the question of the millennium. If we find out the answer, we may find out where we come from, who we are, and what the universe is all about."

"But you haven't told me what it is."

"Whatever it is, it generates an algorithmic tonic chord that does the same thing that Timespan does with its immense power capacity. It bends space-time."

"You mean that pretty little thing that was," she lowered her voice to a whisper, "floating on the floor in Bloomingdale's bra department, is a time machine?"

"Yes, you could say that. We've dated the gold to about the 5th Century BCE on Earth. It has some Aramaic letters inscribed, an unusual floral design, and a vortex. I'm calling it my little Amulet."

"Your Amulet? May I see it again?"

"Not right now, Katie, but I can assure you, it's in a real safe place. Isn't that right, Jorge?"

"Yes, madam. Safe is a useful word. A small word, most assuredly, but a proper word. Simple. Only four letters. Safe, one could say, is being free from danger or risk, or perhaps even being in an enclosed and locked container that affords protection for a person or thing, or, as in that archaic game of baseball that was popular for a few centuries, a player would be safe if he or she reached an area called a bag or a plate, although I don't really see what a plate or a bag filled with dirt has to do with safety unless of course, one would smother a fire with it..."

"...Well, allow me to explain the baseball game to you, Jorge," Joe said as they all walked to the exit. He casually reached up and placed his hand on the android's shoulder. "The game originated in England back in 1744."

"No *way*, Dad," Kate said. "It's an American game."

"*Way*, Katie. The Brits did it first."

Suddenly, Jorge glowed yellow. "Madam, there is a space-time distortion one light year from Timespan."

Lights flashed and dimmed inside the dome. Everyone heard a loud "Whoop, whoop, whoop, whoop," which repeated throughout the large, covered area. Every transparent chamber began to collapse. When they looked up through the vast overhead transparent dome that separated the climate-protected interior from the frozen airless vacuum of space, they saw an astonishing sight: a gigantic gravitational wave was bending space-time. It created an ever-widening field of time distortion. Expanding in size every second, it twisted and turned in on itself. It could send them careening into other dimensions.

Katie said, "What's happening? What's going on? What is that thing?"

Yelling over the shouting, pushing, and confusion, Sara said, "It's a time distortion created when you two bent space-time without any controls. It's an out-of-control time wave. We've got to make a Time Jump, or all of us could be destroyed if Timespan's Tachyon Shield can't reverse it." Turning to Jorge, she screamed, "Jorge, open and cover the three of us. Give me the Amulet." Quickly, she thrusts her entire arm into the middle of the android. Its outer reflective membrane parted with a sucking sound, much like pushing a fist through a bowl of glowing orange Jell-O. As she did this, Jorge's form changed, first flattening like a pancake, then encircling them all in a person-sized silvery-orange ball.

Inside the giant ball, it was silent. They were tightly crammed together. Sara held the golden spinning Amulet, or whatever it was, in her hand, allowing it to dangle from her fingers and twirl wildly. "Now, hold on tight to each other," Sara ordered. Jorge's arms appeared to grow out of the interior's underside and held all of them protectively.

"I'm scared, Daddy."

"I know, honey, I am too."

"OK," Sara said quickly, breathing out. "I'm going to try to return you two to your own time in space-time." She closed her eyes tightly. When she opened them, she stared intently at the tiny spinning Amulet. It became all she saw and all she felt. She became one with it as it rotated faster and faster. Kate and her dad heard Sara repeatedly whisper words over and over again. They sounded like the exact words Kate had heard when she first saw the spinning Amulet.

Sara whispered, "*Echad, Echad, Echad.*" The words grew in intensity and echoed through the sphere's interior. "*Echad, Echad. Echad.*"

They were inside Timespan one moment and then gone the next. It felt like they were free-falling down an out-of-control elevator that went on forever. It pushed them to the right, then to the left, then up and down. They held each other tight, eyes squeezed shut. And they all screamed loud and long.

One second.

Two seconds.

Three-seconds.

Four...

Chapter 3
Port City of Pumbedita, The Abbasid Caliphate

In the year 758 CE, a prosperous city called Pumbedita existed on the shore of the Euphrates River. Traders and merchants from throughout the known world gathered there to buy and sell abundant dates, soft figs, fragrant olive oil, and hearty grains farmed in and around this large agricultural area. It was because of its prime location between the Tigris and Euphrates Rivers in the heart of the Fertile Crescent that stretched from Turkey to Egypt and down into the Persian Gulf that the population grew. Their tall sails billowing in the wind, riverboats would off-load ceramics from one region and take on nuts and dates from Pumbedita. Men and women throughout the Fertile Crescent descended on the ancient city for work. So did thieves and beggars.

It was in this busy milieu that Joseph ben Abba was born. The youngest child of a hardworking merchant family, his father, Solomon, owned a small store in the market area where he sold and traded milk, flour, and olive oil. The family, devout Hebrews, kept the strict dietary laws and the Sabbath and prayed three times a day like many of their neighbors. But Joseph ben Abba was different from the day he was born. He was more subdued than his siblings. Although he made his needs known, he didn't mind playing by himself. Instead of crying, he quietly observed. He learned to talk when he was nine months old, even if it was just a simple yes or no. From that early age, his language ability grew exponentially. It was during his childhood, before he reached age three, that he accidentally discovered a part of existence he assumed everyone else also experienced.

The afternoon was warm as a gentle breeze floated through the small clay brick house. His mother had just put Joseph down for a nap. The child tossed and turned, fidgeting, finding it difficult to sleep. He kept moving his legs. Then, quite suddenly, he found himself floating as if it were the most natural thing in the world. He floated horizontally in the center of his room. He pushed at the air around him with his arms and legs as if in water. He drifted to his bedroom wall. Even though it was made of clay bricks, it offered no resistance. It didn't break or chip. Joseph simply and without a sound passed through. He glided through the chalky painted clay surface. First, the top of his head inched into the wall, followed by his eyebrows and eyes. He saw the mud brick's internal consistency: its granularity, thousands of tiny air pockets, the contours of the very stuff of which it was made. He saw compressed bits and pieces of straw. He noticed tiny shells and stones as he moved through the dry clay. He wasn't scared. It felt natural and safe, like drinking warm milk. Soon, his entire head was outside the wall of his room. He saw the late afternoon sunlight and the shoppers and vendors in the narrow and bustling street rush past him. A dog saw him and barked. Its hair and tail stood straight up as it ran away. Then, in an instant, a flash, a heartbeat, a blink of an eye, something pulled him back into his bedroom. He hovered over his tiny body for a split second and slept the sleep of innocence.

When Joseph was about five, his family moved into a larger mud brick home. His father's business grew as the population of Pumbedita expanded through increased trade. He didn't question his ability to float about unaided, thinking everyone could do it just like he did. Nor did he entirely understand that his sleeping self on the bed and his aware self that was floating above were different aspects of himself. He was not yet an analytical thinker but still a magical thinker. He was himself, Joseph. On one evening, he became bolder. He decided to explore further than he had ever gone before. He pushed up and away, slowly penetrating through the ceiling and up to the roof. It was twilight. A half-moon was already in the sky, with a few stars just beginning to show. As the sun slowly set, casting streaming colors of orange, pink, and purple into a final momentary flare of yellow against the evening sky, Joseph was surprised to see his older sister, Rachel, on the roof kissing her boyfriend, who was a student at the Jewish Academy. Joseph told himself he would have to remember to tease her later. But Joseph was too busy to stop and stare at his sister's kissing, which, on the one hand, disgusted him and, on the other, made him laugh. He was going to see his friend Aaron.

Joseph floated off the roof, making sure to avoid the kissing couple. They didn't notice. He turned and soared over the rooftops to Aaron's house. He entered through an outside wall and floated through the kitchen. His friend's room was on the other side. Aaron was asleep. Joseph tried to wake him, but when he tried to shake his friend's shoulder, his hand simply passed through Aaron's sleeping body. Joseph tried and tried, but Aaron would not wake up. It left Joseph no choice but to explore by himself. What happened next surprised even Joseph. What he wanted more than anything was to see the Earth like the birds experience it from high above the mountains. He moved slowly up from Aaron's bedroom. Effortlessly, he glided through the roof and, gaining speed, up into the night sky. He flew over the city, the river, the mountains and soared even higher. It became dark all around him. Joseph discovered that all he had to do was to think about where he wanted to go, and he found himself going there. He broke through clouds. The higher in the night sky he flew, the smaller the Earth became. Then he thought to himself that he wanted to stop. And he stopped. He looked at the slowly rotating Earth and was awestruck. He had never seen anything more beautiful. He appreciated in a new way the deep blue of the oceans, the green land masses, the white icecaps at the top and the bottom. The Earth was hanging in space, slowly spinning, surrounded by infinite stars floating against a black nothingness that went on forever. Then, he turned and gazed upon the fiercely bright sun. It didn't hurt his eyes the way it did when he tried to look at it from the ground. He thought how amazing it was that his Almighty Lord made all of this. He felt so small in the enormousness of space. Seconds later, feeling a sharp pain in his back, he was pulled down to the Earth, down through the clouds, down through the roof into his bedroom, into his sleeping self, and he dreamed. The house cat jumped off his back and licked its paw.

Joseph couldn't wait to tease his sister Rachel at breakfast the following morning. They were both sitting at a small wooden table in the kitchen. Joseph had a devilish smile on his face. He quietly whispered to his older sister, "So, Rachel, I saw you yesterday kissing Simon. How could you do that? Yuck."

"What do you mean, little brother?" She looked around to make sure her mother wasn't nearby. "I wasn't kissing anyone."

"Saw you on the roof."

"What? How could... that's impossible."

"Impossible? I'm surprised you could even breathe the way you were kissing!"

If looks could kill, then Joseph was a goner. Rachel pushed back her chair, grabbed a drying rag, and twisted it tightly around from tip to tip. "Am I going to get you, little brother!" Joseph laughed and ran around the table, dodging the swipes his older sister aimed at him. He ran right into his mother.

"What's going on here, you two? What did Joseph do now?"

"Nothing, Mother," Rachel said. "It was from before."

Joseph made kissing sounds with his mouth, ducked under his mother's arms, and ran out of the room, laughing.

"Oh, that's it, you little tease." Rachel ran after him. "You better ask Hashem to protect you!" But as she laughed and smiled, she wondered how it was possible. How did Joseph see them? Where was he? He wasn't on the roof. She was sure of that. She didn't think they made any noise. Her mind was full of questions she couldn't answer as she walked back into the kitchen to help her mother prepare the afternoon meal.

The next evening would change Joseph's life forever. He had the same routine ever since he could remember: His mother would tuck him in and put him to bed. Sometimes, his father joined them. His dad had taught him to say the most important blessing in all the Hebrew faith, the Shema. The prayer expresses the enduring belief of the Lord's oneness. Joseph said the prayer every night before he went to bed. This night was no different.

"Sh'ma Yisra'el Adonai Eloheinu Adonai Ehad," Joseph and his mother said together. Then she kissed him on the cheek and asked him not to tease his sisters. When she didn't get a response, she pinched and pulled his cheek hard, laughed a little laugh, shook her head, and left the room.

He made sure that he was under the covers so the cat wouldn't bother him by kneading her paws into his back. He stretched out and got comfortable. Relaxing, he thought of his body lifting, rising through covers that offered no resistance to hover above the bed. In an instant, he was. Then he turned around and saw the room below. He saw himself sleeping in bed and, for the first time, recognized that the sleeping Joseph on the bed, and the conscious translucent-like reflection of himself hovering above, were one and the same. He didn't understand how or why, but deep inside, he instinctively knew that one could not exist without the other.

As he traveled above rooftops and cultivated fields that evening, raindrops fell through him as through a shadow. Higher and higher, he floated above the dark, moisture-filled clouds and aimed for the moon. It took a few seconds until he was there to view it up close for the first time. There were no people, only deep holes from craters and tall hills on a rocky planet devoid of life. So, feeling a little bored, he decided to return to Earth but first fly through it. As he approached it, he traveled faster. The atmosphere gave him no resistance. He plowed through the Earth's crust, mantle, and large outer core and stopped in the unbelievably white-hot molten inner core, the deep central interior of his planet. He was amazed at the dense, bubbling, molten metal. He sped back up to the surface. He traveled through the oceans. He was a child in the playground of life. He swam with fish, went inside a whale, and saw the ocean's corals, sponges, and marine species that humankind wouldn't discover for centuries.

But he wanted more. He traveled out of the solar system and saw the Milky Way galaxy. He looked around and saw more stars

like the sun and more planets than anyone had ever seen. He saw
the immensity of it all. Galaxies upon galaxies: millions of galaxies.
"But is this all there is?" he asked himself. There was no one for
him to play with. Was he the only one who could travel like this?

"Where would you like to go?" A voice he heard in his head
asked.

"Huh?"

"You're not satisfied? You need more?"

"Where are you?"

"Simply desire to be where I am, and you will be there."

Just thinking that he wished to be where the voice was took
him there. Joseph seemed to travel faster than ever, yet he didn't
move. It was more than simply changing location. Things were
different. The Earth was now indistinct. It wasn't the blue and green
planet that he knew. It was more like a shadow of itself, a reflection.
He looked around and saw from a distance a large grey mass of
something that encircled the Earth. From his perspective, it looked
like a jumble of swimming snakes.

"I wouldn't go there if I were you," said the voice.

For the first time, Joseph felt scared.

*"Now, try not to feel scared, or you'll be pulled back into your
body. I'll protect you."*

Joseph relaxed a little, and his fear drained away. *"OK. But
who are you, and where are you?"*

"Why, I'm right behind you."

When Joseph turned around, he saw a stern-looking older
man. The man wore a hairy dark brown animal skin coat, burgundy-
colored turban, and white tunic. He held a long wooden staff in his
left hand that was slightly taller than he was himself. The man had a
long grey beard and grey hair. He was barefoot. Joseph looked at
the elderly man's feet and said, *"You aren't wearing sandals."*

"Neither are you."

"But I'm sleeping."

"And where I'm from, Joseph, I don't need them."

"If you know my name, it's only right that I should know yours."

"Ah, now that sounds like the Talmudist I know and love. I'm Eliyahu, young man."

"I don't know you. I've never met you. How can you know and love me?"

"It's a matter of speech. I will."

"How do you know?"

"It's in the future."

"You can see the future?"

"Of course. You can, too."

"I can?"

"You could, but I'm not going to let you."

"Why would you do that?"

"Because you're too young. You'll get into trouble. You discovered this ability of yours by accident. You'll get it back when you're older. Anyway, it's not nice to spy on your sister."

"You know about that, too?"

"I know a lot. Now, take hold of my hand, and I'll show you that dark grey thing." Joseph held Eliyahu's outstretched hand, and they moved closer to the dark grey mass encircling the Earth. As they got closer, Joseph felt not so much scared but jumpy and nervous.

"What is that?"

"That, Joseph, is a concentration of mankind's evil aspect. The soul catcher."

"Give me a break. I'm five. What does that mean?"

Eliyahu lifted Joseph up and held him close. *"That, dear boy, is a trap. It is everything evil. You see, in our physical life on Earth, we have choices. After a while, the choices we've made in our lives make us feel safe and comfortable. For some people, it becomes easier to hurt others than to love; it is easier to think of self-gratification than to think of and consider other people's feelings. I believe it comes from where humans have evolved, our ancient animal past: the hunter or the hunted. So, when our mortal bodies die, and our souls are released to join the eternal and perhaps return to another life, some of those souls get attracted to the evil, selfishness, or lust that they experienced in their most recent incarnation. It's familiar to them. They enjoyed it. And their souls get trapped there in that withering grey mass forever.*

"Don't they try to get away?"

"Yes, they do try, but they can't. They scream for release. But new souls join them, drowning them out, pushing them down, every hour of every day."

Joseph was silent. He leaned his head against the older man's shoulder and deeply breathed. *"I'm feeling so tired. Like my energy is gone."*

"What would you like to do?"

"I want to go home."

"I'll take you." The change was immediate: where once the Earth was monochromatic, like a shadow of itself, it was now alive with blue and green. Eliyahu quickly glided Joseph into Joseph's room, where the boy's physical body slept. They hovered above.

"Will I see you again?"

"You will, but not until you're much older."

"Will I remember everything?"

"Yes, Joseph, you'll remember everything, but you won't be able to travel like you have just done for a long time."

Joseph looked sad. *"But I'm gonna try."*

"I'm sure you will. I'm counting on it. That's why I want to give you something, so as you get older, you'll remember that what you thought was just a dream was, in fact, real." Eliyahu reached under his tunic, removed an Amulet from around his neck, and put it around the neck of Joseph's non-physical body. The golden Amulet also appeared around the sleeping child's neck as he did.

"What is it?"

"It's called The Hand of El Shaddai. It is more than ancient. It will protect you and keep you safe."

"What do those letters and lines mean on the hand's palm?"

"The symbols are from ancient Aramaic. The letters sound like the one you say every night in your prayers, 'Echad.' It means we are One with our creator and everything in our world. We are not separate from but a part of everything. The lines represent our physical existence in time. But there also are hidden secret words. I will tell you about them now, but you must only reveal them to one other person. You must wait a very long time to reveal them. Will you make that promise to me, Joseph? Do I have your most sacred word?"

With eyes larger than an Assyrian warrior's shield, he stammered, *"Y-yes, I p-promise."*

When Eliyahu bent over and whispered the secrets to Joseph, the child's eyes widened in disbelief. *"Who can I tell it to, Eliyahu, who?"*

"Her name will be Kate."

"Kate? There's no such name as Kate. What's a Kate?"

"It's the name of a girl. And you will meet her. I promise you that. But you won't meet her for a long time.

"Then I promise that I will only tell the secrets to this Kate girl," Joseph said as he tightly gripped the Hand of El Shaddai.

The older man kissed the young boy on one cheek and then the other. *"Thank you, Joseph. Our future depends on you."* As Joseph watched Eliyahu fade away, he quickly rejoined his sleeping body.

Chapter 4
Los Angeles 2076

Their escape from Timespan abruptly ended when Jorge let go of them. They all tumbled to the ground while he quickly vanished into the background. The sound of sirens blaring, people running and screaming, and a police car crashing into another black and white cruiser and then into a third overwhelmed them. They heard the sounds of automatic gunfire everywhere. They didn't know which way to escape. A large silver disc, half of it buried on its side, rose straight up in front of them. It stood sixty feet tall. Blue smoke rose from the damaged craft while laser fire blasted out from it. Large US Army spotlights lit the whole area. Dogs barked. People screamed and ran for cover.

Sara shouted, "Jorge, where are we?"

"Los Angeles, Madam. Same timeline. Nine PM. Echo Park area. Sunset Boulevard, to be exact."

"Well, this sure isn't Manhattan!" Kate said, ducking out of the way behind a blue US Postal Service mailbox. Seconds later, blasts from three green laser lights missed her by inches.

"Say, Katie," Joe said, peeking around the side when the gunfire stopped and the smoke cleared, "Isn't that, you know, what's his name?"

Kate looked, too. "What the...?"

"*Cut. AD's set up for the next scene. Thanks, people,*" said a voice from a loudspeaker. Someone switched the spotlights off, and the film crew started to move around.

A stagehand quickly picked up the fake mailbox they were hiding behind and said, "Hey, you guys were great. Why don't you grab something to eat over at the catering truck?" Kate didn't have to be asked twice.

"I just don't understand how we came to be here," Sara said, clearly exasperated. "It's as if something pulled us off course." They were slowly walking down Sunset Boulevard near Logan. Even Jorge made himself visible by blending in with actors in robot costumes.

"Hey, sweet costume, dude," said a tattooed kid with orange spiked hair who rolled along with them on a skateboard. He patted Jorge on his back.

"Sweet? It is neither sweet nor sour," commented Jorge. "The durable cryogenic multi-phasic polymer grown to manufacture...oh, my mistake. Sweet: A twenty-first-century term meaning attractive, great, or outstanding. Thank you, earthling. My error of a colloquial expression. Never mind." Jorge tried his best to smile.

"Wow, like staying in the moment, or what, huh, dude? Real. Too real. And you're not bad either, space lady." As the skateboarder passed them, they laughed.

"Yeah, space lady," Joe said, "Not bad either."

"Daddy!"

It happened while they approached a used book and collectibles store called Second Sight. Sara's small golden necklace pulled her so hard that she knocked into Joe, almost throwing him off balance. It took all her strength to lower her arm forcibly. Some unseen force pulled her closer and closer to the store's entrance.

"Well, whatever it is that got us off course," Sara said, "I think I know where it is." She looked at Joe and nodded. He carefully turned the old, dented and discolored brass knob on the peeling and faded purple wooden door. Upon opening, it triggered an electric circuit. Instead of the standard buzzer, a small overhead speaker somberly announced, "*Klaatu Barada Nikto,*" as the four walked into the small, dusty, overcrowded store.

Inside, the eerily quiet shop was a hoarder's dream. Upon entering, they ran their fingers over turn-of-the-century dark walnut glass-topped display tables, scratched and scuffed from years of use.

Lining the interior were bookcases with locked leaded glass doors that protected one-of-a-kind volumes on spiritualism, mysticism, Rosicrucianism, Freemasonry, and the Knights Templar. Stacks of old art prints leaned one against the other in wooden crates along the floor. Displayed within the glass-topped tables were small items like rock crystals, ancient trilobites, petrified wood, and antique silver rings. Other shelves and tables contained green and yellow scented candles, soaps, incense, and multi-colored tea tins. The old wooden floorboards squeaked with each footfall. Even though the floor was once covered in fancy, now threadbare red, white, and black oriental rugs, the absolute silence, squeaking, and dank odour unnerved them. The spicy, overpowering scent of heavy patchouli wafting up from a smoking incense burner permeated the store with an unnatural mustiness that failed to mask the smell of rotting decay and death.

"You can't begin to imagine how long I've been waiting for you," whispered a quiet but firm voice from the store's far dark corner. They heard a long, low moan, the kind of sound one might hear from a dying whale. A form slowly appeared from the shadows. For an instant, it was that of an older person or a young woman. It flickered back and forth: male, female, tall, short, as if trying to settle upon what it would be with these beings in this space-time physical reality. It finally chose the form of a round-faced, large black woman with huge breasts who wore a red and white checked apron and tied her hair with a blue scarf. "Bet you weren't expecting me!" she shouted. "Aw, go ahead," she sneered, "You can call me Sugar!"

"Who are you, and what do you want?" Sara demanded.

"I am everything you fear in the darkest corner of your soul: If you fear weakness, I am weakness incarnate; the monster under the bed of your youth; the face leering at you through the window of your teens: all the hate and fear and rage that has ripened in this space-time continuum; this grand experiment of physical reality eating and clawing its way through eons of oozing primordial sludge until now. I am, above all, the creation of thee: Your weakness, your anger, your hate, your fear, your jealousy, and your lust; all the degradation and self-loathing your kind has expressed or thought or felt through the eons, I AM IT. Now, ya gotta admit," it leaned in closer, "don't I look purr-dee?"

Its face and arms began to blister and boil while it morphed into a gelatinous human form. Dark shapes of naked miniature human figures tumbled and thrashed within it, swirling in and around one another like thousands of tightly packed eels starved for oxygen. They screamed in silence with mouths agape, desperately trying to escape their confinement. It extended a gelatinous hand to Sara, palm open, and said in a voice that created a low-pitched sound whose frequency made everyone's guts vibrate, "No more games, old one! I tried to capture the Amulet many times. The last time, this young one grasped at it first. I can't obliterate like I used to. The world would have noticed a large hole at 59th and Lexington."

As hard as she tried to control her arm and keep it down, Sara was no match for the Amulet's enormous power. Now, she knew why. To her horror, as her arm rose and her Amulet strained against its thin gold chain, Sara and the others saw a second Amulet held by the thing's gelatinous snake-like outstretched arm. It was similar in shape to the one Sara had. The Amulets' attraction to each other was earth-shattering. As the Amulets hurled together, they created a light so intensely bright white that no one could look directly at it. The sound was thunderous.

When the light reduced to a soft glow in place of the two small Amulets, a much larger silver and gold one materialized. It was a slender hand about two inches long. The fingers were elongated and feminine. Within the hand's center was embossed a highly stylized spiral. On each of the five fingers were a series of round indented impressions separated from each other by the hand's fourteen digital phalanx. The indentations looked like hundreds of glowing dots. Then, the Amulets' silver fingers curled into a fist. The closed fist morphed into a perfect sphere, obliterating the light from within. What remained was a silver orb whose surface swirled in symmetrical patterns that constantly changed shape from fierce lions and stylized flowers to the internal sectional chambers of seashells and DNA. The creature's massive motion-filled hand expanded, billowing and growing like thunderstorm clouds. It clamped itself around the silver sphere.

"Unfortunately, Sunset and Logan aren't as important," it said sarcastically.

"Jorge! Cover and protect," Sara shouted.

In a fraction of a second, Jorge covered Sara, Joe, and Kate, protecting them from the immense implosion that decimated what was once the quaint Second Sight bookstore. All the bookcases, books, tables, carpets, ceiling, floor, walls, tea, candles, rings, and decades of dust disappeared in a whirlwind of unfathomable swirling destruction. What was once solid lost its atomic cohesion. Electrons lost polarity as sub-atomic bonds broke. Space-time distorted into a screaming vortex of inter-dimensional destruction. Amazingly, the two businesses on each side of the former bookstore, Sushi Rock & Maki and Echo Park Lavanderia, were left unscathed. Jorge remained amid the debris in the shape of a dust-covered silver sphere.

Within the Jorge-ball, it was cramped. Kate hugged the inside wall while Sara and Joe were squashed against each other, which didn't bother Joe one bit. Looking at Sara, Joe said, "You don't look old."

Sara smiled slightly, "I'm not old."

"It said you were old."

"It said I was an 'old one'."

"Hey, in my book, old is old."

"Will you two cut it out? We gotta get outta here," Kate shouted.

Jorge's face coalesced out of the walls inside the curvature. "Kate is right, madam. I've picked up police and fire department sirens. What shall we do? Should I de-cloak?"

"Perhaps you should, Jorge." Sara sounded defeated. "We don't have the Amulet anymore. We can't travel anywhere."

"Hello? How do you think we got into this situation?" Kate said. She waited a few seconds and shouted, "My iCuff, *hello*?"

"Right. Your iCuff. Where is it?" Joe said...

"It's in my side-pack, Joe. Do you think you can reach it?"

"I'll try...my...best," Joe said as he slowly inched his left hand around Sara's waist. He found the side-pack and managed to pry apart the Velcro closure. He reached into the pack and found the device. "Got it. Now, if I can just turn it on."

"Hurry, Daddy."

"I think the battery's dead. It needs to be charged. Jorge, can you charge it?" Before Jorge could answer yes, the entire sphere rolled upside down. Kate screamed. Joe slammed into Sara. They heard voices shouting all around them from the exterior. Outside, a large crowd had gathered and pushed the sphere. Police and fire engines converged on the area.

Jorge created an iCuff charger inside the sphere from his adaptive molecules. The cord looked like a twisting, sidewinding snake about to attack its prey. Joe held the iCuff as still as he could. It was complicated for Jorge to insert it into the iCuff's secondary charging port with the sphere rolling. After several tries, Jorge was finally able to power up the device. His advanced neural systems integrated with the iCuff's audio file that Kate had initially recorded in Bloomingdale's elevator.

"I have accessed the audio file, Madam," Jorge intoned.

"Balance, adjust, and amplify the dynamic harmonics so a distortion wave is not created."

"Where do you want to go, Madam?"

"Take us to Namaste, Jorge."

"Is that in India?" Kate said.

"No, Katie. It's in Ohio."

A question was forming in Joe's mind concerning Ohio when they were flattened against the Jorge-orb's inside wall. Their cellular structure expanded and contracted, speeding through a sonically created wormhole. The protective layer that was Jorge bounced from side to side through the twisting corridor of space-time. They plunged multiple times, like bungee jumpers, off a bridge and back up again before coming to rest. When Jorge returned to his standard shape, they heard a popping sound and tumbled, exhausted, onto sweet-smelling, tall green hay.

When Kate opened her eyes, she was on her back, staring into a moonlit star-filled night. She heard wave upon wave of crickets chirping their songs of love. Slowly, she sat up. The only light was the full moon and, of course, the hundreds, if not thousands, of tiny fireflies hovering in the night sky. Their glowing lower abdomens pulsed bright yellow, silently speaking, "*Come to me. I'm here. Come to me.*" The gentle night breeze felt like tiny, soft kisses against her cheek.

"Welcome to Namaste," Sara said with a smile.

Chapter 5
Pumbedita 758 CE

"What do you mean Eliyahu gave it to you?" Joseph's father said. "He is one of our greatest prophets. He died long ago. Impossible!"

"Ah, so that's why he wasn't wearing sandals," Joseph said.

"Don't be smart with me, young man. Now, tell me the truth."

"I am telling you the truth, Abba. Eliyahu put it around my neck and said it would protect me from harm."

"Perhaps it's true, Solomon," Joseph's mother said. "Maybe it's a sign."

"Give it to me," Solomon said. He flattened his palm in front of Joseph, demanding the Amulet.

"No."

"Then I'll take it." But when he tried to touch it, the Amulet's hidden power knocked him off his feet and sent him flying across the room.

The entire family was silent. Joseph's mother and sisters ran over to Solomon and helped him stand up, ensuring he was not hurt. They all turned and looked at Joseph. They had seen what had happened and were frightened. Joseph was scared, too. He ran over to his father, put his arms around him, and cried. Between tears, he stammered, "I'm s-sorry, Abba. I would n-never hurt you." He buried his head against his father's heaving chest.

Solomon took a deep breath. "I think, my son, we need some advice. We need to see the head Rabbi." Solomon patted his son's back to show him everything would be fine. He hugged and kissed his weeping child.

Although Pumbedita was a small city, there were thirty-three Rabbis. Each Rabbi taught and preached to his small group of followers. The Gaon, or Chief Rabbi of the internationally respected Jewish Academy of Pumbedita, led these rabbis. Over the vast expanse of time, the Academy at Pumbedita orally passed down and eventually made permanent in a combination of early Hebrew and Aramaic writing, what has come to be known as the Babylonian Talmud. The Talmud is a collection of Judaism's Oral Torah, or Old Testament, as well as ethics, history, philosophy, customs, and other questions the Hebrew people would ask their religious leaders to answer. Even more incredible was that hundreds of answers and arguments were saved and passed down from one generation to the next since the destruction of the Temple in Jerusalem. These questions and answers are the essence of the Babylonian Talmud: voices that speak down the corridors of time. In its existence, the Jewish Academy of Pumbedita produced the best Jewish scholars in the Jewish world. Solomon took his son, Joseph ben Abba, to this special place and this head Rabbi, the Gaon of the Jewish Academy.

The narrow streets were dusty and crowded with people and carts that hauled produce. Some of the carts were large enough that donkeys pulled them. Shopkeepers lined the side of the road. Some owned stores as Joseph's father owned; other merchants sold from their pushcarts that offered ripe red tomatoes, yellow lemons, and rich-colored woven baskets. Beggars also lined the streets asking for coins or food. Walking quickly with his father holding his hand, Joseph couldn't help but taste gritty sand in his mouth whenever his sandals kicked up dust. Each time he inhaled, he coughed. Soon, however, the noise and crowds decreased when they reached the imposing Jewish Academy, built on the bank of the Euphrates River.

The school was one of the few in the community. Pillars held up the roof on the second floor while open arches flanked the pillars. Stone steps, worn down in the center by centuries of use, led up the building's side to the second floor's main entrance. Green vines with purple flowers grew along the wall, forming a natural arch over the steps, helping to shelter guests from direct sunlight.

Although it was unusual to have an entrance on the second floor, the Jewish people living at the time found it easily defendable should the need arise. They long remembered being conquered, banished, enslaved, or killed.

Joseph had never been inside such a place. When his father knocked on the old wooden door, he didn't know what to expect. It was afternoon, and he knew prayers and the midday meal would soon end. The door was answered by an older boy whose beard had just started to grow out. He wore a kaftan tied with a sash and leather sandals, much like the other men in Pumbedita. His father spoke quietly to the boy, and they were invited inside and shown to a low bench carved from marble on which they sat. The area inside was dark, lit by only one oil lamp. All around them, it was quiet. Where the street was busy, this place seemed deserted. Joseph was able to see tables with stacks of papyrus covering them. There were drawings on the walls of older men with long beards. Some looked mean, others kind and welcoming. Joseph and his dad turned their heads when they heard footsteps approaching them. One was the older boy who had shown them inside. He walked quickly by the side of an older man who was hooded and wore a long black kaftan tied with a golden sash. Joseph thought that he looked like one of the men in the drawings, the mean one.

As the two men approached, Joseph's father turned to him and said, "Wait here, son. I'll only be a moment," He gave his son's knee a light squeeze before standing up. Joseph began to get a little nervous. He knew they were talking about him. His right leg started to bounce up and down as he unconsciously moved his foot faster and faster. The older man, facing him, bent to the side to look at Joseph and then moved back. Finally, his father turned around and motioned for Joseph to join them. He ran to his father and put his arms around his waist as his father said, "Joseph, I'd like you to meet Rabbi Samuel ben Mari. Rabbi, this is my son, Joseph."

"Shalom, Rabbi," Joseph said.

"Shalom, young man," the Rabbi said. "Your father has told me many interesting things about you. I'd like to hear more. Please, won't you and your father join me in my private study so we can talk?"

Joseph just nodded a little and, with much hesitation, walked with his father to the Rabbi's room. As he viewed more of the second floor, he saw that although the Academy was quiet, it wasn't deserted. There were many rooms filled with men studying manuscripts. Some were even arguing quietly. When they saw the Rabbi pass, they all became quiet, stopped talking, and bowed their heads in acknowledgment. The Rabbi moved his hand, motioning them to continue doing whatever they were doing. Soon, they arrived at the Rabbi's private study and entered. The younger man stood outside the door. The Rabbi arranged three chairs together in a circle, one for himself, and motioned for Joseph's father to sit in the other. Joseph didn't sit in the third chair but leaned against his dad for comfort.

The Rabbi's study looked as if everything had its place. Two oil lamps burned brightly on a large table with neat stacks of manuscripts and rolled-up parchments. There was a small sleeping area for naps and a stone shelf that held a Menorah. The floor was covered with a large wool rug with two lions holding a Torah scroll. "So," the Rabbi said, "I heard you had a visit from Eliyahu."

In a tiny voice, Joseph said, "We sort of met."

"What? I can't hear you." He bent forward a little and, in a low voice, said, "I'm a little hard of hearing, but don't tell my students. They think I hear everything!"

"It's fine, Joseph, just speak up a bit," Solomon said.

"We met looking at the world," Joseph said louder.

"From where were you looking at the world, young man?"

Joseph pointed with one finger up in the air. "From up there."

"On the roof?"

"No, Rabbi, up in the sky. I saw the world from high up in the sky. The Earth looked like a big round stone with green, blue, and white floating against black...blackness and bright white stars...more stars than I ever saw. They were everywhere. And I saw the sun too. It was so bright. But I could look at it. And I saw the moon. It has a lot of holes. I didn't see Eliyahu at first. He saw me first. It was when I saw the dark grey jumble of thunderclouds and snakes."

Solomon looked at his son incredulously. "Snakes in the sky?"

"No, Abba. They weren't snakes. They just looked like snakes from a distance. It was when I moved closer to it that Eliyahu told me to stay away. He said that it was evil. It was the evil aspect of everything man has created, thought, or done. He said it was a trap, a place that traps souls."

The Rabbi and Solomon were silent. Both were trying to absorb everything Joseph had said.

"And then, what happened next?" the Rabbi said.

"Eliyahu gave me this," and Joseph opened the top of his tunic, exposing the now glowing Amulet. The Rabbi reached out to touch it with both hands. "He said that it would protect me and keep me safe."

Solomon shouted, "Rabbi, don't. When I touched it, it threw me across the room like a grain of rice!"

But as the Rabbi's hands moved closer, the Hand of El Shaddai glowed brighter and sent soothing warmth through the older man's stiff fingers, tired arms, and fragile body. It didn't make him look younger, but he experienced more contentment than he had felt in a long time. He smiled. "It is a miracle. I have only heard distant rumors of our Prophet Eliyahu's Hand of El Shaddai, but I never thought I would ever see it." Then, looking at the young boy standing before him, he asked, "And then what happened, Joseph?"

Joseph bowed his head, looked down at the floor, and said quietly, "He told me he would take away my ability to travel like I did for a long time. He said that it would only get me into trouble. He carried me back to where I was sleeping. I went into my body, and he disappeared."

"And he didn't say anything else?"

Joseph didn't look at his father or the Rabbi. He looked at the floor, shuffled his sandals, and took his time answering. "Only that the letters on the hand mean, One. It signifies that we are One with each other, One with everything in the world, and One with our Creator." Joseph looked up into the Rabbi's eyes. He promised Eliyahu that he would keep the ancient secrets, and he did.

It was difficult for Solomon to understand all that his son had spoken. He didn't know if Joseph was sick or was just a little boy who found someone's Amulet in the street and had a bad dream. He was confused and didn't know what to believe. Such talk was foreign to him, like a different language. He wasn't prepared for what the Rabbi said next.

"Solomon, I have known your family for many years. The Amulet that Joseph wears around his neck and the words he has uttered from his mouth cause me both distress and great joy. To have had such an experience at such a young age is remarkable. I would be a foolish old man to dismiss what your son has said as the wild imaginings of a child. We have both felt the Amulet's power." He paused momentarily and gazed at the young boy standing before him. "I would like to accept your son, Joseph, as the youngest student at this Academy. We will teach him the Torah and how to read and write Hebrew and Aramaic, hoping he will one day become a great Rabbi and Jewish scholar. He does not need to live here. He may live at home for now. Bring him in the morning before sunrise and come for him after evening prayers."

Solomon smiled at his son. "How does that sound, Joseph? Would you like to be a student here?"

"I won't be able to help you at the store. You need my help, don't you, papa?"

"We'll be fine, Joseph. What I want to know is how it feels to you. Does it feel right? Is it something that you would like to do?"

"Yes, Abba. It feels right." Joseph smiled and hugged his father. "It feels very right."

Chapter 6
Pumbedita 818 CE

For Joseph ben Abba, time was like an arrow. The Jewish Academy at Pumbedita had expanded during the ensuing years. It now had a large garden with lush green trees and a jungle of colored flowers carefully tended to by his students. He was now the Gaon, the leading Talmudic scholar and Rabbi. Sitting on a carved stone bench near the garden's small reflecting pond, he gazed down upon the image of the older man he had become. He smiled, thinking to himself how the Almighty must be laughing because the mind of the thirty-two-year-old who was inside of himself didn't feel anything like the sixty-five-year-old man he saw reflected on the water's surface. He sighed. For him, it was just yesterday that his father had brought him to meet the famous Rabbi Samuel ben Mari; just yesterday that he began his years of studying the Torah; just yesterday that he had met his wife-to-be, Rebecca; just yesterday that their children were born; just yesterday that his sons and daughters married; just yesterday. Time passed in the blink of an eye. Taking a slow, deep breath, tears came to his eyes thinking about it all: how life unwinds like a ball of thread until the thread runs out, leaving one with memories of a life lived until one's immortal soul re-joins the eternal.

Relaxing in the warm sun, he slowly moved his hand under his tunic. He closed it around the Amulet Eliyahu had given him for protection. The small golden Hand of El Shaddai felt warm against his skin. It had, in its way, brought him protection. It had kept him safe. Eliyahu was right. It helped him to know what people truly felt in their hearts. It helped him help others by giving him a deeper understanding of their problems and the never-ending cycle of existence. Just then, he heard a shuffling behind him.

"Excuse me, Rabbi, but your class is about to start," Aaron said. Aaron was one of his older students and the grandson of his best friend. The young man bent over to help Joseph stand up.

"I used to be able to stand without any help."

"Yes, Rabbi, I know."

"Mind you, it's not that I'm not grateful for your help."

"Yes, Rabbi, thank you."

"It's just that I'm angry that I need it."

"I know, Rabbi, I know," the younger man answered as he helped the famous Gaon through the carved wooden double doors and into the downstairs lecture hall.

The ample interior space accommodated all the students and teachers. As was the custom for centuries, the oldest and most gifted students sat closest to the Gaon in chairs nine rows across and seven rows deep. The younger and less knowledgeable students filled in on the sides and sat looking down from the second floor's balcony. The area was used as a synagogue when not used as a lecture hall. The walls and columns were made of carved stone. Large oil-burning menorahs flanked the Rabbi on both sides, as did marble relief sculptures of roaring lions. Joseph looked out upon the gathered assembly while they quieted down. He was going to give a lecture today on ethics. Points would be debated. Arguments would go back and forth. It was said that the students at Pumbedita could argue a point so precisely that they could thread an elephant through the head of a needle. Others said that if one listens to two Rabbis arguing a Jewish point long enough, one will hear three opinions.

But just as he was about to speak, Joseph stopped and stared in disbelief. Through the far wall floated his old friend, Eliyahu, who he had not seen in sixty years. The elderly prophet hadn't aged a day. He still wore no sandals. Joseph said out loud, "Make room for the old man who is now entering!"[1] Students immediately stopped talking, moved aside, and looked where their Gaon pointed. They were confused since they didn't see or hear anything.

"Shalom, Joseph," Eliyahu said. *"You know, they can't see or hear me. They're going to think you're a crazy old man."*

"Shalom, old friend. Why change their minds? They already think I'm crazy."

Eliyahu stretched out his arm and, with his hand, motioned for Joseph to follow him. *"So, come with me, and we'll talk."*

Joseph asked his assistant to take over his afternoon responsibilities and slowly left the assembly. All eyes followed him. He shuffled up the stairs to his private study and closed the door.

"So, how are you feeling, Joseph?"

"How am I feeling? Everything hurts: Fingers, hips, knees. Why didn't you tell me?"

"You wouldn't have believed me. Anyway, it's only temporary."

Joseph smiled. "So, to what do I owe this honor? You've been keeping away from me. I've called out for you, but no Eliyahu."

"I've been watching from a distance. You've done an admirable job and kept our secret even though you wanted to tell Rebecca and your sons many times. I am proud of you, young man."

"I haven't been a young man for a long time."

"To me, you will always be a young man. You have taught your students well, nurtured others through their sorrow, and helped them enjoy their triumphs. You have kept the faith of our fathers. You are a good and faithful servant, my dear friend." Eliyahu hugged Joseph, but his arms went right through him. *"Ah, I keep forgetting. Well, there will be time for better hugs. For now, rest, dear boy. You'll have special visitors tonight, one of whom will be Kate."*

"At least now I can stop asking if anyone has ever heard of a Kate. My family and students must have thought I was crazy. For sixty years, I've asked if anyone has heard of a girl named Kate. So, where are they from? What should I do?"

"From far away. But don't worry. You'll know what to do." Eliyahu's form began to slowly fade. *"Everything will be as it should. Return to your students. Answer their questions. Have some bread, a little wine, and rest."*

"I haven't seen you in sixty years, and you made me walk up two flights of stairs to tell me that I'm going to have visitors from far away?"

"So, who's perfect?" As Eliyahu disappeared, Joseph began to change. The Amulet he wore on a chain around his neck started to glow. The glow slowly spread through his entire body. His wrinkled skin became smoother and tighter. His eyes regained the blue intensity of his youth. His hair and beard grew slightly longer and turned whiter. The pain in his spine, hips, and knees vanished. He stood straighter. He flexed and cracked his fingers. They didn't hurt anymore. He stretched his arms out and closed both hands into a tight fist. He was amazed. Inside his head, he heard Eliyahu whisper, *"Feel better?"*

"Yes. Yes, I feel great! Thank you, my friend."

"Now, don't run down the stairs, or you'll trip, and I can't fix bones."

Joseph threw open the door and ran down the stairs to his students. When he entered the room, all conversation stopped. All eyes were on him. Then, thunderous applause erupted. Seeing the physical change in their Gaon, the students and teachers yelled in Hebrew, "Baruch Hashem, God is great. It is a miracle!" Joseph ben Abba's reputation as an early Jewish mystic was forever sealed in the annals of time.

Chapter 7
The Namaste Farm, Burton, Ohio 1969

The evening of their arrival, Kate crashed as soon as her head touched the pillow. Seconds later, she found herself in a weird dream. A churning, angry grey-blackness enveloped her in a thickness so dense that if she pushed or kicked as hard as she could, there was no movement, no escape. It was neither hot nor cold but had a firm smoothness that sucked her deeper into a rotating storm of darkness that morphed into the naked bodies of hundreds of thousands of people. They were tumbling and twisting, faces and bodies extending, withering in agonized screams. Their moaning pounded within her head and became louder, like the rhythmic pounding of her heart. Their wails turned into screams. She became the scream. She was screaming, screaming to get out, screaming to be free. Her legs and arms thrashed and pushed. It got her nowhere. She was sucked into an ever-expanding bottomless terror zone where she could not breathe, could not get air. And then she saw her mother, Lauren. Lauren dove quickly down to save her. She pushed through the blackness, shoving the black swirling mass out of the way.

"*Not to my daughter, you don't!*" she hissed through clenched teeth. She rushed through the billowing darkness as bodies of nakedness surrounded her little girl. She grabbed Kate's arm, trying to pull her up and away. Turning, she screamed at her daughter, "Wake up, Kate. Breathe. Wake up. WAKE UP!" But Lauren lost her grip trying to save her daughter from the unending onslaught of evil. She was herself sucked deeper into the black swirling mass of twisting eel-like human torsos, arms, and legs.

"Honey, wake up. You've had a bad nightmare. I'm here. Everything's going to be OK." Her dad hugged her tightly against his chest. Kate shuddered. Her t-shirt was drenched with perspiration. After a moment, she let out a long, deep breath and relaxed a little. She remembered where she was. Impossible experiences roared back into her consciousness. Last night, she had been exhausted. All she wanted to do was sleep. She remembered the old farmhouse, how her dad had carried her to an upstairs bedroom, and how Sara had given her something to wear so she wouldn't be cold. She pulled the light pink rose-patterned sheet up to her chin.

"Dad, I saw mom. She tried to rescue me..."

Sara ran into the bedroom. "Is Katie alright? I heard screaming."

"She's OK. She'll be fine. A nightmare after all of the things we've been through." Joe cradled his daughter in his arms.

"I'm crushed," Kate said, slumping defeated against her father. "Just so bummed. That thing, or whatever it is, really creeped me out. It was in my dream, but it didn't seem like a dream at all, it seemed way more real than any dream. It was just sucking me in, and I couldn't breathe, and mom helped me, she just zoomed in and...and...oh damn it, dad, it got her. That thing or whatever it is has her. It trapped her. She was there. She was with me. I wish she were here. I miss her so much." Kate began to cry. She buried her face in her father's chest. He held her tightly, rocking her gently back and forth.

"I know, honey. I know you do. I miss her, too."

Sara was silent for a moment. She sat down on the bed and gave Kate an understanding touch. She quietly said, "You two have been through so much. I feel so bad. I'll go downstairs and start breakfast. Take your time. Come down when you're ready." She rose to leave.

"What are you wearing?" asked Katie with one eye open. "You look like an earth mother out of the 70s with that tie-dyed top and long skirt."

Sara turned around and slowly grinned, "I have some clothes for you, too. They're in the top dresser drawer. Why don't you put them on before you come down for breakfast? The ones you wore are still in the wash."

The grey clapboard farmhouse that Sara called Namaste was constructed around 1875. Over the years, it had been enlarged and updated, but it still looked and felt old. Inside, the natural wooden doors and door frames became golden brown from many coats of varnish; its linoleum floor was well-worn from years of work boots scraping against the blue and yellow pattern; and its oak table and chairs in the kitchen showed wear from many years of use. A stained-glass shade in a grapevine pattern hung over the table, casting a warm, homey glow throughout the room. Sara set the table for breakfast with a checkered blue and white tablecloth. She was listening to a song by Sly and the Family Stone, broadcast by a local radio station, WMMS, on a combination Zenith AM – FM radio, turntable, and cassette player. The song continued playing as Joe stopped by the open kitchen door and appreciatively watched and listened to Sara singing along with the song while setting the table with forks, knives, and spoons. As she moved around the table, her lengthy hair, tied in a relaxed ponytail, swung back and forth along with her long cotton skirt.

"I haven't heard *Everyday People* in a long time," Joe said. "May I help?"

"Only if you can sing," Sara said, handing him the dishes. Joe saw Sara set the table for four and followed her directions.

Kate stood at the kitchen door, her mouth agape. She wore faded bell bottoms and a loose-fitting blousy top. She couldn't believe it. Her father and Sara were singing!

Sara was the first to spot Kate. She quickly turned down the radio and smoothed imagined tangles from her hair and wrinkles from her skirt. "Hi. Uh, we were just..."

"Whatever," Kate said with a dismissive wave of her hand.

"...Setting the table," coughed her dad.

"Historic," Kate said. "I mean, you actually know the words to that song? It's ancient. Ancient! Too weird."

Suddenly, the back porch's screen door swung open, and a young man dressed in blue work overalls and a new Rolling Stones T-shirt walked in. He was almost six feet tall, had dark hair, a light brown complexion, and a warm, friendly smile. He carried a pail.

"Hi, Sara. Here are the eggs you asked for."

Kate's thoughts were going faster than the speed of sound. *"OMGOMGOMG. He is so hot. Oh. My. God. What a hunk-fest!"*

"Thanks, Tyler. I want you to meet some of my friends. Kate and Joe, this is Tyler Hemings. He lives here with his mom and dad, Amari and Jacob."

Joe said hello, but Kate had a frozen smile on her face. "Katie," Joe said, "This is Tyler. He lives here with his mom and dad. He got us some fresh eggs."

"Well, HI THERE," Kate said. "That's great. You got us some eggs from the store."

"No, from chickens," Tyler said.

"Chickens?"

"It's where eggs come from."

"*Riiight*...chickens...eggs," she raised a finger, "Got it. Well, excuse me. I've got to go text a friend of mine. Sara, where's my iCuff?"

"Your device won't work."

"Why? Is the battery dead? I thought Jorge charged it."

"No, the battery's not dead. It's just that Intel won't create the microprocessor for two more years, and...let's see, there won't be an Internet for twenty."

"What do you mean?"

"See the calendar over there on the wall, Katie?"

"Yeah..."

"Well, it really is 1969."

"Huh? Wow. So, what happened in 1969?"

"I thought you took AP US History?" Joe said.

Kate's face turned red as she got a little uncomfortable defending herself. "Well, I did...or am, but we haven't gotten there yet."

"So, Tyler," Sara said, "Why don't you bring Katie up to date?"

"Sure. Be glad, too." Tyler pulled out a chair and sat down at the table. "Well, there was an awesome music festival in Bethel, New York, called Woodstock. It rained like hell, was overcrowded and cold at night, but people heard great music and had a blast..."

"... I'm up for it!" Kate said, "Let's go!"

Tyler continued despite Kate's interruption. "The New York Mets won the World Series, Richard Nixon became the 37th President of the United States, and Neil Armstrong and Buzz Aldrin became the first humans to walk on the moon and many other things. Toast?"

"Toast? What's so special about 1969 toast?"

"No, please pass the toast. It's in front of you," Tyler said with a smile.

Joe broke the deepening silence. "So, what's this Namaste all about?"

Sara brought over a bowl of scrambled eggs and passed it to Kate. "This farm was named Namaste for a reason. The name is derived from Sanskrit. In many parts of the world, people greet each other by placing their hands together, close to their chest, with their fingers pointing upward, which means Namaste. The word means, "*I bow to the divine spirit in you*" because I recognize the same divine spirit in you as there is in me. We believe that there is this energy, call it what you will, a spirit, a conscious life force in all of us that exists always and forever; that this divine spirit flows through all of nature, through our DNA, our physical bodies, and that it always has and always will."

Tyler added, "A long time ago, Einstein said that energy could neither be created nor destroyed, that it can only change form."

Kate thought out loud, "So, are you saying that there is an energy inside all of us that lasts forever? Is that why I can see my mom in my dreams? I can't touch her, but I can sometimes sense her?"

"Yes, that's what I believe," Sara said.

Joe was curious. "And this farm? Who owns it? What's it all about?"

"This farm was bought decades ago as an investment. Just as in your time, people went to Hawaii or France on vacations; in my time they come here, and places in other time periods like this, more as a refuge, a place to feel the Earth and cherish one's sanity. We have cabins for people to rent, a pond to swim and fish in, and a fruit and jelly stand in the front that needs looking after. My friends, Amari and Jacob, manage it. They took Jorge back to Timespan to get refurbished. He did get a little bounced around during our time travel. They'll bring him back along with a Timepod for us."

"But you said that you think of Namaste as a refuge?" Kate said. "I don't understand. Timespan looked great to me!"

"Well, sweetie, not everything in our time is wonderful. In 3257, it's different. After you live in a pressurized village on the moon or Mars, biologically integrate with protein and quantum technology, or visit distant galaxies, we learned one important thing: we craved that which we lost, our physical senses along with natural, non-technologically assembled food. You can't imagine how simply superb fresh scrambled eggs are, if you've only eaten ones that are molecularly fabricated; if you haven't felt the warm texture, savored the flavor, or smelled the aroma of something that hasn't been available to you for hundreds and hundreds of years, well, you don't know what good is...or real, for that matter."

Tyler added, "And that goes double for a slice of fresh-baked bread with a thick smear of homemade apple butter. What's better than that? *And* no one's in your head!"

"That's enough, Tyler," Sara said.

There was an uncomfortable silence until Joe asked, "Is that what you mean by quantum technology?"

Sara sighed and smiled a sad smile. "Joe, our world, our time, is as different from yours as *off* is to *on*. It's far more involved than simple biological integration with technology. We don't have computers connected to what was once called the Internet. We don't have electronic machines with memory chips, hard drives, or liquid crystal displays. And Katie, we don't have cell phones or iCuffs. We don't need them...because we are them. We are connected at the quantum level to everyone and everything that is everywhere in our timeline of organic living beings, as well as inorganic autonomous and semi-autonomous machines. It's called Quantum Superposition. We're not Homo Sapiens anymore," she paused for a moment and asked, "More coffee?"

"But you look like us," Joe said.

"And we are one hundred percent biological like you and Katie: heart, lungs, pancreas, spleen, the works."

"So, what makes you and Tyler different from my dad and me?"

Tyler looked at Sara, and she nodded her head yes. "It's a small strand of DNA called 5 Prime," he said.

Joe pushed a little more. "So, if the humans living in 3257 aren't Homo sapiens, what are you?"

"Our scientific establishment has named us Homo Sapiens Prime," Jacob Hemings said as he and his wife Amari opened the kitchen's screen door and walked inside. They both joined them at the breakfast table. Kate saw a strong family resemblance between the property managers and their son. Both were tall, with dark hair, almond-shaped eyes, light brown skin, and high cheekbones. Jacob was balding, a little shorter than her dad, and had bright blue eyes. Both wore patched work jeans and faded plaid cotton shirts with snap buttons down the front.

"Where's Jorge?" Kate said.

"We left him in the barn to ensure nothing disturbs the Timepods. He'll put himself in sleep mode until we need him," Amari said. "So, I hear you've been learning about many things."

"We have been receiving quite an education," Joe said. "What I'm interested in is what caused the change in human beings. Was it aliens from another planet?"

"No, it wasn't anything so exotic," Jacob said. "And, anyway, you wouldn't want to swap DNA with the aliens I've met."

"Something far more mundane, I'm afraid," Sara said. "It was a lab accident."

"Now you've got my attention," Kate said as she finished her breakfast. "You guys are a lab experiment run amok? Dish."

Amari smiled. "Almost. "Let me explain it this way. Viruses have been around for a long time. The DNA that makes up a virus is composed of groups of chemical molecular strands attached to sugar and phosphate molecules. Now, viruses are amazing little factories. Over the eons, they have learned how to enter and take over other cells. In the early 20th Century, scientists discovered that a virus's DNA could be chemically cut or separated."

"So why was that so important?" Kate said.

"Because," Sara said, "For the first time, it allowed scientists to remove the harmful parts of a virus, replace the harmful parts of the viral protein with other molecules, and use the virus's amazing ability to chemically attach and enter a cell as a method to deliver the specific proteins right into an infected cell. It would kill, for example, a cancer cell while leaving all the non-cancerous cells alone."

"Well, that's a great thing, right, huh dad?"

"Sounds good to me," Joe said. "So, what went wrong?"

Sara continued. "As I understand it, at a small research institute outside of Lyon, France, scientists were working with this virus that they had made harmless. This was two centuries after the first discovery of genetic splicing. It was an everyday thing. Not even bio-engineered viruses developed in the last hundred years performed as well as the real thing. But what this team added was amazing in its own right: they built upon the D-Wave quantum computer first developed by Canadian researchers. That computer changed the course of computing. The French team's breakthrough was creating the first quantum lattice linkage. They were trying to use the virus to carry the quantum linkage directly into a mouse's brain cells."

"Why?" Kate said.

"Because up until that point," Tyler said, "People had to have either a mechanical linkage or what you would call a Bluetooth link inserted into their craniums to interact with computers and communication devices."

"Ecch. I would NEVER do anything like that!"

"And, Katie, many people chose not to," Amari said. "There was a great debate about a person's right to privacy. Just as in your generation, everything that you 'Liked' or 'Unliked' on social media sites was recorded and sold by companies; just as every Internet site you visited was followed and recorded by still other companies; just as every phone call was tracked by government agencies, many people were afraid of this new technology and the intrusion it would bring into their private lives."

"The French researchers failed, however, to insert a quantum linkage directly into a mouse's brain," Tyler said. "They did try many times. What happened instead was a containment failure, a breach. A seal that surrounded the negative atmospheric enclosure they worked in was imperfect. It had an undetected weakness: a microscopic crease in the thickness of its malleable wall where it attached to a vent. It allowed a few molecules to escape. Seconds before the leak was detected and computerized safety equipment flame-burned and acid-wiped the experiment's enclosure, the scientists unknowingly breathed in a few air molecules that carried particles of the viral quantum linkage. They were immediately quarantined and watched for months. Further research was prohibited."

"You sure know a lot," Kate said.

"I'm a historian."

"Are you messing with me?"

"So, then what happened?" Joe said.

"Then," Sara said, "They didn't die, had no symptoms of any disorder, were released from quarantine, and followed for the rest of their lives. But they did seem to get a lot of colds."

"I have a feeling that that's not the end of the story."

"That's right, Joe, it's not," Jacob said. "The thing that happened to those researchers, the thing that changed the course of human existence, was replicating within their reproductive organs. It inserted itself into their genome, causing a historic modification. It took centuries to pass from one person to another. Around the world, it silently spread from generation to generation. And no one noticed anything. It was a slow revolution. Then, one day, a forensic pathologist was analyzing the brain of a man who died. Throughout his life, this man had severe emotional problems. The researcher was trying to discover why. This researcher noticed an unusual number of neural connections in the man's corpus callosum, that part of our brain that connects the right and left hemispheres. It normally contains about 250 million connections. This person's corpus callosum contained almost ten times that amount. What was most amazing was the shape of the connections: they were a nanoscopic lattice that folded in on itself. It grew off-shoots resembling fibrous plant roots around both right and left hemispheres, making billions of new neural connections. He thought it was a one-in-a-million chance."

"What the researcher saw," Amari said, "was the first Homo Sapiens Prime."

Chapter 8

Geauga County, Ohio, originally part of the great Connecticut Western Reserve was founded in 1806. Its name comes from the Onondaga Indian word that means raccoon. The first Timespan travelers from the future arrived in early October of the Ohio Past year of 1872, about five years after the American Civil War. They were searching for a time and place that was simpler and quieter than their world of the thirty-third Century PC. They bought the 180-acre farm with gold ore, which was common practice in those days. The farm was located just outside of Burton, Ohio. In the early spring of every year, when the ground was still snow-covered, hundreds of tall maple trees would be carefully tapped, buckets hung, and sweet maple sap collected. The precious brown liquid from each bucket would be combined with maple sap from hundreds of other buckets and poured into an immense copper kettle. Since 1872, a giant kettle has been sheltered from the weather inside a log cabin called the Sugar Shack. As the sap boils, it changes into the pride of Burton, Ohio -- sweet maple syrup. Some say it is the best maple syrup this side of Quebec.

In the late summer of 1969, Sara and Joe walked on the same land purchased long ago. In addition to the large two-story grey main farmhouse with a wrap-around veranda and rocking chairs, there was also a two-story red barn with a barn-sized hand-painted sign on one side that everyone could see from the road. It read in tall white, yellow, and blue letters that stretched from the roof to the ground, "Chew Mail Pouch Tobacco, Treat Yourself to the Best." In addition to the barn, there were some sheds, a chicken coop, 5 log cabins for guests, and a large pond stocked with fish, and home to green frogs, electric-blue dragonflies, yellow butterflies, and tall cattails with cigar-shaped soft brown tops. Beyond the pond were the apple orchards where the Namaste Farm raised their Jonathan, Cortland, and Golden Delicious apples that were cooked into their locally loved homemade apple butter. Honeybees buzzed back and forth as Joe reached up and picked two apples, one for him and one for Sara. He shined them on his shirt sleeve and gave her the reddest one.

"So, what now, lady from the thirty-third century?" He bit into his apple, and its juice ran down the corner of his mouth. Sara smiled as she brushed it away with her fingertips. "Stay here forever?"

"I wish that were possible, but…" she took a deep breath and slowly exhaled, "I have to make things right."

"Help me understand what it is you do. What do you need to make right? Katie met you in Bloomingdale's. What was that all about?" They both sat down on the clover-covered grass near the orchard's edge.

"Joe, in my world, my timeline, I'm a research archeologist. I was on an excavation in what people in your time called the Marais area of Paris, France. As we removed rubble from a collapsed building, one of my assistants picked up an energy signature that should not have been there. We unearthed a broken burial chamber at approximately fifty meters under the debris, hidden in what we believe to have been a secret Oratoire or prayer room sub-basement. There were additional tombs scattered around the area. One tomb was covered with a slab of white marble. There were representations carved into the marble of a seven-branched menorah, a lion, an opened right hand with five fingers, an ornamental depiction of a sunflower, and the internal chambers of a seashell. The name carved into the marble slab that covered the tomb was 'Leah Soutine.'"

"That is simply incredible." Joe thought for a moment and followed up with a barrage of questions. "What was inside? What do you think the symbols represent? And what kind of energy field are you talking about?"

"It was a quantum energy field of a type we had never before detected and certainly had not been expecting."

"Fifty meters underground? What caused it?"

"As we painstakingly brushed away centuries of hardened earth and removed the marble slab, we found an intact skeleton. It was the remains of a woman. Atomic dating later placed the time of her death about 1943. She died from old age and had been carefully wrapped in a large white cotton cloth, which was still in like new pristine condition. Neatly folded and placed inside the casket was the French Flag of Resistance with the Cross of Lorraine. Her skeletal hands were clasped before her, protecting a small golden Amulet with words in ancient Aramaic and a spiral carved in the center of its golden palm. The chain was entwined around her ribcage. When the cloth was removed, the Amulet glowed and hovered over her calcified fingers, straining to break free. The powerful energy field was coming from the Amulet. We heard words we had never before heard. We tasted sand in our mouths. We were all shocked."

"I would be too," Joe said, a little shaken. "Was this the same Amulet that Katie first saw in Bloomingdale's?"

"Yes, the same one. I had no idea what I was dealing with. I had to physically strong-arm it into a shielded container and firmly secure the lid before returning it to the lab. It acted as if it were alive. You can't imagine what I went through. Then, it got away from me."

"Got away from you? How is that possible?"

"All I know is that when I returned to the lab and analyzed the metallic structure, it broke away from the holding clips in the atomic force microscope, hovered for a moment, glowed, emitted a high-pitched howl, and disappeared. I tracked it back and forth through time until it stopped in Bloomingdale's. I had to fabricate a period costume, triangulate the coordinates, try to be inconspicuous, and that's when I took it from Katie." She looked straight at him, "You know, Joe, I think it stopped at Bloomingdale's in your timeline because of Katie, but I don't know why."

"What? Because of my daughter? How can that be?"

"I wish I knew," Sara said as her hand touched his. I'm as dumbfounded as you are. It's some power or force that I have never experienced. I need to find out where it comes from. To me, it screams elemental." She firmly squeezed his hand. "You want to find out about it with me?"

"Look, I'm an accountant, a CPA. I feel comfortable with numbers. 2 plus 2 equals four. That I can understand; that I can get my head around. But all this craziness we've been going through is, well, forgive me, a little bit much. Way out of my, uh, comfort zone."

Sara stood up and brushed some grass and earth off her skirt. She began to walk away. "Well, ok. I guess I can understand if you're," she paused for effect and whispered, *chicken*." She ran away from him and laughed. Joe got up and ran after her. When he caught up, he put his arm around her waist and pulled her close.

"I may be a Certified Public Accountant, but I'm no chicken, especially when it comes to my daughter." He intently stared at Sara's beautiful face and slowly brought his lips to hers, giving her a long and passionate kiss. When they parted, he could see that her cheeks were flushed. They touched their foreheads together, and both smiled. "Now, let's go find that kid of mine."

Chapter 9

"**I**'m not going in there. It is too gross. There are fish in there and water spiders and frogs and who-knows-what-else? And the bottom is all muddy-mushy-slimy-gooey and…"

"…Give it a chance, Katie," Tyler said. "Just try it. One foot at a time. Have some faith, ye of little faith."

Kate stood near the edge of the pond wearing a two-piece swimming suit. Looking down at her feet planted firmly in the shallow pond water, she saw tiny tadpoles darting around her toes. Some of the more mature tadpoles had developed legs. Tyler was standing chest-high in the pond water a little further away. "Tyler. It's slippery and gooey. Goo is oozing between my toes. I hate the feeling of oozing mud. And there are live slippery, wiggly things.

"It becomes sandy and stops oozing the further out you get," he yelled. "Tadpoles stay in the shallows. Enjoy them. In my time, all this doesn't exist."

Kate's eyebrows furrowed. Her mouth opened, forming in horror a silent, "*What*?" The hot August summer sun had warmed the water, so it was just the right temperature for fish, frogs, and humans. Around them, the beautiful yellow and black swallowtails and smaller orange and black monarch butterflies fluttered in their up-and-down pattern over fragile Queen Anne's Lace. The delicate ivory-colored lacey flowers looked like fancy parasols on thin, tall green stalks. Camouflaged in the high languid grass, green grasshoppers chirped. Honeybees, their pollen sacs swollen with yellow pollen, buzzed heavily home to their hives, while above, puffy white clouds dotted the bright blue sky. If any day could be the perfect Ohio summer day, this day was it. She slowly moved one foot forward and quietly asked, "Are you kidding me? No more tadpoles, butterflies, or bees?"

Tyler shrugged, "Only in climate-controlled habitats deep underground." He looked in awe at the pond life and smiled while Kate swam through the murky water toward him. She stopped a few feet in front of where he was standing.

"Why?" she asked, smoothing water from her face and hair. "Why only in special places?"

"Why?" he sighed. He thought for a moment, trying to sort out his thoughts. "Good question. At the most basic of levels, we really didn't have a choice. It happened slowly over time. Multi-nationals became stronger than governments. Corporations were given the same rights as individuals in the eyes of the law. But why talk about that? Let's enjoy the present. It's warm and sunny here. Fish, frogs, and birds are alive and thriving."

"I don't think I'd like your world."

"After a while, you get used to it. Sort of like eating breakfast."

"Well," she smiled devilishly, "Right now you're here. And I would suggest that you, oh, I don't know, get ready to eat some *tadpoles*!" With a sudden push of her arm, she splashed a ton of water in his face and laughed.

"Why, you little…" he managed to spit out before she drenched him again and dove under the water. He turned around, looking for her. She popped up a few feet from his right, and he got her back good just as she broke the water. Back and forth, their water fight continued, with Kate screaming and Tyler laughing. They scared away most birds, frogs, fish, and water spiders, leaving the pond with ever-widening circular waves. Near the edge, the tall brown cattails surrounding the pond tilted and bobbed from side to side.

"Truce, truce!" she screamed, "I call a truce!" They both stood facing each other, chest high in water. Catching their breaths, they pushed water droplets from their faces, eyes, and hair while the hot summer sun warmed their skin. "Now, that was fun! Oh look," she pointed with an outstretched arm to a place behind Tyler, "A deer!" As he turned to look at the deer that wasn't there, she took a deep breath, dove under the water, pushed him off balance, and quickly yanked off his swimming trunks. She swiftly reached the grassy shore in a few strokes, almost choking with laughter, his Speedo hanging limp in her hand.

"Hi, you kids having a good time?" Joe said. Sara and her dad held hands as they walked up to the large pond. When Joe noticed that Kate was staring at him, holding Sara's hand, he casually let go of it, and Sara let go of his.

"Oh, yeah, Dad, we're having a great time. It's just awesome. Seems you are, too, huh?" Kate tried to hide Tyler's Speedo behind her back as she eyed Sara and her dad's reaction.

Turning his attention to Tyler, Joe waved and yelled, "Just hangin' out at the pond, Tyler?"

"Yes, sir. You might say that, sir."

"Well, I'm glad to see that you and Katie are getting to know each other. Aren't you, Sara? Aren't you glad?"

"Can't even begin to tell you," she said, trying hard not to smile. "Well, we're going back to the house and get something. Have some work to do. Join us?"

"Not right this moment," Tyler said. "I'm doing some research on, uh, tadpole egg larvae." He bent over and slowly parted the water before him with his hands, studying what wasn't there.

"Yes? Egg larvae," Joe said, followed by a cough. "How interesting."

Sara nodded her head up and down and bit her lip, trying her best to stifle a laugh. "Egg larvae. Well, if there's any place you'll find egg larvae, I'm sure you'll find it here. And you, Katie? Are you going to join us or look for larvae?"

"Oh, I think I'll join you." She smiled and walked between them so they couldn't hold hands as they turned and waved bye to Tyler. They hadn't gone two steps before Kate said, "Hey, catch up with you in a sec. Just got to tell Tyler something. Be right back." She quickly ran to the pond and whispered from the bank, "Egg larvae? All you could think of was egg larvae? Tyler, look," she pointed behind him, "A deer!" He turned around and looked again. She giggled, threw the Speedo at him, and ran to catch up with her dad and Sara. When she realized that a smile had spread across her face, she immediately stopped it, not wanting anyone to think that she could possibly like a nerd brainiac like Tyler, even if he was hot.

That evening, the air felt thick and oppressive as opaque clouds covered the stars and moon with a billowing blanket of dark grey. Overhead, bright white lightning jumped through enormous burnt-charcoal-colored clouds, releasing pent-up energy that sounded like a cavalry charge of pounding hooves. As the storm drew closer, the time between the lightning and the resulting thunder became shorter. Intent on attracting mates, thousands of fireflies quietly flashed their tiny luminescent abdomens off and on, paying no attention to what was happening high above them. The swift barn swallows, blue jays, and black crows that fed on fireflies also continued feasting. But that quickly changed as the first raindrops descended on Namaste. Evil-looking cumulus clouds saturated with accumulated moisture burst, releasing their stored water. Thunderous lightning cracks shook the house, turning the first few scattered drops that plopped onto dry earth into a downpour. The wind roared.

The visitors watched the deluge begin from the safety of the front veranda. "Well, I better go make sure all the windows are closed. Don't want to get wet windowsills," Jacob said, getting up from a wicker rocking chair.

"I'll help you, honey. Don't want my drapes to get wet either," Amari said." They both rushed inside. The wind's increasing force caused the wooden screen door to slam behind them with a loud "bang." More lightning flashes and thunder drums continued as the downpour increased in intensity. Then, Jorge calmly walked up the front porch steps from the yard. He carried a large metallic box and ignored the rain as if it did not exist.

"Good evening, campers," he said. "Always refreshing to get a wash, isn't it? It reminds me of the time I was squirted with stink oil from a wild, and I must say, quite angry Conepatus leuconotus…"

Kate laughed, "What's that? I can't even pronounce it.

"That was Ms. Kate, a livid hog-nosed skunk not happy at my disturbing her while she nursed her grunting furry little offsprings. I stepped on them quite unintentionally, of course, their numbers and genome immediately dwindling, obviously not during the time period we were occupying at the time, but given that time is relative to where one is, certainly not for the skunk perhaps…"

"…Yes, thank you, Jorge," Sara said. Did you bring me the items I requested from Timespan?"

"Yes, Madam. The fabricators made sure they looked old, not the fabricators themselves; of course, they looked just fine, the items…"

Sara took the box from Jorge. "Thank you, Jorge. Why don't we all go inside? We have a lot to talk about."

The living room was warmly lit by colorful stained-glass floor lamps, their light casting an inviting glow of welcome throughout the area. A comfy, burgundy-colored overstuffed sofa, its soft fuzzy fabric well-worn from decades of use, along with a few high-backed wooden chairs, surrounded a low rectangular oak table that held neatly stacked farming magazines. A large handmade ceramic bowl in the table's center contained a few hundred multi-colored M&M's. Next to it rested a well-used copy of The Whole Earth Catalogue. A large oval braided multi-colored cotton rug protected the dark oak living room floor. On the walls were hand-tinted etchings of farm life in the 1800's. Next to the fireplace was a battered galvanized metal tub that held firewood. On the mantle above were pictures of Tyler and his mom and dad. The dining room and, beyond that, the kitchen were separated by the entrance hallway and stairs leading up to the second floor. Joe and Kate sat on the couch while Sara and Tyler took the chairs. Sara placed the box on the floor next to her chair. Jorge stood silently behind, keeping time to the music playing from the hi-fi.

"Katie," Sara said, "we need to do some time traveling."

Pouting, Kate turned to her father. "Dad, I don't want to go back home. Let's stay here a while. We can always get back in time for school on Monday because Monday will happen any time we want it to happen, at least I think so." Turning to Sara, she asked, "Isn't that true, Sara?"

"That's true, Katie, but it's not your father who wants to go."

"It's not?"

"No, it's me."

"Why? It's nice here. You can breathe the air. The hay smells sweet, like honeysuckle. Chickens lay eggs out in that chicken house thing, and they taste like eggs should taste! Even the music's ok, although *everything is totally ancient*." She rolled her eyes.

"I understand your feelings, Katie, but here's why." She looked at Jorge and said, "I'm going to need your help. Please, stand over here for a minute." Sara stood up and walked over to

Jorge. "Now, I'm sure you remember that horrible, sadistic creature that almost destroyed us in Echo Park."

"I won't ever forget it," Kate said.

"Well, do you remember when it took the Amulet from me?"

Joe nodded his head. "I remember. Your small golden Amulet combined with another Amulet that that thing had and transformed itself into a much larger Amulet."

"That's right," Sara said. "And that larger silver Amulet had something on it. I don't know what because I saw it just for an instant before it folded up on itself. I'm hoping that Jorge was able to see it too and store what he experienced." Turning to Jorge, she said, "Can you project an image of that silver hand that we can all see?"

"I will certainly try, Madam. Give it my best shot, so to speak, the good 'old college try, or as *they* say, whoever *they* happen to be at a given time, time being relative, of course; I will certainly run it up the flagpole and see who salutes…"

"…Yes, thank you, Jorge. The image, *please?*" Sara said.

"Yes, Madam, no need to get testy." Jorge projected a three-dimensional image that hovered in the space before them. The silver hand enlarged from two inches to three inches. Jorge adjusted the image contrast and brightness so it was clear and sharp. They all gathered around to have a closer look.

Katie was in awe. "It's so beautiful. Look at the fingers. They're so long and slender. But what are those rows of glowing dots? What do they mean? And that there is a spiral. I've seen that image before in biology class."

Joe was surprised. "You saw that in Mrs. Gardiner's biology class?"

"Yes. It was a shell, well, a nautilus shell cut in half. She had it on her desk. I loved it. It was so symmetrical, so beautiful."

"But what do the dots mean that are on the fingers?" Tyler said. "They begin with just a few, and then they increase. Jorge, analyze the dot pattern. Is it meaningful?"

"I believe that the dots are a binary expression of what has been called the Fibonacci sequence. We see 0,1, 1, 2, 3, 5, 8, 13, 21, 34, 55, 89, and 144 dots or impressions beginning on a proximal phalanx and then moving up to the intermediate phalanx and distal phalanx on each finger. Depending on the starting point, each subsequent number is the sum of the previous two. The numbers represent a ratio. Some people call it a Golden Ratio since it is found throughout nature in plants and animals."

"But how did it get on an Amulet that is so ancient," Tyler said. "The Fibonacci sequence is named after an Italian mathematician who lived around 1200 AD."

Kate wondered aloud, "And how do they glow?"

"And how did it change into a ball?" Joe said.

"And where did it come from? Who made it?" Sara said. "Thank you, Jorge." The android ended the projection, and they all sat down.

"Wow, you actually found the small gold one tied around a skeleton's hand in Paris?" Kate said.

"That's right. And as I started to analyze it, it got away from me. I chased it through time until you found it, or rather, it found you."

"What do you mean, it found me? How can that be? That's just too creepy-weird." Kate shivered, not so much from the cold thunderstorm outside but from the thought that an inanimate object followed her through time.

"I think it is, too. But I also think that you're the key to the mystery." Sara paused a moment to let her words sink in. "Do you want to find out why?"

Kate stood up. "We need to go to Paris. Great! I'm ready."

"No, we're not going to Paris. We're going to Pumbedita. When I analyzed the gold, I also discovered tiny pollen grains within it that are only found in what was once called the Fertile Crescent. I narrowed the exact location down to the ancient city of Pumbedita. And these are the clothes we'll need to wear." Sara bent over and opened the box Jorge had brought back from Timespan. "I had these fabricated especially for us." She handed a package to Kate and Joe.

"Hey, where are mine?" Tyler said. "I want to go."

"You need to stay here and help your mom and dad, Tyler. You're getting about ten new arrivals in a few days."

"Aw, come on, Sara, that's just not fair." He looked sadly at Kate.

"I agree. It's not fair," Kate said. "Tyler could be a lot of help."

"Fair or not, it's what's going to be. Jorge will come with us and look after our safety and the Timepod. Now, open your packages and try on the kaftans."

"Kaftans?" Kate said. "Where is this Pumba pita anyway?"

"It's called Pumbedita. But in your timeline and this one, it's called Fallujah."

"Fallujah!" exclaimed Joe and Kate together.

"I don't speak Fallujian," Kate said.

"Neither do I. How will we know what people are saying?"

Sara laughed momentarily and then said, "They don't speak Fallujian. There's no such thing. Where we're going, the people speak an ancient form of Aramaic."

Kate crossed her arms and pouted. "Well, how am I gonna learn that in a day? I have a hard enough time in French class!"

"Glad you asked." Sara turned to Jorge and said, "Jorge, if you could take a moment to concentrate..."

"Madam, I'll have you know that I can multi-task. Even though I'm enjoying The Dell's rendition of *Oh What a Night*, I am still attentively monitoring your conversation, the weather outside, the perimeter of Namaste, the police frequency of Burton, Ohio, and..."

"Thank you, Jorge. Glad to know you're on top of things."

"Madam, I couldn't be more on top of things than if I were standing behind you, which, of course, I am."

"Then please hand me the molecular biologic."

Jorge's chest area spread apart when he put his hand on his chest. He removed a translucent blue cylinder and handed it to Sara. His appearance then returned to normal.

"What's that thing?" Joe said.

"This cylinder contains something called a neural language enhancer. Tyler, Amari, Jacob, I, and all of us from our time period have something similar within us. It's a natural part of us when we are born. One of the advances our race has developed over many centuries is a genetic mutation to help us understand language."

"You mean you don't have to study French to know it?"

"Yes, that's true," Sara said with a smile.

Kate smiled. "Oh, am I down for that!"

"Now, just hold on a sec, Katie," Joe said.

"But Dad, I'll *ace* French!"

"It's not that simple, Katie," Sara said. "You'll still need to practice the sounds of a language."

"Oh, I can do that. Yep. I can do that. No prob!"

"But is it safe, Sara?"

"Yes, Joe, it's absolutely safe. It doesn't hurt at all. And it will become a natural part of you. Only your language ability will be enhanced. You will more easily understand the symbolic nature of language. Working with this enhanced ability will make you more adept at communication. Think of it as a muscle you want to increase in size. The more weight you put against it, the more repetitions you do, the stronger the muscle becomes. It will be like that with your language ability."

"How does it work?" Kate said. Joe smiled at his daughter.

"Glad you asked," Tyler said. "It's quite simple. Well, maybe not for you, but for me."

"I may start to hate you, Tyler." Kate crossed her arms and glared at him.

"Oh, sorry, Katie. I, uh…"

"Go on, Tyler," Joe said, "now both of you be nice."

"Well, inside the cylinder is a transparent disc about the size of your thumbnail. The disc contains a modified form of a protein called Rqc2. Its unique ability to mimic DNA and RNA was first discovered in 2014. The disc is placed behind your right or left ear, just behind the earlobe. It will feel a bit wet and cold when it touches your skin but dissipates immediately."

"So, what do you do then, put a bandage over it?" Kate said. "I hate bandages."

"No, you won't need any bandages. The disc is made to be absorbed through your skin. It takes about five seconds for your body to absorb it. It's called EMI -- External Molecular Infusion."

"Then what, presto-change-o, you can speak a language?" Joe said.

"No," Sara took a deep breath and continued. "What will happen next takes about a day or two? The protein molecules are encoded to surround the auditory nerves of the ear and then grow to reach into the areas of the cerebral cortex responsible for language. It happens organically, at the molecular level. Over time, the neural pathways between the areas within the brain, called Broca's and Wernicke's areas, become more numerous."

There was a momentary silence as Joe thought about everything Sara had said. Then, he took a deep breath and slowly let it out. "I know nothing about the brain or the two areas you mentioned. I have to take what you are telling us on faith. I don't know you very well at all, but I believe that with all that has happened to us, you would not do anything to harm my daughter or me." Turning to his daughter, he paused and said, "What do you think, Katie?"

Katie looked from Sara to Tyler and back to her dad. "Let's go for it, Dad. Who knows, maybe I'll even pick up Urdu."

The rain had stopped by the time Katie was ready for bed. Her dad and Sara entered the bedroom with moonlight shining through the open window. The window had been opened a bit, and a wonderful just-after-the-rain freshness flowed into the room. A small candle flickered inside a translucent red bowl on the dresser, giving the bedroom a soft, glowing radiance. Sara sat down on the bed while Joe stood at her side.

"Are you ready, Katie?"

"Oui Mademoiselle, s'il vous plait."

Joe chuckled. "She hasn't done anything yet."

"I know. I'm just practicing."

"Ok, sweetie, here goes." Sara placed one end of the blue translucent tube against Kate's neck just below her ear and put her thumb over the opposite end. A sensor on the tube recognized Sara's specific genetic code. It moved an internal chamber, releasing a clear, absorbable protein disc against Katie's skin. The tube glowed blue, and the color vanished as quickly as it appeared. Sara removed the tube.

"How do you feel, Katie?" Sara said.

"What? That's it?"

"Yes."

"You mean that's really it? I can touch it now?"

"Touch away."

Kate put her hand to the back of her ear. "I don't feel anything."

"That's because it's already inside you. When you wake up, who knows, maybe you can talk to dogs!"

"Really?"

"Nah."

"Darn, and I thought I would amaze my friends. Now, it's your turn, dad."

"Already had it done, sweetie. I was the test guinea pig for our family." He bent over and gave her a kiss goodnight on her forehead. "Bonne nuit, Cherie!"

"Dad! You've already learned French?"

"Uh, not quite, hon," he replied, messing her hair. "I already knew how to say goodnight in French. See you tomorrow, sweetie." Joe and Sara quietly left the bedroom, leaving Kate with her thoughts.

As she relaxed, puffed the pillows, and made a comfy cocoon for herself, she wondered how this new language ability would change her life. Did it mean that she wouldn't need to study verb conjugations? Would the change happen quickly? What would it feel like? Closing her eyes, she mumbled, "Too bad about those dogs. Always wondered what they thought..."

Chapter 10

B oth Joe and Katie slept for over two days. Sara and Jorge watched over them to ensure their breathing was regular and deep. Joe snored loud enough to wake the cows. During their lengthy sleep, significant changes occurred in their auditory cortex. Fragile neural fibers grew from recently introduced stem cells. They extended internally from one ear to the other and then up, branching like veins of a maple leaf, nature's example of the Fibonacci sequence. They multiplied, expanding higher and further into the most profound centers of the brain. Under the direction of encoded manufactured proteins, molecules created balanced neural pathways and connections. If left to natural selection, genetics, or an accidental laboratory accident, the enhancement would not have evolved for thousands of years.

While one molecule attached to another, branched paths connected and crossed. Auditory and visual memories within both Joe and Kate replayed in their dreams. Their REM sleep became more profound and colorful. Their dreams felt like hearing a philharmonic orchestra perform Mahler's Resurrection Symphony. With each slow breath inhaled and slowly exhaled, tight muscles in their necks, arms, hands, thighs, calves, legs, and feet let go and relaxed. Joe heard himself crying as a baby; Kate smiled, hearing the first tinkling sound of her crib's windup mobile that played *Twinkle, Twinkle, Little Star.* Joe listened to his mother Susan's laughter, and Kate heard again the soothing song her mother Lauren sang to her when she was frightened. Joe heard the crack of the bat as he hit a pitch to third base, and Kate heard the audience's applause when she took her first bow at her ballet class's recital. There were sounds of laughter and tears, sounds and sights of candles being blown out on birthday cakes, sounds from waves crashing on sandy Maui beaches, and above all, the sounds of voices from people they loved.

They both heard the clanging at the exact same time. In Joe's dream, it became the incessant ringing of an office building's fire alarm -- in Kate's, it was a weird-sounding school bell. As they awoke and became more aware of their surroundings, they realized where they were. The clanging was the sound from a weathered cast iron farm bell. It stood high on a grey wooden post outside the kitchen's back door. Kate tried to muffle the bell's loud clang by burying her head under her pillow. Joe just exhaled a deep breath and grunted. After thirty seconds, the ringing stopped.

"Good day, sir," Jorge said. "I trust you have had a satisfactory sleep?"

"Oh, hi, Jorge. Yes. Fine. Really had some dreams, though. What time is it?"

"About noon on the third day, sir. May I help you up?"

"What? I've been sleeping for three days?"

"Not exactly. More like two and a half days." Jorge offered his hand, "Here, let me help you sit up."

"No, of course not. I'll just..." Joe tried to get up but had a difficult time. "Well, maybe I can use your help." He put his feet on the floor. "Two and a half days, you say? I must stink. Better shower and shave."

"We'd rather you wouldn't bathe, sir. Where you're going, it is best that you haven't bathed or shaved for several days. Perhaps for even a few weeks."

"Really?"

"Oh, yes, sir. You'll fit right in!"

"Can't wait. How's my daughter?"

"She's fine, sir. As you most aptly described, she stinks, too. Sara is with her."

In an adjoining bedroom, Sara sat on the bed talking with Kate, who was still hiding her head under the pillow. "Time to get up, sweetie. We're going to go into town today to buy some things." Sara shook her gently. "You'll be able to test out your new language skills."

"Go away. I just want to stay in bed. I was having a wonderful dream about Tyl..." Kate quickly realized what she was about to say and stopped before she said anything more.

Sara smiled and whispered in her ear, "I won't tell a soul."

"Promise?" came the muffled reply.

"Won't tell a soul what?" Joe said as he walked into the bedroom to check on his daughter.

"Oh, it's nothing. Just girl talk," Sara smiled and squeezed Kate's leg.

"Glad to see you're up," Joe said. "Hungry? Ready for pancakes, maple syrup, fresh milk, and coffee?"

Kate sat up quickly. "Totally. I'm starving. Like, I could eat a thousand pancakes." She took a quick sniff of her armpits. "Oo-we nas-ty. Better take a shower first."

"Nope. We can't take any showers, Katie."

"And no perfume, either. You and your Dad can take a dip in the pond later. But, where we're going, it's better if you smell like everyone else," Sara said.

"You mean they actually like foul-smelling people in Burton, Ohio?"

"No, not in Burton," Sara laughed. "When we travel back in time, the three of us will need to not only look like everyone else but smell like everyone, too."

In the lazy flower-child summer of 1969, Burton, Ohio, like many other small Ohio townships and villages, had a large grassy-green, tree-shaded common area right in the town's center. The community used it for picnics, holiday celebrations, or relaxation. Unlike other Ohio towns, the grassy commons also had an old-time log cabin sugar shack that still produced maple syrup every spring. Flanking the commons were antique shops, gift stores, mom-and-pop clothing stores, and Belle's Colonial Restaurant, home of world-famous apple, peach, blueberry, and pumpkin pies. Burton was also a place where cultures met. Families from Cleveland would visit on weekends to go antiquing or to buy freshly picked apples; Amish farmers would ride in their horse-drawn black buggies to stock up on needed supplies; and hippies would stroll through town dancing and handing out flowers while listening to 'The Age of Aquarius' blasting from their cassette players.

The fall season brought thousands of visitors to enjoy the Apple Butter Festival, where hot, cinnamon-flavored apple butter would simmer in large wood-fired copper kettles. Freshly pressed Apple Cider could be enjoyed, hot or cold, along with thick slices of freshly made bread slathered with sweet-tasting apple butter.

Winter brought its own beauty of fluffy white snow blanketing the ground. The tall maple trees, whose branches were dusted with the puffy-white snowflakes, looked like a ballerina's outstretched arms. During the day, sunlight sparkled off the white snow, reflecting dazzling bright sunshine from millions of ice crystals. Throughout the Christmas season, garlands of evergreens wrapped with bows of red satin entwined fences and gates. Tiny colored lights of red, green, blue, orange, yellow, and white were strung around storefront windows. They twinkled off and on, giving Burton, Ohio, such a joyous, magical feeling that even Ebenezer Scrooge, simply by looking, would have turned into the happiest person on earth.

The early springtime drew thousands of visitors to Burton's famous Maple Sugar Festival. Visitors could watch maple syrup made in the town's Sugar Shack or enjoy Ohio maple syrup served over hot pancakes, cold snow, or as candy on a stick.

But on this particular hot, humid, and sweltering August day, Sara drove the farm's old white Ford County Squire station wagon over Ohio's State Route 87. Joe sat in front with Sara, and Kate sat in the back with Tyler, but only after Kate's incessant pleading had convinced Sara to let him come along. Sara stopped the wagon at the curb on East Park Street, just across from Burton's historic park. As Kate left the rear passenger seat, she saw an Amish horse and buggy pass them by. The men inside the buggy were dressed in dark overalls and blue shirts. The older man wore a long dark beard and a yellow straw hat. The two younger boys, about the same age as Kate, wore similar work clothes and hats. Their beards were just beginning to grow out. Kate took a deep breath, inhaling the sweet country air. A slight breeze had just started to offer some relief from the blistering summer heat.

"I wonder if Burton is the same in my time as it is now," Kate said.

"I'm sure it's pretty close to what it is now," Sara said. "There are more people, I bet, but just about the same. And that reminds me," she said, bringing them all close to her. She spoke in a quiet voice. "There are some important rules about traveling in the past. The most important is to make no changes."

"What do you mean?" Joe said.

"If you change the past, you will alter the future, maybe even your future. You cannot predict what the impact of that change will be. So, don't cause an accident, and don't save anyone's life. You may interact with people but only in a way that will not change the future. You can't tell them to buy Microsoft when it is created; you can't start a bank account for yourself now and collect it and the interest in the future; you can't tell anyone which team won the World's Series so they can win a bet; you can't affect the future in any way. It will create a paradox in the time continuum that is deadly. Deadly. Do you understand?" Joe and Kate nodded their heads in agreement.

"Ok. Now, let's see if your new language centers are working."

"How will we know?" Kate said.

"Oh, you'll know," Tyler said. We'll keep it a surprise."

Kate didn't have long to wait. The two Amish brothers that Kate had seen earlier in the horse and buggy were outside leaning against an old red brick two-story building with a hardware store on the ground floor. They were watching their family's horse and buggy while their father went inside. As Kate passed them on the sidewalk, she heard one of them say in Pennsylvania Dutch, *"I sure would like to get that one alone in the hayloft. I bet she wouldn't put up a fight. See how she looks at me? Probably wants it right now."* The boy's younger brother just snickered.

Kate turned red in the face and stopped one second later. She slowly turned around. Her fists were curled by her side into a tight ball, ready to throw a punch. Walking up to the Amish boy who spoke, she said through clenched teeth in perfect Pennsylvania Dutch, *"You would be lucky to get a kiss from a fat-lipped hairy cross-eyed cow, you pimply-faced fool."* She poked him in the chest three times as she said it. He quickly stopped smirking. He and his brother looked shocked, knowing she understood Pennsylvania Dutch, a language only spoken by the Amish. *"So, you want it right now, huh? I'll give it to you right now. With my fist, I'll give it to you!"* Kate was nose-to-nose with him. She held her fist up to his now colorless face.

Joe ran over before she hit the boy and said to him in Pennsylvania Dutch, *"You owe my daughter an apology, young man. That is no way to speak to any young woman."*

"Ya, ya, yessir. I'm sorry. I'm sorry, mam. Sorry," the older boy said. Both boys took their hats off their heads and held them in their hands, heads bowed. Quickly, they turned and piled one over

the other as they rushed into the safety of their buggy. They didn't look back as Joe, his arm proudly around Kate's shoulders, joined Sara and Tyler.

"And that, Katie and Joe, is how your new language ability works," Sara said as she beamed at Kate. "You stood up for yourself really well."

"I was gonna smash that dufus right in the face, I swear."

"Well, I'm proud of you and glad you didn't," Joe said. "You did the right thing by telling him off, in Pennsylvania Dutch no less."

"Yeah, pretty cool," Tyler said. "Pret-ty cool."

"Pretty cool? Where did you get 'pretty cool' from? No one says 'pretty cool' anymore," Kate said as she walked ahead of him.

"They did in 1969," Tyler whispered, running to catch up with her. "Hey, slow down. What's the matter?"

"Oh, those guys got me so mad. I hate it when someone tries to make me feel less than I am. Just looks at me as an object. Something to use and throw away." She stopped and turned to Tyler. "That's not who I am."

"I know." Silence. He looked at her. More silence.

"Good." She put her arm through his, patted his hand, and smiled sweetly. They walked down the cement-grey sidewalk together with the summer sun shining brightly. "Now, let's go get a slice of that famous apple pie at Belle's."

That evening, departure time for the ancient past had arrived. Their costumes had the look and feel of garments used, patched, and handed down from generation to generation. Joe's outer beige kaftan was made of roughly spun wool. He tied a faded brown sash around his waist to hold it around his body. Old-looking leather sandals covered his feet, while a faded tan turban was wrapped around his head. Sara and Kate wore similar-looking long-sleeved woolen kaftans that almost touched the floor. Sara's light brown hooded garment was tied with a dark brown sash; Kate's faded blue kaftan, also hooded, was tied with a darker blue sash. Both wore leather sandals. Embedded inside their sandals and woven into the woolen fabric of all the kaftans were hidden location devices. If they were to get separated, Jorge could find them. They took wool blankets for warmth and gold for trade. Looking like thousands of other travelers to Pumbedita in 818 CE, no one would mistake them for wealthy merchants or nobility.

Located behind Namaste's red barn, hidden from the road and off to the right, was an oversized garage that, at times, was used to protect expensive farm machinery from Ohio's severe weather. Unlike any other garage that existed in Northeast Ohio, this nondescript farm building was a transfer station for Timepods. It was powered by a quantum device called a De Broglie-Bohm Generator, buried deep underground when Namaste was first built. Louis de Broglie and Tyler Bohm developed the theory of wave function as defined by Bohmian mechanics. Inside, the only noticeable difference was the floor and support structure. If one took the time to look at the surfaces, one would see upon close examination a ripple effect similar to the ripples on a shark's skin. These overlapping ripples acted like a heat sink, which would absorb and quickly dissipate heat caused by the Bohmian wave mechanics of transferring through time. The unique surfaces had a hardness factor greater than 10 to the 4th power on the Mohs Expanded Scale of hardness. When Sara, Joe, and Kate opened the garage door, they saw Jorge standing by their Timepod waiting for them. Amari, Jacob, and Tyler were also there to give them hugs and send them off.

"I'll miss you," Kate said as she gave Tyler a big hug.

"Have a great time, and try not to punch anyone. You'll tell me all about it when you get back." He gave her a quick hug in return.

"Bye, sweeties. See you on the flip-flop," Sara said to Amari, giving her and Jacob each a big hug.

"Be safe," Amari said.

"You'll have to hurry, folks. We're expecting another Timepod arrival momentarily," Jacob said. "Please, step onto your Pod. As soon as the other one arrives, you'll be off."

They waved goodbye. Tyler, Amari, and Jacob stepped to the side. Through the transparent dome, Kate saw another Timepod appear a few feet from their own. Inside the new Timepod was a family of five. One was a girl about her own age. She was tall, had long blonde hair, and a perfect figure. She wore one of those tight-fitting white jumpsuits Sara had first worn at Timespan. Kate saw a large smile spread across Tyler's face. She placed her hands and face against the Pod's transparent curved surface, pounded her fists against the curved dome, and shouted, "Tyler!" But Tyler couldn't hear her. The world outside faded away. Burton, Ohio, of 1969 was gone.

Chapter 11
Port City of Pumbedita, Sasanian Empire, 818 CE

W hat is now commonly referred to as "The Morris-Thorne
Time Tunnel" was first postulated by Michael Morris
and Kip Thorne in March of 1987 at the California
Institute of Technology in Pasadena, California. Their academic
paper, "Wormholes in Space time and Their Use for Interstellar
Travel: A Tool for Teaching General Relativity[2]," was published in
1988. Within the academic community, it generated significant
controversy. It took two thousand years to prove their thesis true
and another five hundred to make what eventually became known
as Timespan commercially operational. Kate Levy didn't care
anything about Morris-Thorne or the power to create a stable
traversable wormhole in space time. All she knew was that some
tall blonde from the future had stepped out of a Timepod into a
past that she, Kate, had just left, and Tyler didn't look miserable
about it at all.

Kate was still leaning against the interior of the Timepod's
large, curved surface when the blackness outside changed to
brilliant sunlight. A large grey horse was running straight at them.
When the pod fully materialized, they were shocked to see that the
horse's front end was on one side of the Timepod, and the back end
was on the other. The middle was squashed underneath the giant
machine. They had landed in the middle of a dirt street on market
day. Hundreds of people dressed in long robes and tunics were
staring at them. People began to scream. Baskets full of vegetables
and fruit were pushed aside and overturned. Tables crashed to the
ground. Women grabbed their children and covered their eyes.
Others stood dumbfounded, unable to comprehend what they were
seeing.

Sara shouted but didn't need to since she and Jorge
telepathically connected at the quantum level. "Jorge, adjust the

space time axis. Get us out of here!" Suddenly, they heard a crackling sound followed by a localized wind that inverted and drew into itself. In seconds, the bright sunlight changed into a murky brown. They had materialized in water. As they drifted down, they came face-to-face with a school of large, ugly fish with very sharp teeth.

"Whoa. Those some mean-looking fish or what?" Kate said.

"I believe, Miss, that those are called Muskellunge, a species of large trout once found abundantly in the Euphrates River," Jorge said.

"Jorge, what happened? Why did we land where people could see us? Why are we now in the water? This is serious. Run a diagnostic."

"Yes, Madam, of course, I have. I am at a loss to understand. Nothing shows as abnormal. I have never miscalculated before. But something is exerting a slight resistance within an internal theta wave generator. I am still determining what it is. I will monitor it. I deeply regret the incident in the marketplace."

"Thank you, Jorge. Please monitor any significant changes in the timeline compared to our recorded experience."

"Will it hurt our ability to return?" Joe said.

"It shouldn't. But it could change the world we all return to. We'll just have to wait and see." Turning to Jorge, Sara said, "Why didn't we land in the cave in the hills above the town as we had planned?"

"I discovered while we were in flux that the cave we had intended to use for our arrival was recently adopted by a family of nomadic goat herders. I had but nanoseconds to alter our dimensional course. Unfortunately, we were seen by hundreds of people, killed a horse, and now the heat we have generated has caused two hundred and seven trout to be boiled, along with other aquatic life and amphibians."

The school of trout that had surrounded the Timepod turned belly up and rose slowly to the surface. Watching the dead trout and following them with his eyes, Joe drolly said, "Make that two hundred and fourteen."

"The temporal time here is 1100, Jorge. Bring us forward to 0200, slowly raise the pod, and move it to shore at an area that will be safe and out of view," Sara said.

Jorge did as he was told, finding a secluded spot along the Euphrates River with trees and tall cattails 300 meters from Pumbedita. The area was deserted. He directed the Timepod to the riverbank using its gravity wave-producing Kuo Drive, named after a 20th-century physicist whose research team first detected gravitational waves. Then, he helped Kate, Joe, and Sara off the hovering platform. Jorge initiated the Timepod's light diffraction and infrasound generators to keep the pod hidden and people or animals away. If anyone or anything should happen to stumble upon it, a low pounding 7-cycle sonic wave would make them feel sick, discouraging them from getting closer.

The night was quiet, warm, and filled with bright starlight. Walking deliberately and carefully together, they saw scattered campfires in the distance. Waves of chirping crickets, like the ones Kate first heard at Namaste, followed them down the dirt road that paralleled the river. Jorge walked behind them, invisible, cloaked by his light diffraction unit.

"Are you sensing the Amulet's frequency signature, Jorge?" Sara asked.

"I am Madam. It is just a kilometer beyond the port up ahead. We should be there in about an hour. But I am also sensing humans watching us. They are on both sides of the road. There are more of them as we get closer to the port."

Kate put her arm around her father and held him close. They slowed their pace and listened. It was then that they heard a baby's cry. In the starlight, they saw an infant lying in the middle of the dirt road. Kate broke away from her father and ran to the helpless child.

"Katie. Wait. Don't go there," Joe whispered as loudly as he could without shouting. Sara and Joe quickly ran after her. When they reached Katie, she was cradling the infant in her arms.

"Daddy, look, it's so tiny. Why would anyone leave a baby in the road?" In seconds, she had her answer. From both sides of the road, thirty men encircled them. A woman rushed from the roadside and snatched her crying baby away from the now frightened Kate and quickly ran away to comfort her infant. Two men grabbed a struggling Sara. Two more held Kate. One put a knife to Joe's throat.

The heavy man holding the knife said in Assyrian in a low, deep voice, "Be a fool and I rape your women and kill you and your family. Now, give me your gold."

Sara pretended to faint and fell hard to the left, catching the two men who held her off balance and pulling them forward. She doubled over, flipped, and kicked hard, hitting the men in their stomachs and knocking both to the ground. Joe grabbed the knife hand of the man in front of him and pushed it to the side. With his right hand, he punched him in the jaw. To his surprise, he knocked the heavy man out. Kate bent and did a back flip as she had learned in karate class, surprising the men holding her. Her dad was on top of the men in seconds, hammered them with uppercuts to the jaw, and again, to his absolute amazement, knocked them both out. He looked at his fist and couldn't believe the power of his punch.

The remainder of the robbers descended upon them. Joe was a CPA on steroids, a whirlwind of pain delivery, falling first to the ground, then kicking and knocking the robbers, one after another, senseless. He punched the thieves before they could punch him, knocking them stone-cold out. He kicked them in the butt and sent them flying. Sara, a martial arts expert, protected herself and Kate with defensive moves, allowing Joe to take out all thirty without getting a scratch.

"You are some CPA, Joe Levy!" Sara said.

"Amazing, Dad. I never knew you could fight like that. Where have you been hiding?"

"I, uh, I don't really know what came over me. I just knew I had to protect you, that's all, and I guess everything else was just, uh, animal instinct."

"Well, that's some instinct, Dad. I mean, look around. Those guys are out!"

"Yeah, they sure are, aren't they," Joe said with just a little pride.

"Too bad Jorge missed all the action, huh, Dad?"

"Absolutely. Where is he?"

"Oh, I, um, sent him to scout ahead to find the Amulet's location," Sara said.

"Really, I didn't hear you say that?" Kate said.

"You didn't?"

"I didn't either," said Joe.

"Oh, well, you must have missed it. Anyway, we're connected at a quantum level. He always looks ahead. I wonder what's taking him so long?"

"Just got back, madam," Jorge said, spooking them a little as he allowed his head to become visible. "Yes, just this moment returned. The coast, as they say, is clear." Jorge looked around at the bodies scattered on the ground. "Well, it looks as if you have been busy now, doesn't it? But we better move along. Don't want to be around when these ruffians awaken, now, do we, Madam?"

"No, certainly not." Sara cleared her throat. "Ab-so-lute-ly not. Jorge, lead the way since you've just returned from, uh, wherever it is that we're going." She turned and looked down at Kate, "Careful, you don't want to step on that fellow's finger, Katie. That's right. Step around it."

As they walked toward town, they didn't encounter any other robbers. If they had been able to look down at their position from high above, they would have seen bodies lying on the ground for the next kilometer and a half. Jorge was highly accurate with his sub-sonic neural neutralizer. Joe, however, was oblivious. He was still enjoying the glow of winning the battle and having Kate and Sara's respect. On approaching the outskirts, Jorge became totally invisible. The town of Pumbedita was quiet. It seemed as if even the birds were asleep. Although they kept in the shadows, a few dogs did bark when they noticed strangers passing.

Sara whispered, not knowing where Jorge was, "Is the signal getting stronger, Jorge?"

"It has changed direction, madam."

"Changed direction? How could that be?"

"I meant that it seems to be coming from above us, from up there on your right." He reappeared for a moment and pointed. "There, on the second floor of that building. It's powerful there. Do you want me to investigate?"

"No, Jorge, we'll all go. It's why we're here." Sara gathered Joe and Kate around her in a tight little circle and whispered to them, "Ok, group. We've had a little excitement, and I'd like to avoid having any more, even though your dad, our very own certified public accountant, defender, and champion of the poor, has helped us greatly."

"Thank you, thank you," Joe said. "I was just doing my duty as father and friend."

"And it was appreciated. But now we've come to the reason we're here: to find out more about the Amulet's power and see if we can obtain it. We still have a few more hours to use the cover of darkness. We don't know what we'll find on the second floor of that building. We need to be extremely quiet. You've seen what some people are like."

"Yeah, they'd as soon kill us as say hello," Kate said.

"That's right. Now, follow me." Sara placed one finger to her lips, "Shhh." She led Kate and Joe up the building's side steps. They passed under a canopy of flowering vines and were careful not to tip over potted plants. Jorge followed behind. Just as Sara was about to see if she could open the door, it swung open. A soft glow, like the glow from the moon, flooded over them. Standing at the door and blocking their way was an old man wearing a long white kaftan and turban. His skin was smooth, like a baby's skin. His white beard was long enough to reach the middle of his chest. His eyes were bright blue, alive with intelligence and life. But the most fantastic thing of all was that he glowed, just like moonlight, he glowed.

"Shalom," he whispered in Hebrew. "I am Rabbi Joseph ben Abba. I have been expecting you. Come quickly, but be quiet." He soundlessly ushered his surprised guests inside and locked the door.

Chapter 12

Silent as a ghost; he led his visitors through the darkened corridors and into his private study. A small oil lamp, its flame flickering, illuminated the room with a soft glow. The day's events had left him physically changed and emotionally stunned, but more alert and more in the moment than he had ever felt since childhood. He sat in a high-backed chair and motioned for his guests to join him. His bright blue eyes slowly looked from one to the other. Eliyahu had visited him a few hours before. Now, he realized his old friend was again stirring the cauldron. A thought formed in his conscious mind that his life was about to undergo a change as dramatic as the one that happened when his father took him to meet Rabbi Samuel ben Mari sixty years ago. He took a slow, deep breath, exhaled, placed both hands on his knees, and, leaning forward, asked quietly, "Now, who is this Kate person?"

Their surprise was absolute. The time travelers looked at each other and couldn't believe what they had just heard. Kate was the first to speak. "I'm Kate."

"And I'm Kate's father, Joe."

"And I'm their friend, Sara."

"Well, welcome to the Pumbedita Hebrew Academy. And who is that metal man hiding in the corner, trying hard not to be seen?"

"But how?" Sara said. "You can't possibly see Jorge. We can't see Jorge."

"I can sense everything. But what is Jorge? Turkish? Did you bring a soldier from Turkey into this Jewish Academy?"

"A soldier from *ancient* Turkey? I should say not," Jorge answered belligerently. He fully appeared in all his glory for everyone to see. "I am a..."

"...Jorge," Sara said. "Thank you. Enough."

"...not a soldier from Turkey, ancient or otherwise," he spat out before Sara's harsh glare and silent scream silenced him. Everyone was quiet.

"I do not think the word amazement could even begin to relay my shock or astonishment to you." The old Rabbi stared silently at Jorge, completely awestruck. "Eliyahu told me to expect visitors from far away, but it wasn't until just a moment ago I realized that what he meant by far didn't mean distance."

Sara spoke in a soft, kind voice. "I don't know who Eliyahu is, Rabbi, or how he knew we would arrive here, but you are correct. He didn't mean distance."

"If you mean," Jorge said without asking, "Eliyahu or Elijah, from the Old Hebrew Testament, Eliyahu the Prophet was said to be an angel in human form that clothed himself in animal fur..."

"...What do you mean by 'Old Hebrew Testament?'" Rabbi Joseph ben Abba shouted as he arose from his chair and walked closer to examine Jorge. "There is nothing, *old*, about the law..."

"Well, I didn't mean to imply or infer that there was anything old other than to distinguish it from the New Testament, as it is commonly called," Jorge said.

"...What? There is a New Testament, too?" the Rabbi interrupted. "We haven't finished documenting our laws and ethics. How can there be anything more than the Law? The Torah? The five books of Moses? Now, you tell me there's something else, something new?"

Kate tugged at the kaftan the Rabbi wore. "It won't be New for a long, long time Rabbi. Maybe, not ever. Maybe all of us will be gone in the blink of an eye. That's why we're here and came to see you." The elderly Rabbi touched Kate's head and smoothed her hair. He smiled wistfully and returned to his chair.

Sara stood and gathered Jorge, Joe, and Kate around her. "We are from far away, Rabbi: far away in distance, yes, but especially far away in time. We are from a possible future that may become permanent or never be created. That is what is so difficult and dangerous about journeying into our past from our present. You and everything you know in your historical record are also integral to our historical record. Everything will deviate if we make one misstep here or accidentally change one significant aspect in this time and place. That means everything within our recorded history will change from what it has always been. Our very existence, our world, is a continuation of physical, emotional, and historical experiences from you, your time, your world, and your history. We have come from what will be your future, our present, into your present, which is our historical past. We have taken this tremendous risk, where we could accidentally destroy everything: our history, our accomplishments, our very existence in the universe, to journey here and meet with you due to an extreme threat to our existence that not even we understand."

"Ah, I am beginning to understand the strange things I have heard this day."

"What things are those, Rabbi?" Joe said.

"Why, the horse flattened right in the primary market area this morning. And the sizeable round silver ball, taller and bigger than this room, that people reported caused the animal's death.

"Yes, Rabbi," Sara said, "I am sorry to say that was us. We were in our, um, traveling cart. There was a horrible error upon our arrival. We instantly corrected it. And Jorge immediately reviewed his self-contained recorded history with the historical sync-pulse, uh, written book from the future to learn about any deviations of recorded history from your time forward. There were none. We were extremely fortunate."

"And now you say you need my help? How can I, an old man who has only studied what you consider ancient history, possibly help people from a civilization as advanced as yours? What has happened that is so horrific that you come to me?"

Silence. At first, no one spoke. Then Katie said, "We came here because an ancient evil has become powerful. It has to do with an Amulet I found at Bloomingdale's. The evil thing took it."

"Bloomingdale's?" the Rabbi said. "What is a Bloomingdale's?"

"It's a big indoor market we call a department store," Kate said.

"But the place where the Amulet arrived doesn't matter," Sara said. "What's important is that the Amulet can travel through time. For some reason, it was attracted to Kate. We don't know why."

"That is amazing," the Rabbi said.

"My team of researchers found the Amulet thousands of years from now. It was buried deep underground in a tomb in a city called Paris. It was caught around the skeletal bones of a woman who had died in 1943, thousands of years earlier than our time period. We discovered it because our time travel technology was diverted off course by it. The Amulet emitted a powerful signal, similar to the one artificially created when we travel through time. We have never encountered an energy source like it. We still need to understand it.

"And you think I do?" the Rabbi said.

"It's here in this very room, Sir Rabbi," Jorge said.

"What does it look like?"

"It looks like this." Kate held out her hand with her palm upright. "It's made out of gold and has ancient letters and symbols inscribed on it."

Joseph ben Abba placed his hands over his chest, untied the top part of his robe, and pushed aside his undergarment. "You must mean this." He let the Amulet rest against his clothes. "Is this what you have been searching for?"

"Yes, that's it," Kate whispered in awe. "That's the Amulet that came to me. And that is when I saw you. You were in

Bloomingdale's bra department. I tasted sand in my mouth. I heard the loud wind. I remember your blue eyes. But what does it mean?"

"How can it do the things it does?" Sara said. "What powers it?"

The old Rabbi tucked the Amulet back under his robe and smiled. "The question of its meaning is the most important question you will ever learn. You ask me how and why it does the things that it can do. I may be able to point you in the right direction, but I am not sure that even I comprehend it."

"But it's extremely powerful," Sara said. "It has gotten into the control of..."

"It does not matter." Rabbi Joseph ben Abba waved her off. "What is most important is what it represents." He reached out his arm, took hold of Kate's hand, and turned it toward her so she looked at her palm. Her fingers were extended, mimicking the Amulet's shape. "This is a simple exercise. All of you look at your hands." Everyone looked at the palm of their hands, even Jorge. "Now, answer this simple question: Who is looking at your hand?"

Jorge quickly responded, "My internal sensory apparatus is scanning the molecularly assembled appendage, constantly measuring its internal and external dynamics."

"Yes, I am sure that is true," the Rabbi said.

Under her breath, Sara quietly said to Joe, "Obviously, the old man has dementia. We need to humor him." To the Rabbi, she said, "Why, I'm looking at my hand, am I not? Who else would be looking at it?"

"I have to agree, Rabbi," Joe said, "I'm looking at my hand. It's attached to my wrist, which is attached to my arm..."

"Yes, and that is an easy answer to the question, but it is not the true answer." Turning to Kate, he said, "You have not said anything, dear."

"I don't know, Rabbi. I'm in high school. I lost my mother. I've been through a nightmare of pain. And now a vile, ugly wickedness almost killed us, and I'm tired and hungry. If I knew who was looking at my hand other than me, I'd tell you."

"Forgive me," he hurriedly said and rushed out the door. Moments later, he returned with a young man following close behind. "Aaron, these are my friends. They arrived from far away during the night. Please find them food to eat and beds to sleep in. Make sure they are not disturbed." He looked at Sara, Joe, and Kate and said, "Please forgive an old man for being such a poor host. Follow Aaron. He will show you to your rooms and bring food and water to revive you. Just rest. There will be time enough tomorrow to talk."

They all thanked the Rabbi. But before leaving the room, Kate turned to him and asked, "What do you call it, Rabbi? The Amulet. Does it have a name?"

Rabbi Joseph ben Abba placed his hand over his chest and smiled, "It is called the Hand of El Shaddai, Kate."

"What does that mean?"

"It means, my young friend, the Hand of God."

Chapter 13

For Joseph ben Abba, it was nothing less than a miracle. Later that evening, after sixty years of trying in vain, he could finally do what he had done when he was but five. He saw his sleeping self. Awareness flooded through him. Suddenly, he felt lighter than air. The old Joseph ben Abba remembered the feelings of freedom he experienced as a five-year-old child. Hovering above his still-sleeping body, he felt reborn and youthful, with muscles that no longer hurt and fingers that bent without pain. He simply needed to think where he wanted to travel, and he was there. He soared through the ceiling and into the early morning light with joy. Arms outstretched, he twisted and turned high above the rooftops. He flew, remembering what it was like when he was young, joyfully savoring each moment, like when he fell in love for the first time-- as if tomorrow was an eternity away.

"I do not understand this at all," Sara grumbled as she sat on the edge of the bed, looking at her hands. It was early morning, and she, Joe, and Jorge were in a small, simply furnished room. An opening in the wall allowed a minimum of outside light to enter. In the background, they could hear the students reciting their morning prayers. "I mean, what is it he is trying to convey to us? I know it's important to him, but I just don't get it."

"And I have checked all available stone carvings, partial parchments, ancient manuscripts, early printed literature, the AGI/Google Digital Archive, extensive worldwide quantum memories, and have found no reference to, '*Who is looking at your hand*' anywhere, Madam," Jorge said.

"But it must be important," Joe said. "He did infer that it wouldn't be an easy question to answer. Perhaps we need to look at it from his point-of-view instead of historically or scientifically."

This time, Sara rolled her eyes, "Meaning what?"

"Well, meaning that he is an early religious leader. Religion is the center of his life. Perhaps we need to look at it from a theological perspective?" Just then, Katie walked into the room, looking at her hands.

"Dirty nails, I presume, Miss?" Jorge said. Sara and Joe stifled their laughter.

Kate stared at him with a look that could melt his impervious molecular structure. "Jorge, you are one weird robot."

"I could take offense to that, Miss. But *I* already know who is looking at *my* hands."

"Where did you get him, Sara? Can he be unplugged?"

"Nah, gonna keep him around. He reconstructs great garlic mashed potatoes."

"Oh, you're wearing that same nail polish you wore in Bloomingdale's. It changes colors. I wanted to ask you about it."

"Can we please stop with the nail polish and mashed potatoes for a minute?" Joe said exasperatedly. We're living in ancient history, traveling through time, and almost getting ourselves killed. Now, let's get it together here, huh?"

"Ok. You're right, dad. Sorry. Now, what were you saying?"

"What I was getting at is that I think we're on the wrong track. Maybe what the Rabbi asked us is something like a Buddhist koan."

"That is rather insightful for a human of the twenty-first century," Jorge said. "Perhaps you have hit on something, as the ancient saying goes. A koan is a question that a Buddhist teacher asks his students. The answer to the question gives the student insight."

"What kind of insight?" Sara said.

Joe thought momentarily and smiled a smile tinged with regret and longing. "Well, that there is no duality, difference, or separation between the subject and object. That we are one."

"It sounds as if you know Buddhism," Sara said.

"I studied comparative religion at Columbia. Seeing the Buddhist nature in things, the oneness of all things, its connectedness, is central to Buddhism."

"Good morning!" The Rabbi was standing in the room's entranceway. "Excuse me for interrupting. What language are you speaking?"

"It's called English," Sara said in Hebrew. "It's our native tongue. But forgive us. It's rude to speak in a language you do not understand."

"How many languages do you speak? Last night, you spoke Hebrew as if you were born to it. This morning, I was told you also spoke Assyrian like a native."

"Thank you, Rabbi. We can communicate in all languages. It makes life simpler and causes less misunderstanding between people."

"Yes, indeed. The world is a miraculous place. I am constantly amazed. So, what have you discovered?"

"We've been talking about looking at our hands," Kate said.

"And what have you found out?"

"Well," Joe said, "We, uh, or I was thinking about how we are all one."

"And that is a good and noble thought. We are indeed one. But *one* is not the answer to *who is looking at your hand.*"

Joe looked disappointed. "It's not?"

"Do not worry. You will discover it in your own time. The world will bring you messages when you least expect it."

"But Rabbi, we can't stay here long," Sara said.

"I understand completely. But please, give an old man a little more time, which shouldn't be a problem, right?"

Sara smiled, "No, Rabbi, it won't be a problem."

"Then, I have a wonderful day planned for you! Sara, you, and Joe can experience a day in Pumbedita. Two of our students and their wives will accompany you. It's no Babylon, but it will give you a greater understanding of this time and place."

"That sounds like fun, Dad. We can go shopping!" Kate said excitedly.

"Katie," the Rabbi said, "I would like you to stay here with me. I need you to understand some things you can only understand through experience. I want you to learn about the Hand of El Shaddai, but I can only do that here where it is private, quiet, and safe."

"But shopping sounds like so much fun."

Joe had a worried look on his face. "Will she be safe here, Rabbi?"

"Yes, of course."

"I'll stay with them, too," Jorge said. "If either of you need me, I'll know."

The Rabbi looked surprised. "Can he be in two places at once?"

"No," laughed Sara, "but sometimes it sure seems like that."

Kate ran up to her dad. "Promise you'll buy something for me? Something really hot? Sara, make him promise! Who knows when we'll ever be back here?"

"You have my word, daughter dearest."

"If there's anything *hot* in Pumbedita, we'll buy it," Sara added. "You never know what you'll find. It may be a dried goat bladder. People of this period used them as canteens."

"Oh, gross me out or what? I'm a pescatarian."

Chapter 14

When she was much older, Kate would look back upon this day wistfully. Just as there are forks in the road for a traveler, directions that will take one this way or that, so there are forks in the road for a soul. If there is one thing in life for sure, it is that one is offered a series of choices. Some people would disagree, saying, "*It is fate. It is meant to be. The Lord has a plan.*" Others believe just as strongly, "*It is our choice.*" Still others will say, "*It is chance,*" to choose one direction or another. The truth within all three positions is that change occurs whichever way one travels, be it fate, chance, or choice. Our life action is put in motion: experiences will be created, the game will be played, and one's life will be lived.

The private garden cared for and appreciated by the staff and students of the Jewish Academy was lush with fruit-bearing trees, blossoming flowers, and ripening vegetables. It also enjoyed the safety and privacy offered by high stone walls. Sunlight filtered through the leafy trees while a slight breeze caused delicate branches to sway languidly back and forth, casting a dancing mosaic of dark and light on the ground. A few paths, filled with tiny, rounded river rocks, allowed visitors to treasure tranquil meditative garden walks. While Sara and her dad were occupied with a shopping excursion, Kate and the Rabbi sat on a large blue blanket placed on the ground. A woven straw basket containing locally grown grapes, dates, and nuts rested within easy reach, while a tall tree with a sturdy trunk to lean against offered them back support. Jorge, invisible, stood guard silently nearby. Aaron, a senior member of the Rabbi's staff, stood in front.

"Is there anything else I can get for you, Rabbi?" Aaron said.

"No, Aaron. Thank you. Everything is fine. Just make sure we are not disturbed."

"But people may talk, Rabbi. Our Rabbi, here in the garden with a young girl..."

"...People will always talk thinking that they know what I do or do not do; misinterpreting things that I say, they talk and talk. They have talked about me while I am alive and will talk about me when I am dead."

"May the Lord forbid..."

"...Everyone dies, Aaron, even Rabbis. That is why there are graves."

"But..."

"...It is fine, Aaron, really. You may go. Go and study. Aaron nodded in acknowledgment and left them, looking back worriedly in concern just once. The elderly Rabbi relaxed and took a deep breath. He reached out to Kate and gently patted her hand. "Kate, allow me to make a special treat for you."

"A special treat just for me?"

"Yes. It is something that I made for my own children when they were small and even not so small," he smiled.

"What is it?"

"It's good. Wait, you'll see." Kate watched as Joseph ben Abba reached into the basket of fruit and nuts and removed a soft, brown, ripe date. Then, he carefully split the date down its length, opened it, and removed the long seed pit. Holding the opened date in the center of his left hand, Rabbi Joseph looked closely at a few crunchy almonds in the basket, chose one, and placed it inside the date where its pit had developed. He gently drew the date's sides together, gave them a slight squeeze to cover the almond, and handed the fruit and nut combination to Kate. "Here, a special treat just for you!"

"Thank you." Kate looked at the date. "What do you call it?" She placed half into her mouth and bit down.

"My children and grandchildren call it their 'Papa's Special Treat'.

Kate smiled, quickly chewed and finished the rest. "It's wonderful. May I have another?"

"Of course. And I will make one for myself, too." He happily made a few more and put them in the basket. "So, Kate, have you given any more thought to my question?"

"Well, we were all discussing it and don't know what you want us to say. But I have a question for you."

"Oh?" the Rabbi sounded surprised. "And what would that be?"

"Those letters on the Amulet, The Hand of El Shaddai, what do those letters mean?"

"That is an easy one to answer. Those letters are written in ancient Aramaic. When repeated in the proper sequence, they sound like the Hebrew word, Echad, meaning *one*."

"Do you mean one, like the number one?"

"That is it exactly. Mystery solved!"

"But when Sara said the word, Echad, like really totally weird stuff began to happen. So, why didn't weird stuff happen right now when you said it?"

"Because The Hand of El Shaddai is smarter than that."

"So, you're not going to tell me the answer to the question, 'Who is looking at my hand' when I'm looking at my hand?"

"No, you're just going to have to experience and understand it for yourself," the Rabbi smiled. As he said those words, he reached out and gently held Kate's hand in his own. The change for Kate was instantaneous. She suddenly realized she was floating in a sitting position, slightly removed from her physical self. It was the strangest sensation. Her mind flashed on an early memory of the same feeling when she was four years old in her first big-girl bed. She found herself floating near the ceiling. The memory quickly faded away. And now, here she was in a beautiful private garden. She had the same type of glow that the Rabbi had. She stretched out her legs from a folded position. Rabbi Joseph was smiling and holding her hand. He spoke to her but didn't move his mouth. She heard the words he was saying inside her head.

"Are you alright, Katie?"

"Are you kidding? I'm floating in the air, and I'm sitting on the ground, and every thought I have, you can hear, and I can hear you, and this is so sick..."

"Sick? Are you sick?"

"Oh, no, no, just totally lit!"

"Fire? Where?"

"Sorry. I mean amazing."

"No problem. I probably thought the same thing when it first happened to me, but, uh, used different words." The Rabbi smiled a knowing smile.

Kate looked closely at the garden around her. Everything she saw was connected: the trees, flowers, fruits, vegetables, and all the growing living things around her were alive with an energy she had never imagined. Kate sensed how the Earth gave these plants unique plant life energy. She looked at a leaf as if seeing it for the first time: its ridges and indentations. Her consciousness entered the leaf, and she saw its cellular structure and how chlorophyll changed sunlight into sugar for nourishment. When she tried to touch it, her finger went right through it as if it wasn't there, yet she could see that it was green, but a softer green, like looking at it through a mist. When she tried to touch a tree branch, or trunk, her hand moved through them as if they weren't there. She sensed everything in the garden: its shape and form, the aliveness within through mist-like color, but could not feel their solidness. Even the large decorative rocks and small, smooth, rounded river stones had a slow pulsating energy that she could see and sense but not touch or feel. Jorge was the only thing in the garden that didn't have this energy, this aliveness that every other thing had. His entire form was solid black. It was as if he was outside the world, where the aliveness flowed around him but not through him. She understood fundamentally that his energy was not connected to anything else. It made her feel sad.

Sensing her sadness, the Rabbi explained, *"Jorge is different. He is constructed from the physical world, but unlike us and every other living thing, he is not part of the eternal. Jorge is a creation of mankind's hands and minds. He does beautiful things, amazing things. But he will only exist in the physical world of here and now. Do you understand?"*

"I...I think so."

"Tell me, would you like to go on a little excursion?"

"Sure! But won't Jorge stop us, want to come with us, or see us go?"

As he spoke, they slowly rose above the quiet garden until their toes reached the last leaf on the highest branch of the tallest tree. *"All Jorge knows is that we are sitting on the ground under a tree eating dates with almonds. But now, our consciousness is outside of our regular time and space. We are in a place where there is no time. This is what our eternal selves, our eternal spirits, the essence that makes us human, can accomplish. We can pull out of our physical bodies. We, my dear Kate, are the true time-travelers. Are you ready to swim with the fish, travel through the Earth's center, or see the brightest star?"*

"Huh?"

"Good. I thought so. Just keep your hand close to mine. I won't go too fast." He lied. The Earth went by in a blur. With Rabbi Joseph's help, like a driving instructor teaching a new student how to drive a car, they shot high into the sky, then suddenly turned, breaking all traffic laws, and plummeted towards the Earth like a shooting star. The mammoth blue ocean grew closer. They cut through its surface as if it wasn't there. It was the most exhilarating feeling Kate had ever experienced. Through the ocean, they raced, outrunning everything that swam in the sea: sharks were left in the

proverbial dust, and schools of fish that in a flash could turn first one way and then another seemed slower than snails. Suddenly, an absurdly giant blue whale appeared. As they approached it they slowed down and kept pace with it. Joseph looked at Kate to see her reaction and said, *"Let us glide through it."*

"What are you talking about, glide through?"

"Like this." And keeping pace with the colossal mammal, Joseph ben Abba pulled Kate through the whale's outer epidermis and into the lipid-rich fiber-laced hypodermis known as blubber. Moving slowly within the body, they saw the calm, rhythmic thumping of the mammal's heart, blood flowing through its veins. Happily, they noticed it was pregnant with a baby calf about to be born. They departed through the whale's other side and sped into a deep ocean trench. They hurtled through the Earth's outer crust, mantle, and liquid outer core and stopped inside the center of Earth's solid inner core.

"This is so awesome!"

"Are you ready for more, Kate?"

"Y-yes, but how..."

Before Kate could think of another word, they sped through the core, mantle, and crust, up through the deep ocean water, and high into the sky. They aimed for the stars and stopped so far from the Earth that the planet looked like a small blueberry held at arm's length. Around them were billions upon billions of stars that glowed from the deep and dark immensity of space, like diamonds scattered in a haphazard jumble across a never-ending black velvet foreverness.

"If I had breath to take away," Rabbi Joseph thought to her, *"this would take it away."*

Kate gazed at the stars above the Earth with wonder and awe. Then, another thought came to her. *"Yes, and that's another question I have. Am I dreaming, or are we dead? We're not breathing. How can that be? And we didn't get wet or taste the salty water in the ocean. My hair didn't even get messed up, which in itself is amazing, and I didn't smell anything or even hurl inside of that whale like I did in biology class when I had to dissect a frog..."*

"That is all true, Kate. I am unsure what hurling or dissecting means, but I will take your word for it. To answer your questions, you and I are not dead or dreaming. Our bodies breathe in and out, and our hearts beat while we sit under that beautiful tree in the garden. Jorge is watching over us, keeping us safe. But as you have experienced, there is a difference between our physical bodies in the garden and our non-physical or eternal selves here."

"But we look alike. We look exactly the same as we look...in...our physical...selves..."

"Ah, you are beginning to understand."

"You mean we are more than our physical bodies...we are...more."

"Yes, Katie, we are much more."

"So, when you put my hand in front of me and asked me, 'Who is looking at your hand?' the true answer would be that my eternal self, my spirit or soul, or whatever you want to call it, is looking at my hand. Isn't that right, Rabbi?"

"That is exactly right, Kate. Exactly, perfectly right."

"Phew, that will have to sink in for a while. I have within me an eternal spirit."

"You are an eternal soul."

"But why does my eternal self look exactly like my physical self?"

"Well, that is a good question. I believe the reason is that our physical world is powerfully compelling. Our senses of touch, taste, sight, hearing, and smell influence us. Combined, they make us forget what we truly are. We are more than our physical bodies. Our eternal spirit is obscured with layers of physical reality. Think

of it this way: when we are pulled into physical reality at birth, we accept all the conventions of physical reality. Our eternal self, our immortal soul, merges with the new physical body formed within our mother's body. While we exist in the physical world, we are that physical body. Only in the physical world do we enjoy the amazing, almost overpowering senses of physical touch, taste, sight, hearing, and smell. It is here and only here in the physical world that we can express our feelings of physical love and feelings of emotion within the physical nature of existence."

"But sometimes it hurts so much, like when my mother died. I didn't have a chance to say goodbye. It's not fair."

Rabbi Joseph tied to ease her pain and looked at her tenderly, trying his best to comfort her. *"Ahh, yes, my dear Kate. That is the extreme misery of the physical world: physical and emotional pain. And no, it is not fair. I am so sorry."* They slowly moved closer to the Earth.

"But I must save her, Rabbi Joseph. I have to save my mother from that evil vile thing that has sucked her in and trapped her if it is the last thing I ever do!"

Pointing to a grey swirling mass near the Earth, he said, *"Do you mean the evil aspect of mankind over there? The Soul Catcher?"*

"Yes, that must be it. But it's much smaller now. In my time, it is powerful. It assumed a human-like form and talked to us. It tried to destroy us after it took the Amulet I found. I'm sure it's what grabbed my mother. Why is it there?"

"It is part of the nature of creation and the nature of humanity. For physical reality to exist, there is both creation and destruction, life and death, the good and evil aspects. What I believe, which could not have been foreseen when physical reality was created, was that the evil aspect would become conscious of its existence. You told me it has become self-aware. It has to do with the tremendous power the attraction of the physical has over us."

"Well, powerful or not, I've got to destroy it!"

"You cannot. It is impossible. It is elemental."

"What? What do you mean, impossible?" Kate curled her fists by her side and flung herself far away from Joseph ben Abba. He quickly followed.

"It is impossible to destroy it, Kate. Its essence is eternal souls who were more attracted to the evil they had recently experienced in their physical existence than the forgotten love of the divine. They quickly realize, however, that the only second chance they truly have is in rebirth, but by then, it is too late for them. Layer upon layer of other souls trap them. The only way to defeat the evil aspect is to weaken it by releasing trapped souls. It will be perilous. If it has become as powerful as you say, if it has become aware, you could become trapped for all eternity. What it craves is power and control."

"How can I possibly weaken it? Are you going to help me? It already took an Amulet from me."

"That is because the Hand of El Shaddai it took from you was not of you, one with you, or a living part of you. The Evil Aspect can collect as many sacred Amulets as it wants, but they will turn in on themselves. They will lock their powers away."

"This is the first time you've said the Hand of El Shaddai was sacred. What makes it sacred? What gives it so much power?"

"Sacred things become sacred by the beliefs of people. Over the eons, the Hand of El Shaddai was endowed with power by sincere and honest beliefs from millions of souls. My absolute conviction is that it was created from someone or something not of this Earth: that it comes from that place where souls are born." Joseph paused for a moment. *"Ah, now I understand. I see what my friend Eliyahu meant when he told me I would know what to do when the time came."*

Joseph ben Abba smiled at his memory. He bent his head forward, removed the Hand of El Shaddai from around his neck, and placed it around Kate's. *"It is yours now, dear Kate. I'm giving it to you freely like Eliyahu gave it to me over sixty years ago. It has served me well. I trust it will serve you well, too."* He gave her a hug, but his arms went right through her. *"Ah, I always forget."*

"I, I don't know what to say, Rabbi. It's such a wonderful gift. Thank you." She went to give him a kiss, but her head went right through his. *"That is just too weird. But how come the Amulet didn't fall away? How come it's still hanging around my neck?"*

"Because it and the special power it radiates can only be freely given and received, one to another, in the non-physical realm. It is a hint from whence it came."

"Will I have it when we return to the garden?"

"It is already there."

"Then let's go back. I can't wait..."

"Well, in a bit. But first, there are some things you need to know. Some, uh, secrets."

"What kind of secrets?" Kate placed her hand around the Amulet.

"Three, actually, and some secret words. The Hand of El Shaddai is in the shape of a hand to remind you of the question I asked when I forced you to look at the palm of your own hand."

"You mean, 'Who is looking at my hand?'"

"That is right. It sounds simple, but it is not. You now realize that the truest answer to the question is: your eternal self, your spirit, your forever essence, or the life force within you, is looking at your hand. Understanding that you are more than your physical body and that your consciousness can exist outside your physical body is a great advancement in your life on Earth. It will change your relationship with the world and everyone in it."

"I understand that I am more than my physical body. I mean, how else could I be here and do this?" She thought to herself for a

moment. *"But you know, I've been thinking about that a lot. How can I be here and do this, and everything else we've done, and my flesh and blood body is down on Earth in a garden? How do we get back? And..."*

"I see what you mean, Kate, forgive me. I take it all for granted. As long as our physical bodies are alive, as long as we live and breathe, our immortal selves are still one with and connected to our physical bodies. And that brings me to the second secret. Look at the Hand of El Shaddai."

"OK, I'm looking."

"The second secret you already know. It comprises ancient Aramaic letters that make the sound of the Hebrew word, Echad. In Hebrew, Echad means one that we have one God, and we are one with God. But it also has a broader meaning. It means that the differences we think we see in each other, the color of our skin or the shape of the eye, are not eternal differences but only cosmetic. We need to welcome diversity instead of fear it. The word is pronounced Echad. Can you say it?"

"Echad." When Kate repeated the word, the Amulet glowed. *"Ah, pretty awesome. It lights up."*

"Yes, it is, as you say, pretty awesome. Simply think about what you want to do or where you want to go, and the Hand of El Shaddai will know. And that brings me to the third secret. It is important, powerful, and deeply hidden. It was whispered to me by the Prophet Eliyahu when he gave me this Amulet over sixty years ago. Will you promise me that you will never tell anyone else the third secret except the person to whom you give the Hand of El Shaddai? Do you promise, Kate?"

Kate looked away, would have bit her lip if she could, and then answered, *"Yes, Rabbi Joseph, I promise."* The elderly Rabbi told Kate the third secret and the remaining secret words. Her eyes and mouth opened wide. Although she had not been good at keeping secrets for most of her life, she knew it was necessary this time. These secrets she would keep.

"Ready to return, Kate?"

"Ready, Rabbi."

"Then, take my hand and learn how it's done!" She placed her smaller hand within Rabbi Joseph's. *Now, all you need do is think, 'Return to my body,' and you will return.*

"And will I be able to get back out again?"

"You must practice with the Amulet to learn how it is done, but I will help you. We traveled all afternoon while resting under the shade tree. Now, let us go back and see if Jorge has missed us."

It would have been nice if there had been a sound, but there was none. Just silence. Visually, however, things happened quite fast. It was like speeding up a movie at one hundred miles an hour. The Earth grew larger, hurtling toward them in a whir of soft, misty green and blue hues that suddenly became garden-bright green and bright blue as they miraculously reattached to their physical bodies. Kate rubbed her fingers across the soft blue blanket they sat upon, breathed in the perfumed-scented garden air, and saw its deep, luminous colors through her physical eyes. She reached out for a large green grape, felt its soft, plump smoothness, placed it gently in her mouth, and slowly bit through its outer skin, allowing its sweet juices to linger over her tongue. At the same time, she sensed the fruit's soothing bouquet float up through her nose. It felt glorious: simple pleasures of the physical world. She quickly wolfed down three at once, allowing the sugary juice to escape from the corners of her mouth as if experiencing the novelty of grapes for the first time.

"Would you like a grape before Kate devours them all, Jorge?"

"No, thank you, Sir Rabbi. I do not need the type of energy stored as an organic sugar within a small cellulose sack-like membrane. My energy requirements are quite different, although if pressed, taking for granted that you understand the word's multiple meanings, I could convert the sugars within grapes into alcohol, on let us say, an industrial level, but not for this operating unit's singular use."

"Ah, how unfortunate," the Rabbi said. "Knowledge without sensory appreciation."

"It is what I am."

"Are there more of your kind where you are from?"

"Yes, Sir Rabbi. We are numerous and available in all shapes and forms for any type of task. For example..."

"That's quite all right, Jorge, I don't need to know. I wouldn't understand it anyway. Wherever you are from, the world must be a wonderful place. You are wonderful. But I am old and tired. I think I should go inside and rest a while." The Rabbi was helped up with an assist from Jorge's invisible hand.

"But I thought..." Kate said.

"...You just rest here, Katie." Rabbi Joseph gave Kate's hand a knowing squeeze. I won't be away long." As if on cue, Aaron came rushing out to help the elderly Rabbi walk inside the school. "Enjoy the day, Kate. I'll be with you soon."

Kate reached out for one of the Rabbi's special date and almond treats and slowly enjoyed its sweetness. Then she closed her eyes, relaxed, and wondered, *"Now, how does this thing work?"*

It didn't take long to find out. She heard the Rabbi's voice inside her head, *"Just think to yourself, Katie, 'Echad, out-of-body,' and see what happens."*

She opened one eye and looked around to ensure the Rabbi wasn't in front of her and that his voice was inside her head. Then she closed her eyes, squirmed, relaxed as best she could, and did as he instructed. She said to herself, *"Echad, out-of-body."* But nothing happened.

"Try again, Katie. Relax. See yourself reclining against the garden tree and say the words once more. Take long, quiet, regular breaths. Slow your whole body down. The Amulet will help you.

There is no hurry. Just think to yourself, 'Echad, out-of-body' over and over."

Kate slowed her body rhythms down. Her breathing became quiet and regular. Her heartbeat slowed. She focused on the words, and then, without really trying, she saw herself relaxing against the tall garden tree. She knew she wasn't dreaming. She was out of her physical body, surrounded by the soft, mist-like garden beauty. She saw the Rabbi at her side. The grey solidness of Jorge was standing guard next to her. And she saw something else, too. There was some connection, like a shadow of light that stretched from her physical body to her non-physical self. She didn't even need to ask the question before the Rabbi answered.

"That thin string of light, Katie, is the connection that binds your soul to your physical body. As long as your body is alive in the physical world, its connection can never be severed or lost, no matter what. It's how your non-physical self, your forever consciousness, will find its temporal physical body when it wants to return."

"In other words, it's how I will be able to return to the garden here."

"That's right. Now, where are you going to take me?"

"I take you? You're the Rabbi."

"But it is your adventure. Where do you want to go?"

"Well, I want to go home."

Joseph ben Abba placed his hand slightly below hers and said, *"Just think where you want to go and say the words, Echad, and see what happens."*

"Echad." And the world Kate and the Rabbi knew, the beautiful garden outside the Jewish Academy of Pumbedita with its tall trees and tranquility, faded away into a swirl of misty colors. They were sucked up into a tornado of light and hues that spun faster than the blades of a blender. Flashes of bright red and electric

*blue lightning followed the arc of the curving swirl as they shot
through time and space, tugging them right and left, up and down,
until their position had no meaning. Then it did. Like an elevator
descending at the velocity of a Lamborghini race car screaming
around a Formula One track, they stopped. "Oh no!"* Kate
screamed.

"Kate. What's wrong? What is this place?" The Rabbi looked
around, confused and a little fearful. They were in a small room.
Piles of clothes were scattered in little mounds across the floor.
Light streamed in between the metal blades of an opened mini-
blind.

*"Ohh, it's my bedroom. I forgot how I left it. Didn't think I
was gonna, uh, ever bring anyone here. Just don't look, don't look.
See, I'll pick things up."* Kate bent over and tried to clean up the
piles of discarded clothing, but her hands kept going through the
little moguls of jeans, tops, and handbags. It was as if she were a
ghost, unable to grab a thing. *"Damn! Well, it is a little, uh,
crowded, I guess."* She thought to herself, *"Dad is gonna kill me."*
She looked at the Rabbi, smiled meekly, put her hand on his, and
said, *"I have a great idea. Let me take you to someplace that's happy
and wonderful. Something that you've never seen..."*

"Well, I've never seen anything like this..."

But before he could think another thought, Kate squeezed her
eyes shut and thought of a place she knew he would love, because
out of all the places in New York City, she loved it too.

"Echad," she thought in her mind. The instant it takes a
thought to pass and then is gone forever, they silently were pulled to
a place where soft white snow covered the ground. It was early
evening. Stars sparkled in the darkened sky overhead. Tall buildings
surrounded them. They saw children wrapped warmly in winter
clothes that protected them from the night's winter chill. The clang
of a hand bell from a woman dressed as a Salvation Army Santa
rung out on their left. Crowds of shoppers carrying packages
wrapped in bright colors of red, green, gold, blue, and white rushed

past them. One little girl made a snowball, packed it tight, and threw it at her father. At the same time, Christmas music echoed from speakers on their right and left, directing the Rockefeller Center crowd toward a large outdoor ice-skating rink. Towering above the ice skaters was a huge evergreen tree. Every inch of its branches was decorated with thousands of twinkling-colored lights that warmly glowed the seasonal welcome of peace and harmony. Under the tree rested the famous brightly gilded statue of Prometheus, bringing fire to the world. Skating around the crowded ice rink were children and adults who wore hats and long knitted scarves to help them keep warm. The air from their breaths made them all look like little steam engines, puffing white smoke at each exhale while sounds of Christmas music joyously played in the background.

Rabbi Joseph was astounded, amazed, gob-socked, and flabbergasted. He gazed up at the tall buildings in awe, breathed in the colors from thousands of Christmas lights that adorned display windows and tall evergreen trees, marveled at the large leafy-red poinsettias with ribbons of gold, and stared happily at the smiling, laughing people as they rushed past him and through him. He felt the joy in their hearts. *"This is wonderful! What is this place? This time?"*

"It's Christmas Eve, Rabbi Joseph. Rockefeller Center. New York City. It's the beginning of a holiday that is celebrated all over the world. People give each other presents."

"Christmas? I don't think I've ever heard of it. Is it new?"

"Not exactly. It's been celebrated for hundreds of years. It celebrates the birth of Jesus Christ. That's why it's called Christmas. Jesus said that we all should love our neighbor as we would want to be loved."

"I don't believe I have ever heard his name." They strolled further down the sidewalk between two tall buildings that helped obstruct the blustery winter wind. They stopped once they reached the ice skating rink to watch the skaters twirl and dance on the ice.

"History says that he was born Yeshua of Nazareth. Christian people all over the world celebrate his birth on Christmas Day."

"What? Are you telling me that your world celebrates the birth of the Jewish Rabbi, Yeshua of Nazareth? I have heard of him. He was an ancient Rabbi, teacher, and preacher. Baruch Hashem! God is Great! I never could have imagined that there would ever be a worldwide holiday honoring a Jewish Rabbi, where people are happy, give gifts, and love one another. How wonderful! It is truly a time of loving your neighbor as yourself. Thank you for showing me this. I'm going to have to ask Eliyahu about him. Who's pulling on my sleeve?

"Pulling on your sleeve, Rabbi? No one here can pull on your sleeve. Uh oh."

"Quick, I'm being awoken. Take my hand..."

Chapter 15

"I assure you, madam," Jorge said matter-of-factly, "when they were in the garden, they didn't move at all. They just sat under a tree and talked. And they also consumed a large quantity of locally grown fruit and nuts. They offered me some..."

"And you are certain there was no anomaly, nothing out-of-the-ordinary?" Sara intently probed.

"The only thing I sensed was a slight fluctuation, a nanosecond at most, in the Amulet's energy signature. Nothing before or after, just..."

"Just what, Jorge?"

"It seemed as if it wasn't there for a moment, and then it was. Most peculiar."

"And that's all?"

"That, and they held hands a lot."

"Held hands?"

"Yes. It seemed they didn't want to let go of each other. But then the Rabbi got tired and went inside for a rest. Kate remained in the garden and fell asleep."

"I will always cherish my goat bladder, Dad, really. I mean, how many other goat bladders from Pumbedita will there be in New York City? And one so large...and... so smelly." She held it up, dangling down arms-length away, and pinched her nose with her other hand to stop the dead-goat stench fouling the Rabbi's study.

"Well, maybe it does need a little more time to cure," Joe said.

"To cure what? A disease?"

"The farmer did say it might be a good idea to keep it in the sun for a few more days. But he assured me that it would last in the hot desert for years and that it was from one of his prized goats. I didn't notice the smell until we got inside."

"I'm sure it must have blended in with the outside."

"Well, we were walking into a strong headwind."

"Oh, Dad, I'm only teasing. Thank you for my bladder. I will never leave home without it. Or maybe," she whispered, "I'll re-gift it." Kate gave her dad a big hug as Sara and Jorge entered the room.

"And what is it you won't ever leave home without?" Sara asked.

"My beautiful new stinky bladder." Kate held it up for all to admire. "And I've got a surprise for all of you."

"What's that, honey?" Joe asked.

"The Rabbi gave me a present, too." Kate happily showed them her Amulet, the Hand of El Shaddai that hung around her neck. "Isn't it great!"

Sara's smile froze on her face. She answered with enormous restraint, staccato-like, "Yes, honey, that's just great." She slowly reached out with one finger to touch it, and the Amulet glowed with a warm white light. It quickly expanded with an intensity that seemed like a sunrise within the room but then changed into a blinding desert brilliance. Moments later, it quickly faded. To everyone who witnessed the surprise surge of light, it looked as if Sara was flung across the room and only stopped when her body was pinned against the far wall. Joe and Jorge rushed over to help her as the Rabbi entered.

"Sara, are you hurt?" Joe said.

"Madam, what happened?"

Kate ran over to Rabbi Joseph and hugged him around his waist, not knowing what else to do.

"No, no, I'm fine," Sara said. "Just, well, surprised. Astounded, really."

"Astounded?" Joe said. "All I saw was a power surge that knocked you across the room."

"But that's just it. It didn't throw me anywhere. It was incredible. My finger was almost touching the Amulet; the next moment, I was here. The very next moment! No physical thrust. No push. I wasn't tossed. I was just there one moment in time and here the next." Kate ran from the Rabbi and hugged Sara.

"I'm sorry, Sara. I would never hurt you, I..."

"Oh, no, sweetie, it's not your fault. I'm fine. Everything's ok. I'm not hurt. No broken bones. I'm just amazed. I..." She stopped momentarily as the scientist in her was searching for the right words. She looked at each person near her and quietly said, "It took tremendous energy to do what it did and not harm me or any of you." She looked at the Amulet. "Something so small and so incredibly powerful."

The Rabbi walked over to Kate and gently touched her shoulder. "The Hand of El Shaddai can do amazing things."

"But where does the power come from?" Sara said. "I didn't feel threatened by it, but now that I think about it, I sensed a focused intelligence. Oh, what's the word? It had awareness and purposefulness. And I felt the word, 'no' in a gentle way."

"It talked to you?" Joe said.

"No. It didn't talk to me while it collapsed space-time to move me seven-and-a-half feet."

"Well, you don't have to get snippy."

"I wasn't getting snippy." She looked from Joe to his daughter and continued, "I just sensed that it wasn't mine to touch."

Everyone was silent. Kate raised one hand to the Amulet dangling from the necklace around her neck and protectively enclosed it with her fingers. Jorge broke the silence.

"If I may suggest, Madam, perhaps we should now consider a time to depart, now that Kate has her bladder."

Rabbi Joseph laughed, "You should go into politics, Jorge."

"Ah, politics, yes, it was a noble occupation. I wouldn't call it a profession, but as one's time should be used constructively, one must do something, mustn't one? I would have made a wonderful contender in the battle between wits and nitwits, myself being absolutely brilliant."

"And modest," Kate said.

"Why, thank you, dear girl. That's the second compliment I've received in one thousand years, the first being: My, isn't it shiny."

The elder Rabbi moved to his desk, sat, and addressed them. "Sara, I know that you came here for the Amulet. It now belongs to Kate. I do not know where it will take her and you, but wherever it takes you, know in your heart-of-hearts that it was meant to be. Now, how will you return to your own time and place?"

"We have a device that will take us there," Sara said.

"Is it the same device that squashed the horse and killed hundreds of fish?"

"Uh, unfortunately, yes, a slight temporal mistake."

"I'm unfamiliar with the word temporal, but I know the word mistake, so I understand. May I accompany you to your device?"

"Yes, of course, Rabbi."

Later that night, Rabbi Joseph ben Abba directed Aaron to load the Jewish Academy's donkey cart. He prepared some of his special dates with almonds for them to take on their departure. Aaron drove the cart, with Kate sitting between the young man and the older Rabbi on the wooden front seat. Sara, Joe, and Jorge were in the back. As they slowly creaked across rutted mud-worn paths bordering the Euphrates River, Kate leaned against the Rabbi, and he put his arm protectively around her.

"I'm going to miss you, Rabbi Joseph."

"And I will miss you, dear Kate. Remember the words I taught you. They are powerful. And remember the secrets as I will always cherish our time together."

"I will, Rabbi. I will. I promise." They rode on in silence, with moonlight guiding the way. As they approached the grove of trees where the transport platform had been hidden, Sara asked Aaron to stop the cart. Jorge had been constantly scanning the area for danger. He made sure there would be no surprises. They quietly got down from the cart.

Before Kate walked into tall grass and cattails, she turned to Rabbi Joseph and asked, "Will I ever see you again, Rabbi Joseph?"

"If it is meant to be." He bent over and whispered in her ear, "Perhaps, in that other place we travel to, if not this?" He kissed her on her forehead.

"Yes," she whispered, "in that other place." She stood on her tiptoes and kissed him on his bearded cheek. He handed her a basket of sweets just for her. He hugged everyone, even Jorge.

"Take good care of them, Jorge."

"Oh, most assuredly, Sir Rabbi, most assuredly, as the Lord is my witness."

"He is." The old Rabbi sighed and slowly turned, walking to the cart where Aaron awaited him. He wanted to remember his friends from the future as he experienced them, alive and vibrant. *"People from the future,"* he thought to himself. *"How amazing."* He shook his head in disbelief. As he placed his hands upon the old wooden cart, Aaron helped him up. Just as he was about to sit, they both heard a loud, high-pitched whine and then an abrupt crack, like a lightning discharge. The donkey became frightened and reared up on its hind legs, trying to escape. Then silence. The sounds of crickets slowly returned to normal. He knew his visitors were gone.

"Come, Aaron. Turn the cart around. If we do not hurry, we will miss morning prayers. And please, dear boy, watch out for those bumps."

"But our guests, Rabbi. We cannot just leave them out here."

"Oh, they will be fine, Aaron. They will be fine. They are used to traveling in the dark."

Chapter 16
3257 PC

Even though their eyelids were tightly squeezed shut against the intense white light that surrounded them, the pain they experienced was overwhelming. Blinding light seeped through the outer layers of thin, protective skin. In microseconds, the radiant energy shot past the cornea and through the gelatinous vitreous humor to the optic nerve. Not even placing her hands against her eyes helped Kate or her father escape the crushing onslaught of agony brought on by the brilliant beam. Vibrational wave after vibrational wave caused by the penetrating electromagnetic radiation made the thin hair on their arms rise and fall, like rolling waves during a fierce ocean storm.

"It will be over in a few more seconds," Sara shouted. "Steady. Almost finished." And as suddenly as the light started, it stopped.

"What the hell was that?" Joe said, rubbing his eyes.

"We facetiously call it a Time Scrub. Everyone must get disinfected whenever we travel from Earth's ancient past into Earth's far future. We don't want to bring anything bad back with us."

"Not that it would matter," quipped Jorge to Kate. Sara gave him a stern look.

"But, welcome to my home. Welcome to 3257 PC."

As Kate's eyes adjusted to the sudden lowered light level, she saw they were all still standing on the Time Platform. The platform had materialized inside what looked to Kate like a large circular room in the shape of a white bubble. She couldn't tell by looking up where it ended. Unlike the crowded Timespan, this room was empty except for the platform and them. "PC?" Kate said, rubbing the skin on her arms. "You mean politically correct? Everything is politically correct here?"

"No, Kate. Not exactly." Sara paused, deciding whether to tell the truth. "It means Post Cataclysm."

"What?" asked Joe and Kate at the same time.

"You've said enough and done enough damage already, Dr. Lazarus," a male voice said with disdain. It came from a man standing at the far end of the room. He had entered through a circular opening that was there one moment, then gone the next. As he slowly walked over to them, his soft-soled maroon slippers made a quiet padding sound on the hardened floor. Tall and slender, with a light tan complexion and slightly slanted eyes, he wore a loose-fitting light grey tunic that covered him from his collarbone to his slippers. The overall impression was that he floated. Joe and Kate looked at Sara, trying to judge her expression, but her face showed no emotion.

When the man arrived at the platform's edge, Sara calmly said to Kate and Joe, "This is Albert Beck, Terrestrial Governor for Earth of the Beck Consortium. Albert, this is..."

"...I know who they are," Beck interrupted with a dismissive wave of his hand. He ignored Kate and her father and stared straight at Sara. "What I want to know is if you have accomplished your mission. You claimed to have found a new energy source. Where is it? I don't detect anything. No energy signature, except the one coming from your Android. All I know is that you created a massive space-time distortion that could have obliterated the known universe..."

"...I think that was my fault, Sir," Kate said. "You see, I was trying to find Sara, who I thought was the fashion jewelry buyer at Bloomingdales, so we used my iCuff to..." Joe quickly put his left hand over Kate's mouth to silence her. Albert Beck glared at her, trying to control his growing uncontrollable fury. His mouth twitched spasmodically.

"Very nice to meet you, sir," Joe said, extending his hand. "I'm Kate's father, Joe Levy."

"Yes. Wonderful." He looked hard at Sara. "Why did you bring these ancients here? To show them what their future Earth looks like in person?"

"No, I uh..."

"Well, I'll be glad to show them." He stepped back from the Timepod, spread his arms wide, and shouted, "Behold!"

Suddenly, the interior of the room changed. It was as if they were floating high above Earth. In whatever way it was created, the images covered a three-hundred-sixty-degree field around them. The clarity of the view that showed the Earth, sun, moon, and stars was intense and startling. Joe was awestruck. The displayed images felt so alive that he thought he could reach out and touch them.

"Ah yes, the wonderful world you came from. Earth in all its supreme glory!" Beck's sarcasm was unmistakable. "The water planet. Home to millions of ignorant humans, not much smarter than the crawling insects on which they stepped. Indeed. How simply magnificent!"

As the view of Earth grew more prominent, the point of view reversed, shifting to the unending darkness of outer space. Beck continued his discourse.

"It was in the year 2352 that the James Webb Space Telescope discovered an unusual image. With its enhanced infrared processors, it found an object that no one knew existed. Oh, some astronomers had hypothesized that there might be a colossal asteroid left over from the moon's creation, but it was only speculation. Eventually, it was concluded that a gigantic remnant of the moon would collide with the Earth. Governments tried to calm their increasingly anxious public. For the first time, politicians, dictators, and talking heads worked together on a common goal: to destroy the asteroid and protect Earth. Terrorist groups that had become the bane of modern existence stopped being the first stories in the news. But governments weren't the only entities concerned about how the Earth would be impacted. Corporations were, too."

"Oh, I bet they were," Kate said.

"You want to get in my face, young lady? Fine. Let me show you your new world." He roughly grabbed Kate by her arm and pulled her off the platform.

"Take your hands off my daughter," Joe said, jumping off the Timepod.

"Stand back, Levy," Beck threatened. "I'd just as soon stop your heart as keep you alive."

"Albert, stop it. The edicts. They're from the distant past."

"You had your chance," he snapped at her. "We'll do it my way now." He turned around and hurriedly pulled Kate across the floor. The images around them faded to white. While they were walking to the far wall, Kate looked to make sure that Jorge was with them. He wasn't. He hadn't moved from the pod's platform. As the wall in front of them opened, Beck forcibly dragged her into a dimly lit tunnel. Kate turned to Sara and whispered, "Jorge is not with us."

"I know; Arnold turned him off."

"He can do that?"

"Oh, yes," Sara whispered. "He can do anything he wants." The passageway, made from the same material as the large dome in which their Timepod appeared, connected to a clear, elongated tube that Joe thought looked like a long balcony. From his vantage point, he saw hundreds of other tubes crisscrossing each other both above and below them. They were attached to a wide cylindrical vertical core that radiated in all directions. Some of the tubes were opaque, others transparent. Within the clear ones, he saw people moving back and forth.

"Welcome home," Beck sarcastically intoned. "Fortress Earth, or what's left of it. Built a mile below the surface."

"What?" Kate said. "Why do you live underground?"

"We live underground because everything on the surface is dead," Sara said. "An international effort from countries around the globe tried numerous times to blast the asteroid apart to change its course. Dozens of rockets were aimed at it with enough bombs to destroy hundreds of planets. And although the object was diminished, more fragments were created."

Beck continued, "That's when Beck International Corporation decided that the only way to save our species was to go deep underground. We had years to plan the ten underground storage systems spread out in countries around the globe. We sold shares in them for future generations. We called them Safehomes. Has a nice ring to it, no?"

"But only if you had enough money, huh, Albert?" Sara said. "Only if you had enough money would you and your loved ones have a chance for survival."

Beck looked at her with disdain. "No one gets a free ride. Corporations are in business to make a profit. It's what capitalism is all about. We help duly elected governments to stay in power. If you could pay the price or were judged to be indispensable, you got in; if you couldn't or weren't, you were, as they used to say, *on the topside*. The plan, of course, was only to be underground for a few years. No one expected asteroid segments to crash into containment pools for spent fuel rods. A few nuclear-generating plants were hit in France. Plutonium began to spread over Europe. People, crops, and livestock on the surface started dying."

"And that gave some religious fundamentalists and terrorists their final solution. Those same groups who kept the Middle Eastern conflict active in your time, Joe, joined forces.

Beck cut in, "The same old hatreds that tried to bring duly elected governments down in your time, who protested corporate profit, who tried to get Citizens United overturned, got access to dirty bombs and planted them at nuclear power plants in every country. Jihadists joined hands with white supremacists. The detonations spread plutonium around the world. It poisoned the land and sea for hundreds of thousands of years." Beck looked around triumphantly. "They thought they would bury us underground. They thought these underground refuges would become our tombs," he snorted.

"Sort of like payback but big-time, huh, Beck?" Joe said. "Not that they were angry that you saved your own skin and forced them to exist in a poisoned hellish anarchy?"

"If they had the smarts, if they had the money, they could have saved themselves," Beck answered as he sauntered towards Joe. When they were an inch away, he slowly said through clenched teeth, "You know, I'm starting not to like you." He quickly reached out with one hand and placed it around Joe's neck. As he did so, he lifted him two feet off the floor and squeezed his hand tighter. Joe kicked his feet, trying to escape and break Beck's hold. With two hands, he grabbed the arm that was holding him. Joe's face reddened as his air supply was cut off.

"Albert," Sara screamed, "Stop it! You'll kill him." She tried to break his grip, but Beck pushed her away with a flick of his wrist.

"Get away from my dad," screamed Kate as she ran towards Beck. She kicked him as she had been taught in karate class, right between his legs. That got his attention.

"Why, you little bitch," Beck sneered. He released Joe, roughly tossing him across the floor. His hand reached out to Kate's kaftan and pulled the front of it down. The golden Hand of El Shaddai dangled from around her neck. "Can we cut to the chase now? Can we end this subterfuge?" He turned to Sara. "Is this the power source you think will somehow disperse the plutonium? This little thing? This piece of jewelry? Are you all mad?"

"Albert," Sara quietly said, "Please don't touch it."

Kate squirmed and threw punches at him right and left. She kicked him and tried to get away, but it had no effect. Joe got up, rubbed his sore neck, took a couple of quick breaths to gulp some air, and lunged at Albert.

"What? Don't touch this tiny thing?" When Beck grabbed the small Amulet, they all saw a bright white light and heard a loud crack. Albert Beck was there one moment and transported the next, landing halfway through the clear tube surrounding them. Parts of him stuck out from the tube's wall. One leg was bent at the knee, and the twitching part of one foot was on one side of the curved tube. The other parts of his body were on the other side of the curved tube, dangling an unimaginable distance from the bottom; an arm bent at the elbow had a hand whose fingers twitched. His body was severed, twisted, and contorted, where half of his mid-section was bent. His head, thrown back, was cut in half with his mouth agape, cranium on one side, and face on the other. The wall had sliced him. About two-thirds of his body slowly slid down along the curved interior surface, making a squeaking sound. The remaining parts oozed off the exterior, bouncing off other tubes on their way downward to wherever the central core began.

"Holy crap," Kate said. She ran to her father and quickly put both arms tightly around him.

"My god, Albert, what have you done to yourself?" Sara said to no one in particular. "What have you done?"

"Where's the blood? There's no blood," Joe yelled. "What the hell's going on here?" He and Kate rushed over to where an arm had sloughed down to the floor and examined it with Sara. It was like no arm they had ever seen. "No bones. No blood." He stuck his finger into the gelatinous, yellow slime-like substance. Some of it dripped off his fingers and onto the floor, where it evaporated.

Sara said, "I've seen that substance before in a lab. It's a nutrient-rich environment for nano-bots. But once set, nano-bots can't alter their purpose. That would take reprogramming by chemical protein sequencers." She picked up the arm to examine it. "But that may be just what's happening here."

"It is called a Synth," Jorge said, standing behind them.

"Jorge, you're alive!" Kate ran over to him and gave him a big hug. "I thought he turned you off."

"He shut down my ability to move but didn't turn me off. In doing so, we shared a deep connection for a few seconds; perhaps I am exaggerating; nanosecond is more correct. Yes. Yes, I should logically strive to be more accurate, accuracy being of primary importance in most occupations, as Joe can certainly attest since he is a CPA, and..."

"Yes, thank you, Jorge. I'm glad that you are with us," Sara said. "Now, tell me about Synths."

"Synths are an advanced form of synthetic or laboratory-created autonomous life form. This particular one, some of whose parts we see lying before us, had the emotional, psychological, intellectual, and memory of the Homo Sapiens Prime known as Albert Beck."

"Why didn't I know about this work? Why was I kept in the dark?"

"Albert compartmentalized everything. It was on a need-to-know basis," Jorge said. "At least, given the available information, that is what I have deduced. The process was developed at another Safehome. I don't know where."

They were all quiet for a moment. Then Joe said, "Does this mean the bastard's dead?"

"Dead may be a relative term in his case. He is certainly quickly dissolving." The Synth's remaining nanostructure turned to dust and disappeared, leaving only light grey fabric and one maroon slipper. "He could have made clones. It depends," Sara said.

"What does it depend on?" Kate said.

"If there has been an advance in this technology, and if he could somehow upload his essence and experiences into a quantum computer somewhere, clones could be possible. I just don't know enough about this. But we can't wait another moment to find out. Let's get to my lab. I'll grab items that we may need. I have a Timepod there. We may not have much time. Hurry."

"Just a second," Joe said. He reached out and grabbed Sara's hand. "I have to know one thing."

She stopped and turned around. "What's that?"

"How do Kate and I know you aren't a Synth?"

"Joe. Katie. I'm not a Synth. Please, believe me. We need to go!"

"My dad is right, Sara." Kate placed her hand around the Amulet while looking straight and hard at Sara and said, "I'll destroy this now, Sara. I'm the only one who can. Now, please prove it."

For a moment, there was silence. Then Sara asked, "Do you trust Jorge?"

Kate looked at her father, and he nodded once. "Yes," Kate said. "We trust Jorge."

Sara held out her arm to Jorge and said, "Jorge, I want you to take a sample of my blood, analyze it, and tell all of us what you find."

"Yes, Madam." Silently, he held Sara's right hand in his. Jorge's other hand became a sharp tool that quickly punctured Sara's fingertip. In seconds, a small drop of blood appeared on the surface. The puncturing tool dissolved into a thin golden suction tube that took up the small blood sample, which then disappeared into Jorge's hand. The hand became transparent. They all watched as the analysis happened in real-time. A readout appeared on the flattened surface: Name: Sara Lazarus, Age: 332...

"Three hundred and thirty-two?" Joe said. "Are you kidding me?"

Sara smiled a slight smile. "We've learned how to extend our lifespans."

The readout continued. Blood Type: O positive, Homo Sapiens Prime. Then Jorge asked, "Would you like your complete genetic code, Madam?"

"I don't know. Why don't you ask them?" Sara said, turning to Joe and his daughter.

"No, I'm satisfied. Aren't you satisfied, Dad?" When she didn't get an answer, she poked him in the ribs with her elbow and asked louder, "DAD?"

"Huh? No, I'm fine with, uh, three hundred thirty-two? Really?"

"Ancients. You get so hung up with age." Sara calmly licked another blood drop away that had formed on her finger. "Now, stay close and follow me."

"*What happened to my quantum connection?*" screamed Albert Beck's reconstructed voice. The sound echoed throughout a large laboratory within Safehome Four, built two miles under Pretoria, South Africa, due to that region's stability from catastrophic earthquakes. Inside the mammoth semicircular dome, which could easily have accommodated the Statue of Liberty, were translucent and opaque surfaces that visually monitored quantum links throughout the system. At floor level within the dome's center was an enclosed thick-walled rectangular tub, similar in form to a twentieth-century isolation tank. The submersion tank was full of a yellowish semi-gelatinous substance with a dark reddish mass floating in its center. Scientists carefully monitored the dense mass as it slowly coalesced, molecule by molecule. "*I said, what happened to my quantum connection? I'm blind!*

"Uh, we don't know, sir." The lead female scientist, Dr. Takahashi, responded to the disembodied voice emanating from the three-dimensional translucent image formed in front of her. "All we know is that all contact has been lost..."

"*...Lost? How do you lose a quantum connection? How do you lose a Synth?*"

"We don't know, sir. All we know is that all contact has been lost from Safehome One. It went dark." The scientist moved her head and hands in quick, jerky movements. Each time there was motion, the image changed or enlarged on the plane facing her. One picture showed all of the Safehomes. Six showed a positive quantum connection with each one. Only Safehome-One was offline.

"*Well, get me out of here. Get me my Synth!*"

"We don't have a Synth to download you into, sir. Our resources are extremely limited. The Quantum Molecular Sequencer has begun fabricating a Synth for Commander Shao of Safehome Eight. It cannot be reversed or stopped."

"*So, I'll look like him. I don't care. Tell the Commander it's an extreme global emergency. I'm sure he'll understand. And if he doesn't, I don't care!*"

"Yes, sir, but..."

"*No buts, just do it. And find out what the hell happened to my Synth. We both know this must be my last cranial content duplication. No one can have more than eight, or the original data becomes corrupted. It will degrade too much.*"

"But, sir, I..."

"*Do it, Doctor Takahashi, or you'll be a topsider within two seconds. Do I make myself clear?*"

"Yes, sir. Extremely clear, sir. It will be as you desire," the scientist said. As she ended the connection, a self-satisfied smile spread across her face. She looked at the Synth growing in the submersion tank. It would take about thirty days. She hoped to live long enough to see Beck integrate and become conscious.

❖

"Everything looks so sterile here, so orderly," Kate said. "How can you tolerate it?" Kate and her father were standing in the middle of Sara's laboratory in Safehome One. At the same time, Sara and Jorge were busy gathering together items Sara thought they would need. All the lab's equipment was stored in white-colored drawers, cabinets, and closets that silently opened and closed at the slightest touch. Large translucent panels floated over work areas.

"True. If it weren't for the Timepods, we'd be lunatics. But we can make some alterations." Turning to Jorge, Sara said, "Put us in a rainforest, Jorge." As soon as she said the words, the circular interior walls changed into a realistic-looking Amazon rainforest. "It helps, but it's not the real deal. It's not like Namaste. All the species of frogs, butterflies, and plants alive and growing on the farm are in a deep freeze down here. All the seeds for apple trees and sweetcorn are frozen in Safehomes around the globe. They won't be re-animated for hundreds of thousands of years."

"Who could live that long?" Joe said.

"Well, we're going to give it the good old college try, as you used to say in your time. I'm brought out of suspended animation every ten years. All of us down here take turns. If we all lived at the same time, we wouldn't be able to feed ourselves. That's why we travel to different times via Timespan and the Timepods." Suddenly, the lab's power flickered. Every source of illumination was extinguished. Beyond the lab's entrance door, they heard a constant loud pinging sound. Thin, pulsating green lines embedded in the floor, which had not been visible while the room was illuminated, revealed themselves, showing the way to the exit. The small Amulet that dangled around Kate's neck began to glow.

"We need to leave. No time to change clothes." Sara said. "We don't want to be detected. Follow me." She quickly ushered them into a smaller room adjacent to her large laboratory. It held only one thing: a wall-to-wall Timepod. It was charged up and ready to go.

Sara silently thought, "*You know where to go, Jorge.*"

"*Yes, Madam.* Hold on, everyone!" The Timepods' semicircular protective shield hardened around them, becoming a sphere. The entire globe became a reflective mirrored surface that glowed. One moment, they were there; the next instant, nothing was there.

Chapter 17
Burton, Ohio 1969

"I know where we're going," Kate said in a know-it-all tone of voice.

Joe smiled slightly and glanced at Sara. "Really? Since when were you upgraded to Homo Sapiens Prime?"

"It's just logical, that's all. But I won't talk to Tyler or acknowledge his existence."

"Oh, really," Sara said with a slight smile. "Why's that?"

"Because of the way he smiled and hugged that thin blonde-haired girl when we left, that's why." Kate crossed her arms. "I was going to give him this water bladder, but now I don't think I will."

"Hold on, please," Jorge said. "Materializing in a few moments. December 25th, 1969."

"Hey," Kate happily smiled, "It's Christmas. How great is that!"

A hard bump threw them to the Timepod's floor. When the semicircular walls disappeared, the smell of burnt wood was the first thing that hit them in the face. Namaste was gone.

"Oh my god, no," screamed an anguished Sara as she jumped off the slightly tilted Timepod and ran to what was once the quaint farmhouse, now a burnt and blackened ruin. Split timbers jutted into the air; others still smoldered in a jigsaw jumble on the frozen Earth. The once proud farm bell lay on one side with numerous cracks; the other side was half melted by the intense heat that almost incinerated it. Crushed next to it was a twisted piece of metal with a winter scene of a sleigh pulled by horses. Everywhere she turned, everywhere she looked, were burnt-out buildings. The barn sheds, and cabins were smoldering heaps of scorched and splintered wood surrounded by compacted ash-grey snow and ice that held the frozen imprints left by fire fighter's boots.

Joe and Kate ran over to comfort her. "Sara, I am so sorry," Joe said. "I don't know what to say. This is horrible!"

"Sara," Kate sobbed, "I...I..." and she tightly hugged her.

"Between tears, Sara silently spoke to Jorge, "*Jorge, scan for survivors or any remains.*"

"*Yes, Madam,*" he silently replied. "*By the way, you should know that there is a Burton, Ohio, police car that has spotted us and is heading our way.*"

They all heard a siren and a whoop, whoop as the white patrol car pulled slowly up the long driveway. Its snow tires made a crunching sound as it stopped just feet from where they stood. They could see the officer talking into a palm-sized microphone. He wore a blue uniform and a thick woolen navy-blue winter jacket. As he stepped out of the patrol car, his greeting was polite but suspicious. They hadn't had a chance to change out of the long robes they had worn in Pumbedita. As he walked closer, he wrinkled his nose and quickly stepped back. Coughing and wheezing, he grabbed a folded white handkerchief from his back pocket and held it over his nose. The stink almost made him retch. It reminded him of a dead goat.

"Merry Christmas, folks," the gray-haired, slightly overweight police officer said. "Don't remember seeing you around these parts. What are you doing here at a burned-out farm on Christmas Day?" He parted his coat with one hand and casually rested his fingers around his sidearm.

"Uh, well, officer," Joe said, "we were hired to be part of, uh, a nativity scene and sing Christmas carols for the guests here." Kate looked at her father as if he were nuts.

"Christmas carols," the officer repeated. "Well, if that doesn't sound just like Amari and Jacob. They were the sweetest of folks." The police officer's eyes teared up. A tear ran down his cheek.

Trying to hold back tears herself, Sara asked, "When did this happen, officer? Are there any survivors?"

"Happened late last night, best we can tell," he said, trying without luck to regain his composure. "I just saw them not hours before. Brought them some Christmas cookies that the wife baked. The explosions woke up the whole town. You know, we do have a volunteer fire department, and they all got here as fast as they could, but by the time we got the engines out and everything, there wasn't much left. Don't know what happened. Far as we could tell, it must have been a gas leak. But funny thing is we never smelled any. After we put out the fire, we couldn't find hide nor hair of a soul. Phew, you smell that stink?" he asked. "That dead animal smell would choke the Pope for a month of Sundays. Did you know them well?"

"Uh, no officer," Joe said. "We didn't know them well."

"I'm going to have to ask you folks to leave here. It's just too dangerous. It's a suspicious fire, and we're still investigating." He looked around over the snow-covered ground. "Now, please forgive me, but I know you didn't fly here. I don't see any tire tracks. Where's your car?"

"Oh, it's just around back," Joe said.

"Really?" the officer asked as he loosened the gun strap holding his service revolver. "Why don't you take me to it? As far as I know, there's only one way in, and I know you sure didn't drive by me. You have an ID I can take a gander at?"

Sara, Joe, and Kate looked at each other and slowly walked to the back. "It's in the car," Sara answered. She silently sent a message to Jorge: "*Jorge, stun the man. I can't take it anymore.*"

The Burton, Ohio, police officer stood frozen. Jorge quickly returned the service revolver to its holster and removed the officer's nightstick from the belt ring. Then, he carried the officer to his patrol car and gently placed him in the front seat, putting his safety lap belt around his waist, and rejoined the group.

"Were you able to find anything, Jorge? Anything?" Pleaded Sara.

"I only found a few cells. No bodies. Nothing. Anything and everything from the future has been obliterated."

"Well, this has got to be the work of Albert Beck," Sara said. "He must have another Synth clone trying to cut off our escape. We'll just have to prepare better. Outflank him. Be smarter. He will stop at nothing to get the Amulet. Let's get back to the pod."

Due to the burnt wooden beams below it, the Timepod had settled at an angle. Jorge began to power it up, and the curved sides formed a transparent semicircle. "Where to now?" Joe said.

"Same time, same temporal coordinates, but seventy-five days in the past, Jorge."

"Madam, you know we can't tamper with..."

"...Beck knows it too," Sara shouted. "How can we allow him to, what, I don't know, destroy the known universe? How do we know that he hasn't caused a time distortion whose ripples will change life as we know it forever? I can't believe that life on Earth was created for us to destroy. It doesn't make any sense. We must try and save Namaste. We have an obligation to save Amari, Jacob, and Tyler. It is essential for our survival as a species. Humanity was not meant to live underground."

Kate softly said, "Jorge, please. Just this once."

"Katie. It violates everything I have promised to hold sacrosanct. If we change the past in any manner, we will most assuredly change the future."

There was a momentary silence when Sara said, "But hasn't someone or something changed the future already?"

Joe interrupted, "Look, I don't know if Albert Beck is responsible for this destruction. The only thing we do know is that this devastation was so complete, so utterly total, that not even you could find any remains except fragments from a couple of cells, which I'm sure by now you have been able to identify."

"Yes, that's true," Jorge said. "The fragmentary cellular structures match that of Amari, Jacob, Tyler, and fifteen other people."

"Tyler!" Kate screamed. She hit Jorge with both hands on his chest. "Ouch. That hurt. Take us back!" She put both hands under each armpit for comfort and glowered at the Android.

"If we can prevent innocent people from being destroyed," Sara said, "shouldn't we do our best to do it? Do we exist simply to observe? Where is the justice?"

Jorge took a moment to consider. "On one condition," he said.

"What's that?" Kate put both hands on her hips and had an angry look on her face.

"So as not to alter in any manner historical future timelines, not one of us can tell Amari, Jacob, or Tyler what we have seen or experienced here at this sad place today when we travel back into the past. You must give me your most sacred promise as if you were promising Rabbi Joseph ben Abba."

"Did Rabbi Joseph do something to you?' Sara said.

"He didn't do anything to me. But he did give me a new appreciation for integrity, justice, and kindness." Jorge looked at Sara and continued, "Those qualities were only a subset of my primary programming. Now, do you agree with my conditions? It's taking all my effort to override the programming that forces me to digress if you know what I mean, and I am quite certain you know what I mean."

"Yes," they answered. Moments later, the Timepod disappeared, taking them seventy-five days into the past.

Chapter 18
Safehome Four, 3257 PE

It took weeks to download, check, and re-check the 8.7 Zettabytes of Albert Beck's memories and knowledge into the quantum neural network of Beck's new Synth. Data flowed back and forth from one quantum matrix to another. It began slowly. As the Synth's neural connections grew, more data was layered molecule by molecule, one upon another. Inorganic neural connections duplicated organic neural connections as nucleotide-sized nano-bots became function-specific. The Synth's toes and fingers twitched as nano-neural networks extended, connected, and responded to artificially induced quantum cranial stimuli. What grew in the underground, derisively named birthing tank, was an unholy alliance between science and technology.

Finally, the last kilobyte of data from that which was once Albert Beck's mind was delivered and sealed into the Synth's quantum neural-nanorobotic brain. Then, the newly downloaded and independent quantum brain took time to organize itself. It became conscious of its fingers, hands, and arms. Its legs flexed spasmodically. The tank slowly emptied the yellowish gel-like fluid. As sensitive skin cells were exposed to oxygen, they transferred messages back and forth to the neural cortex along newly created pathways. Within nanoseconds, tiny goose bumps appeared on the skin's surface. His Synth's eyes quickly opened as growth medium drained from around its face, enabling it to see the world for the first time. The eyes were bright green. Expelling gel medium out of its mouth, Albert Beck's new Synth tried to sit up but slipped. Two technicians ran over to help it sit up and acclimate to its new body and surroundings.

"What the hell are these?" Albert Beck screamed as he held in his hands the two large breasts protruding from his hairless chest. He spat liquid from his mouth and stood up, shaking the gel substance from his body. His Synth had long red hair, cinnamon-colored skin, a slender body with a narrow waist, and stood six feet tall. Its face had high cheekbones, piercing green eyes, long lashes, and full lips. Its hands were delicate, with long fingers and small wrists. The Synth's musculature was lithe like a ballet dancer. "What the hell is going on, Doctor? I'm in a woman's body. You think this is a joke, Doctor? I don't see you laughing!"

"No. No, sir, it's, uh, no joke. It's the synth body that Commander Shao ordered. The one I told you about that had already been programmed into the tank," stammered Dr. Takahashi. "Once the process starts, it cannot be aborted."

Beck's new Synth climbed out of the tank as a technician offered it a robe to cover its naked body. It tossed the robe aside. Turning to the scientist, it grabbed her around her neck and pulled her close. A thin sensing device slipped from her hand and fell to the floor. "I remember, Doctor. I remember everything very clearly. It's the only thing that is keeping you alive." He tossed her like a ragdoll onto the floor. "I think that I'll go pay Commander Shao a visit. I'm sure you've already informed him. Perhaps he thinks the joke is on me? But no one jokes at my expense. In the meantime, prepare an Albert Beck synth body for me. I'll return for it." He started to walk toward the circular opening that led out of the lab but stopped at a scanning device.

"But we've never done a synth-to-synth transfer. I don't know if it will work," the scientist shouted after him.

"For your sake, and your family's sake; for your entire line whose eggs and sperm are stored frozen in our vaults, I hope it will." To the scanning device, he said, "This is Albert Beck Synth Eight. Copy my voice print and scan this body. Prepare clothing for a free-spirited hippie female circa 1969.

"Yes, mam," came the reply.

"Mam. I think I like that. Yes, it has a certain ring to it." While the device scanned his body measurements, he thought, *"As if I don't know where they'll go. They'll go to where they feel safe.*

They'll never see me coming." He walked out the door. Under his breath, he muttered, "But first, I pay a visit to Commander Shao."

In the year 3257 PC, most of the underground population looked similar. Over the centuries, intermarriage between people whose skin color was different shades of brown or various shades of white, whose eye shape was rounded or slanted, whose hair color was dark brown or light blonde, whose eye color was light blue, green, hazel, or dark brown, all those cosmetic differences blended together. Variations in height between people of all genetic backgrounds became standardized to a consistent norm. Although civilization on Earth did experience a time when genetic manipulation was widespread among the wealthiest of the population, eventually, that too was outlawed and forbidden due to the possibility of a genetic catastrophe. Under the ground, anti-procreation laws were strictly enforced. Families fortunate enough to survive underground for an unknown future would take turns traveling into the past via Timespan or in suspended hibernation deep within one of the Safehomes. Each Safehome had a commander appointed by the Beck Consortium. Safehome Eight was no different.

Commander Shao felt something he hadn't felt in over two centuries: agitation. Pacing back and forth in his luxuriously recreated 18th-century private quarters, he felt trapped. The ornately furnished French period of Louis the Sixteenth could not alleviate his tension. Although he was judge and jury over the conduct of all the inhabitants of Safehome Eight, only one person was judge and jury over his own conduct, and that person was moments away. He knew he had taken advantage of his position of power to have a synth created for his private amusements. Synths were going to be the saviors of humanity. They were going to make it possible to live again on the surface. Did he really think Albert Beck wouldn't discover what he had done? A primitive emotional response descended over him. He had to escape. He grabbed a clear plastic tube and placed one end against his neck, releasing a chemical stimulant that caused his senses to be heightened. He quickly threw a few sentimental items into a pouch and raced to the door. It opened with a slight hiss.

"Hi, sugar," said the smiling six-foot-tall red-haired woman blocking his way. Quickly, her smile turned into a pout as she sweetly asked, "In a rushy-rush, are we?" She lifted one leg up and kicked him in the chest, sending him flying back into the room. He landed hard on the floor. In seconds, she was on top of him, pinning his hands. "Is this what you wanted? These hips? These breasts?" She bent over him, her long red hair cascading down the sides of her face. "These lips?" she teased. She released his hands and smacked him in the face once, twice, three times.

"Albert. I'm s-sorry."

"You're sorry? You weak little..." In a flash, she was off of him; one hand grabbed his neck, and her other hand grabbed Shao's crotch and threw him across the room as if he weighed nothing at all. He landed hard on an ancient harpsichord, breaking it apart. The pieces scattered like splinters over the floor. She towered over him. "Now, get up. We may not need to make a civilization of synths."

"What do you mean?"

She yanked him up with disgust. "While I have been working on the Synth project to protect our species, Dr. Sara Lazarus has discovered a new energy source. Her energy source may make the Earth habitable, not in three-hundred-thousand years, but now. We may not need to download our consciousness into these fabricated Synths for survival. As Synths, humanity will end at Homo Sapiens Prime. It won't have any chance to progress. It will be static and die as our cellular structure diminishes each time we transport or enter cryogenic suspension. Sara Lazarus's new discovery is our best chance at long-term survival. Right now, I believe Sara and the energy source are in 1969. You and I are going to go there and retrieve it. Now, clean yourself up and fabricate clothes to make you look like a pot-smoking, free-love hippie in 1969." She walked closer to him and pinched his cheek. "We'll be boyfriend and girlfriend. Won't that be fun?"

Chapter 19
Namaste, December 24, 1969

"Welcome to Namaste, Commander Shao!" Jacob exclaimed as the farm's two newest visitors stepped off their Timepod. He extended his hand to shake the Commanders. "It's not often that we are honored by a visit from a Safehome Commander. And on the day before Christmas, no less!"

"Thank you, my friend. Please, allow me to introduce my..."

"Security Assistant, Ruby Jones," interrupted Albert's Synth. She gave Jacob's hand a firm shake. As she did, the long leather fringe sewn onto her beige suede coat swung back and forth.

Jacob smiled and said, "Well, I'm sure there won't be any security problems here at Namaste. We are a safe refuge here in 1969."

"And I'm here to make sure it stays that way for the Commander," Ruby said with her most sincere smile.

"Yes. Of course. I'll help you with your bags. Amari is just putting the finishing touches on Christmas Eve dinner for everyone, so please follow me to the house where you can relax and join our other guests."

Although the Ohio winter sun was bright, the temperature outside felt like arctic cold. The strong wind didn't help. It sent a shiver through anyone brave enough to venture outdoors. The trio trudged silently over the fields, their boots crunching as they strode slowly across the newly fallen snow. The old farmhouse was decorated along its roofline with long strings of multi-colored Christmas lights. Within each bedroom window glowed tall electric candles with flickering bulbs that looked as if they were real flames. Each candle was encircled by a small green wreath. Commander Shao and his security assistant followed Jacob up the freshly shoveled front flagstone walk and the snow-cleared flight of grey-painted wooden steps to the porch. Jacob opened the squeaky wooden oak front door. A hand-made holly-berry wreath, its silver Christmas bells tinkling, knocked against the door's beveled glass surface as it was pulled shut. They walked into the hall that separated the living room from the dining room and put their winter coats on the antique oak hall tree in the vestibule.

It was warm inside and smelled of freshly baked bread, oven-roasted turkey, and smoke from the living room fireplace. Long tapered candles throughout the downstairs warmed the area in a soft, gentle glow. A freshly cut pine tree added its pungent Christmas scent. The tree was draped in red, yellow, blue, orange, and white twinkling lights. A long string of fluffy-white popcorn circled the tree from the star at the top to the long branches at the bottom, where presents had been set. Some branches even held red and white striped candy canes. Fighting for space between the lights, popcorn-on-a-string, and candy canes were tiny hand-made corn-husk angels, each cinched at their waists with slim ribbons of gold.

Introductions were made around the large oval dinner table covered in a bright red tablecloth with red and green plaid napkins. Brightly polished silver, which was only used for special occasions, and lead crystal stemware was set at each place for guests to enjoy. The table's centerpiece was a miniature Santa with a bag of presents in a sleigh pulled by reindeer that Jacob had made. While each of the fifteen people stood up and told a little about their background, Albert Beck's Synth scanned the room and quickly saw that Sara, Joe, and Kate were not in attendance. Christmas music played in the background as Tyler helped his mother carry in never-ending platters of gastronomic delights.

Amari had outdone herself: steaming garlic-mashed potatoes, hot yams with brown sugar and melted butter, string beans with button-sized pearl onions and mushrooms, sliced ham marinated in raisins, cloves, and honey, Amari's famous melt-in-your-mouth stuffing with onions, carrots, and peas, and of course, the piece-de-resistance, a giant perfectly cooked golden turkey. Everyone applauded as Tyler placed the bird before his dad for carving.

While the group focused on watching Jacob slice the turkey, telling him what a fantastic job he was doing, Beck's Synth slipped a palm-sized Quantum Inverter she had hidden within the folds of her long skirt and attached the device to the table's underside. She didn't even allow herself a half smile. She cooed, "Jacob, you are definitely up for the Carver of the Year award! Such smoothness. Such dexterity!" The Synth raised a glass of wine for a toast, "To Jacob, Amari, and their son Tyler, for preparing such a wonderful and hospitable Christmas Eve dinner! Hugs and kisses to you all!"

The group happily responded, "*Here, here!*" and "*To Jacob and Amari.*" Ruby smiled broadly as holiday songs from WKSU FM's Christmas program provided joyous commercial free music from the kitchen's radio.

After the dishes were cleared from the fabulous meal, Amari entered the dining room with pies in both hands. Like a schoolteacher to her first-grade class, she said, "Now, I did tell you to leave room for dessert." Tyler followed with two more pies. The guests groaned.

"Impossible, I can't do it," a guest said.

Another admitted, "I'm going to burst if I eat another thing."

But Amari wasn't having any of it. "Well, you can choose apple, cherry, pumpkin, or our famous Shaker lemon. But, if you're too full, I can take them away..."

Some guests decided to take their pie into the living room and sing Christmas carols. At the same time, Tyler accompanied them on the old upright piano. Others remained seated around the dining room table, too stuffed to move. Jacob came into the living room and added more logs to the fire. "Don't want this fire to get too low. It gets cold here in Ohio." But just then, the doorbell rang. Jacob got up to see who it was. "Now, who in tarnation can that be on Christmas Eve?"

An older, slightly overweight policeman was at the door. "Why, Sergeant Scott, Merry Christmas! Come on in and have some of Amari's pies!"

The policeman walked into the house, knocked the snow off his boots, and removed his hat. Commander Shao and Ruby, on the couch, joined the others in saying, "Merry Christmas, Sergeant Scott."

"Well, a Merry Christmas to you folks, too. I just stopped by to give you some Christmas cookies the wife baked." He handed Jacob a tin of homemade cookies. A Christmas scene of laughing children in a horse-drawn sleigh was imprinted on the tin. The colorful Christmas cookies were protected by a covering of clear Saran Wrap.

"Now, Scotty, don't go. It's Christmas Eve. Let me warm you up with some coffee. I know how you love Amari's pie."

"Oh, Jacob, I can't. Got to skidoodle. Have a few more deliveries to make. But you give the misses a big Christmas hug for me. Just between you and me, Christmas Eve is kind of slow 'round here. 'Cept, of course, for reports of a large red sleigh and reindeer in the sky. But thank you, my friend. 'Night, folks. Merry Christmas!"

"Merry Christmas," said Ruby and waved. The smile remained on her face a little too long.

One by one, each guest said goodnight. Some slowly walked upstairs to their bedrooms on the second floor while others put on heavy winter coats to keep themselves warm as they rushed to the guest cabins outside. Ruby and Commander Shao were still sitting on the overstuffed couch, watching the fire's last glowing dark red embers snap and pop. The burning embers in the fireplace and the colorful Christmas tree lights were the comfy room's only illumination. Amari, Jacob, and Tyler were the last to bid them a good night.

"We're so happy you could join us for Christmas at Namaste," Amari said. "I hope you come back again."

"Thank you for your warm hospitality. I will tell everyone in Safehome Eight to prioritize it!"

"Yes, thank you for your kindness," Ruby said. "I think I'm going to need to walk some of this meal off," she laughed. "Would it be a problem if the Commander and I take a walk outside before we retire? It would be a real treat for us."

"Why, of course, not at all," Jacob said. "It is beautiful this time of night. Quiet and serene. No one will bother you."

"I'm counting on it," Ruby smiled.

"If you'd like me to go with you and give you a quick tour," Tyler said, "I'd be happy to."

"Oh, you needn't trouble yourself, Tyler. We'll be fine," Ruby said.

Tyler smiled shyly. "Really, it's no trouble at all. It would be my pleasure."

"In that case, lead the way," Shao said.

Tyler got his winter coat as Jacob and Amari trudged upstairs after a long day of cooking and entertaining. While Tyler was distracted, Ruby tossed a Quantum Inverter among the Christmas presents under the tree.

"What a nice surprise you will be," she whispered to the bomb. "Such a cutie!" she patted a wrapped present next to the implosive device and smiled.

Walking outside at zero degrees, their exhales became like human smokestacks puffing out little clouds of steam. The frozen snow crunched under their boots as Tyler showed them one outside building and then another. Within each building, Ruby hid a Quantum Inverter. They were programmed to activate in groups of three, with each group separated by fifteen seconds. The destruction caused by an Inverter is irreversible.

The Quantum Inverter was unintentionally discovered by Böoth-Heideger at the University of Leipzig when they accidentally created a randomized wormhole within the University's Tokamak reactor. They learned that a quantum wormhole expands exponentially and inverts upon itself due to protonic wobble, creating additional wormholes until a critical mass is reached. When that point is achieved, all matter within fifty meters is drawn into the created wormholes and forcefully spewed back out. The particle size depends on the length of the contractions, the number of quantum wormholes generated, the mass, and the strength of the atomic bonds.

The last structure they arrived at was a mid-sized barn. "This, of course," Tyler said as he swung open the barn's door, "is the pod arrival and departure chamber. We obviously fabricated it to look like a barn."

"And where are the pods?" Ruby said.

"Oh, they're underground being charged. Let me show you." Tyler turned a switch mounted on a thick vertical beam. The center floor area, which looked like planked wood, changed into a smooth surface that swiftly opened wide, turning out like an iris. A Timepod silently rose up from the floor below.

Ruby exclaimed, "This is simply incredible. I mean, it even smells like a barn. There's hay on the floor, and look over here."

Turning away from Tyler, she approached a large wooden barrel, exclaiming, "You even have farm tools!" She tossed another Quantum Inverter into the hay.

But she wasn't smooth enough or fast enough for Tyler. Out of the corner of his eye, he saw her toss something. "What the hell is that?" he asked, running over to the hay-covered floor. He stopped immediately when he saw it. He knew what it was. "What? An Inverter? Who are you?" The Synth allowed him access to its mind. A look of utter shock came over his face. "Albert Beck?"

Swiftly, the Synth grabbed the metal pitchfork that rested against the wooden barrel and viciously swung it deep into Tyler's chest. The fork's five tines punctured his heart and lungs and exited out the back. His knees buckled. Blood came up out of his mouth. His arms and legs twitched spasmodically as Beck's Synth lifted the pitchfork high into the air.

"Bu...but...why...?" Tyler was able to spit out.

"Because I'm a mean bastard, and you're in my way, that's why!" Ruby savagely flung the impaled, bleeding youth across the floor. Casually, she tossed a dozen more Quantum Inverters into the sub-basement. "This building will take more than one." Then she turned and looked for Commander Shao.

Shao could not believe what he had just seen. He quickly looked one way and then the other, trying to figure out if he could escape. Making a run for the door, Ruby caught him by his shirt. She threw him back into the room so hard that he slid along the smooth floor and bumped against the Timepod. The Synth ran to a wall that held tools and found just what she wanted: a curved sickle. Casually, she walked back to the cowering man.

"Wha, what are you going to do?" asked the frightened Shao. "Have you gone crazy? I'm Commander of Safehome Eight!"

"What am I going to do, Shao?" She bent down and was nose-to-nose with him. She smiled and pushed her left hand's long, slender fingers through his hair. She gripped his hair firmly. "Well, my friend, as they say, it's payback time." She quickly stood up and pulled him up with her. His feet dangled four inches above the floor. Shao's eyes grew wide, realizing the impending horror.

"No! No!" he screamed, "You need me." His feet flailed. He tried to use both hands to remove her one hand that held him by his hair. "I, I helped you here. I can help you anywhere."

"I work alone." With the sickle held firmly in her right hand, she reached back and, with one powerful stroke, sliced his neck so completely that his body crumpled to the ground, spraying bright red blood over the floor. It happened so fast that his vocal cords made a gurgling sound. "Sorry. Didn't quite catch that." She tossed Shao's severed head aside and stepped up onto the Timepod's platform. She glanced down at herself. "Now, look at me. You've ruined my blouse!" She smeared drops of blood across the fabric and flicked her long red hair back, removing it from her face and eyes. "Now, where shall we start our hunt?" she asked out loud. "Where is that naughty little android?" Moments later, the Timepod disappeared, and the detonations began.

The first blast was preceded by an otherworldly high-pitched whine that grew in intensity until the entire farmhouse structure imploded into the Earth and then, moments later, exploded with such a powerful force that many people later said they were able to feel the shockwaves on their skin. Pieces of wood and metal rained down. The first blast triggered the second, and the second blast triggered the third. By the time the local volunteer fire department arrived, there was only burning wood and twisted metal. No survivors. No bodies. No buildings. Namaste was gone.

Chapter 20
October 12, 1969

Some Ohioans may argue about what the most beautiful time of year is. To some, it's the fluffy white snow and joyous lights of the Christmas season; to others, it's tall, green-stemmed tulips, trumpeting yellow daffodils, or the sweet taste of maple syrup in spring; still others love the lazy days of lemonade summers, just picked sweet corn flawlessly roasted, and spectacular fireworks celebrating the 4th of July. Sara's favorite was autumn: when leaves that were once bright green change into hues of orange marmalades, burgundy reds, bubble gum pinks, and mustard yellows, all tenaciously holding onto the quickly vanishing veins of key lime green so as not to forget what just departed. In Ohio, nature's autumn crazy quilt is nothing if not miraculous. And on this particular Sunday, October 12, 1969, the leaves were at their peak: at their most intensely stupendous, colorful perfection.

The Timepod materialized in the barn. It was not yet eight in the morning, but Sara knew everyone would be up as Joe and Jorge swung open the barn's large wooden-like doors; bright early-morning sunshine washed over them. Outside, stacks of golden bales of hay, morning dew still clinging, and sunlight streaming through tall sugar maple, birch, and oak trees turned their abundant leaves into thousands of multi-colored stained-glass windows. Amari heard the pod appear and walked out of the kitchen's rear door, drying her hands on her checkered apron. When she saw who it was, she screamed and ran towards them with arms opened wide.

"Why didn't you tell me you were on your way?" She quickly stepped back and pulled her apron up to her nose. "Boy, do you stink, woman!" She saw Sara was crying and became concerned. "Why the tears, honey?"

"Oh, I, we're just so happy to be back," Sara said, wiping the tears from her eyes.

"Well, let me give you all a big hug and a bath! You go first, Katie. You smell the worst!"

"Oh, it's the goat bladder. I'm used to it now, but I guess it needs to be in the sun a little bit more."

Walking back to the farmhouse, Amari put her arms around Kate's shoulders. She smiled, "Sweetie, I don't think any amount of sunlight is going to take that much stink off that thing, but you can try. Hang it on the clothesline before you come inside."

As they walked into the kitchen, Joe said, "Where's Jacob and Tyler?"

"Oh, they've been up and out early. It's the last day of the Apple Butter Festival over at Century Village, and they've gone to stock up our display tent. Once you get washed up and get something in your bellies, we'll drive over and help them."

"Excuse me, madam," Jorge said, "but I've just received a coded quantum message alert that Albert Beck, Terrestrial Governor for Earth, has suspended all time travel until further notice."

"That's highly unusual," Amari said. "I wonder why?"

Sara had a worried look on her face. "When did you receive it, Jorge?"

"Just as we walked into the kitchen, madam. I immediately shut down all power systems, not of twentieth-century technology."

Silently, Sara asked Jorge, "*Do you think he will be able to track our displacement signature?*"

"*It's only a matter of time, madam.*"

"*Then we must prepare, Jorge. Make sure that Katie is always safe.*"

"*Yes, of course, madam.*"

"It is highly unusual, Amari. But I'm sure it's all for our welfare, Sara said. "Anyway, let's not concern ourselves. There's nothing we can do about it anyway. Let's get cleaned up and enjoy the day. Who knows how long we will be here, right Joe?"

"Absolutely. Shave and shower, or shower and shave. It doesn't matter to me. You go first, Katie. The stink from the bladder must have rubbed off on you. But do me a favor. Please don't use up all the hot water, okay? You and your thirty-minute showers."

"Dad, I never use up all the hot water. I always leave you *some*!" she said, laughing as she ran up the stairs.

An hour and a half later, their breakfast was almost done, and the kitchen radio was tuned to WMMS. "Okay, everyone, we gotta get going," Amari said as she clicked off the radio. "Just put the dishes in the sink; we'll take care of them when we get back." She looked at her watch. "By now, Jacob and Tyler must be wondering where I am."

Sara, Kate, and her dad pushed back their chairs. Joe shoved a last bite of pancake into his mouth, and Sara took a quick sip of tea before clearing the table. Since it was the middle of October, they were all dressed in warm wool jackets and hats. Even though it was sunny, it was still cold. The old station wagon had a little trouble starting up, so Jorge lifted the hood and put his hand on the battery to give it a quick jump charge. "Not too much, Jorge or you'll blow the damn thing up!" Amari yelled. When the car finally turned over, they headed toward the site of Burton's famous Apple Butter Festival at the Century Village Museum.

Most museums are buildings that showcase different types of art from various centuries. Unlike a building that houses art,

Century Village could only be compared to an area like Historic
Colonial Williamsburg in Virginia, but in a more down-home, laid-
back way. The area contains about twenty-four historic buildings that
authentically recreate what life in a Western Reserve village was like
in 1789. A small wooden church, one-room schoolhouse, library,
Marshall's office, blacksmith shop, general store, barn, and weaver's
house were all either existing where they stood or taken down and
reassembled on sixty-five rolling acres in Burton, Ohio. The
interiors contained original art and functioning items from the 18th
and 19th centuries.

There are famous food festivals all over the United States:
Mount Olive, North Carolina has its incredible Pickle Festival,
where one can taste their famous fried pickle, available in both
spears and sliced chips; not to be out-done, Gilroy, California has
their, smell-it-from-five-miles-away Garlic Festival, where one can
sample their surprisingly good garlic ice cream and garlic fries.
However, the Burton, Ohio Apple Butter Festival, which has been
held in Burton since about 1947, is more about comfort food. It
began when World War II was over, and families wanted to go
somewhere close and enjoy themselves safely and in the simple life
experiences of days gone by. Caravans of families drive from Ohio,
Pennsylvania, West Virginia, and Indiana. In a way, it's like what the
families from Sara's time do. The people from the future Earth of
3257 go back in time when living was simpler, when everyone didn't
know each other's thoughts, and when life was not as frenetic or
confined.

Amari drove through the back roads to Century Village. She
wanted no part of the miles of bumper-to-bumper cars slowly
inching along State Route 87. It was fine with Kate, Sara, and Joe.
Everywhere they looked, it was like a painting come to life: colorful
fall foliage and grazing dairy cows protected behind grey weathered
fences on one side of the road, and fields of orange pumpkins with
children laughing and carrying ones almost too big for them to hold
on the opposite side. After a few minutes, she slowly drove the old
station wagon into the area for exhibitor parking, just missing a big

rut that would have taken out an axel. When she found a parking space and turned off the ignition, the old car chugged for a few seconds and then died. They all got out, stretched, and took a deep breath. Unlike the re-circulated air inside a Safehome or the polluted air of Manhattan, the mid-morning October air of Burton smelled fresh and sweet and crisp, just like baked apples sprinkled with nutmeg and cinnamon.

The very first thing one notices upon entering the bustling Apple Butter Festival are rows of copper pots so large that the word cauldron seems humbling. Each massive, thick-walled, hand-wrought copper cauldron sits upon fires continually stoked by hearty souls that magically slip hand-chopped wood logs under their heavy, demanding, squat bodies. Within each gaping top opening is a searing mixture of boiling apples, apple cider, cloves, and cinnamon that churn and froth like dancers lost in a tango's final crescendo. Each boiling caldron is carefully watched over and constantly stirred by individual cooks who take immense pride in perfecting their family's secret apple butter recipes.

Since the festival's creation, other attractions have been added to the festivities. Along one side of the cooking area are large white tents. Tents are essential in October in Northeast Ohio because one never knows when it will rain. Under some tents, merchants sell homemade thick-sliced bread topped with a generous serving of freshly made hot apple butter so dense that it wouldn't dare drip down any of the four sides. For a modest charge, one may add homemade peanut butter, freshly cut bananas, or hot roasted pecans that will turn, as mother nature transforms a caterpillar into a butterfly, a simple snack into a gastronomic delight.

Further down in another tent, one can find honest, sweet apple cider for sale, hot or cold, filtered or not. In another area covered with yellow straw, a merchant stands in a sea of bright orange pumpkins, just waiting for a child to find and take home his or her special one. There are pumpkin coloring and cutting contests, sack races, pony rides, and down-home fiddle music, which one can only hear at county fairs. There was also a large green and white banner in front of one tent that proclaimed:

Namaste Farms of Burton, Ohio,

Famous Apple Butter and Shaker Lemon Pies.

Jacob and Tyler were swamped selling Mason jars full of the farm's apple butter and whole lemon pies to the crowd standing five deep in front of their tent. At first, they didn't see Amari, Sara, Kate, and Joe. Jorge had, of course, been invisible since they left the farm. It wasn't until the four walked behind the long, green-draped selling table that Jacob looked up and said, "Well, it's about time you got here!"

"I beg your pardon, mister, high and mighty," Amari said, "we had early-morning visitors."

"Well, I'll be..." Jacob happily stopped what he was doing and hugged everyone. "Great to have you all back. Can't wait to hear all about it." He quickly looked around, saw what he needed, and handed them all green aprons. "But first, put on these aprons and start selling. We sure can use your help."

"Hi," Kate said to Tyler, unable to look him straight in the eye.

"Uh, hi. How's it going?"

Her eyes began to tear up. "Uh, okay, I guess. Good to see you."

"What's the matter? Why are you crying?"

"Oh, it's nothing, really. It's just so beautiful here and..." She couldn't stand it anymore and quickly turned and gave him a long hug. He hugged her back the best he could with one arm while holding a slice of lemon pie on a paper plate in his other hand. She broke away and said, "I was so pissed at you!"

"Huh? Are you nuts or something? What'd I do?"

"I saw how you looked at that tall, long-haired blonde girl. I saw the smile on your face as we left."

"Hey, I'm a guy. What-do-you-want-from-me?"

"*Hey, I'm a guy,*" Kate repeated, trying her best to sound like a jock. "Hey, watdoyawantfromme, huh? I'm a guy, huh?" She stretched her arms apart, raised her thumbs up, pointed them out to the side, and nodded her head up and down like a bobblehead doll. Then she grabbed her crotch.

"What is with you, woman?"

"Nothing!" Kate shouted as she removed her apron, threw it on the ground, and ran out of the tent in tears.

Amari and Jacob looked at each other in bewilderment. Then they looked at Sara and Joe, who both looked worried. Amari asked, "What's going on here? Is there something you're not telling us?"

"We'll talk later." Turning to Tyler, she said, "Tyler, why don't you go after her?"

"What did I do? What did I do?"

"You didn't do anything. She's been through a lot. Just go find her and try to show her around. *And you watch them too, Jorge,*" Sara added silently.

"*Of course, Madam.*"

"Come on, Joe, let's sell some apple butter," Sara softly said as she brushed a strand of dark hair away from her face, trying to cover up wiping away her own tears.

Tyler stopped at the tent across from theirs and bought two cups of steaming hot apple cider before he searched for Katie. The festival was crowded with thousands of people: families with strollers, kids running this way and that in a jumble of laughter, bobbing heads, knit caps, and plaid shirts. He found her leaning against a weathered grey fence post, watching children ride ponies around a circular ring.

"Want to go riding?"

"Leave me alone," she replied and turned her head away.

"I bring sweet and spicy magical potion as an offering of atonement for being a horny guy." From behind, he held a cup of hot cider under her nose. She tried really hard not to smile and turned around to face him, head lowered.

"Thanks." She smelled the spiced cider and took a sip. "When I was a little girl, we drove up to Connecticut on Sundays. At least once every October. My mom knew a family that owned an apple orchard in Cheshire. They also made stained glass sun catchers. I still have one in my room."

"It sounds like a good memory."

"It is." She took a deep breath. "I miss my mom a lot. It was one of the things that we did together as a family."

"You up for a walk and talk?" She nodded yes, and he timidly reached to hold her hand. She stopped. Quickly put her arm around and through his and leaned close against him. He smiled. Her touch made him feel like a million bucks. "So, you had a tough time?"

"You might say that." She whispered in his ear, "I killed Albert Beck."

"You wa-what," he stammered. Are you kidding me?"

"Nope. Sliced and diced. Didn't mean to."

"And Sara and your dad know?"

"They were there." She took a long sip of apple cider. "When he tried to take the Amulet from around my neck, he was sliced in half. Well, maybe quarters. Yeah, more like quarters."

"That is so dark! A lot of blood and guts, huh?"

"Nope. Not a drop."

"Wa, wait, wait, wait. If someone is sliced in half..."

"Quarters."

"Okay. Whatever. Quarters. There has got to be blood."

"Well, there would have been if he wasn't a Synth."

"What the hell's that?"

And she told him everything that had happened to her except, of course, his, his family's, and Namaste's destruction. She held him tight as his eyes opened wide in disbelief. After about an hour of mostly a one-way conversation, interrupted now and then by his "Wows!" and "Well, close the front door!" They found themselves away from the festival's crowds, sitting on the football-field-sized tree-lined center green near Burton's famous log cabin Sugar Shack. Kate was talked out. The entire ground area where they sat was covered by a crazy quilt created from fallen multi-colored maple leaves. She picked one up in silence and twirled the leaf's stem around and around between her thumb and forefinger.

"I don't know what to say. It just sounds so amazing."

"I know. It's all so strange. Time travel. Back and forth. And this amazing Amulet of mine."

"May I see it?"

"Sure. Look, but don't touch, or you'll be blasted into that log cabin over there." She showed him the Hand of El Shaddai, which glowed in the afternoon sun.

"Amazing." He gently touched her cheek and smiled. Slowly, Tyler bent his head and kissed her tenderly. She closed her eyes and kissed him back. It was her first real kiss. She stopped twirling the leaf. She put her arms around him and drew him to her. She thought to herself how nice he smelled and how happy she felt. Then suddenly, they both heard a " *WHOOP WHOOP.*" Parting simultaneously, they saw the white patrol car from the Burton, Ohio, PD pull up to where they were.

"Hi, Sargent Scott." Tyler waved as a red blush spread over his face. Kate waved, too, as the older police officer smiled and slowly drove away.

"I guess we better be getting back," Kate said with a smile.

"I guess so." He stood up and offered his hand to help her up. He pulled her to him and kissed her long and hard. "I'm glad you're back safe and sound."

She bit her lower lip and smiled. "I am, too." They slowly walked together hand-in-hand, stopping to kiss now and then, back to the Apple Butter Festival.

As he invisibly observed them from across the street, Jorge silently communicated to Sara, "*Madam, all is well in Burton, Ohio, or as they so aptly phrased it in 1969, suck-face has commenced and has been accepted by both parties, predicated, of course, upon steadily increasing concentrations of endorphins.*"

Chapter 21

That evening, as a slight breeze whispered between the ash and maple trees, gently encouraging more colorful leaves to release and float towards the Earth, autumn calm settled over Geauga County. Burton's yearly Apple Butter Festival was over; the merchants packed up their tents and sold their remaining food or craft items. The unsold pumpkins were placed in wooden crates and taken to other pumpkin patches; the fires that had once heated boiling hand-wrought copper caldrons were put to rest, and thousands of visitors returned to their homes. Around the town square, store displays were decorated with cut-out flying black bats, witches on broomsticks, evil-looking orange pumpkins, and wispy white ghosts for Burton's next celebration, Halloween. And the last dinner dishes were dried and put away in Namaste's cozy kitchen.

"Well, I think that was the best festival ever," Jacob said. "I mean, we sold out. Simply sold out."

"You mean we don't have any more lemon pies or apple butter?" Kate said.

"Hey, that is simply not allowed," Tyler said. "If I have to go back in time and get some..."

"...Now, we'll have none of that, young man. Whoever heard of going back in time for pie!" Amari said. "I've saved one for us. Now, you four scoot, go on. I'll bring it into the living room. Your dad and I will finish up here."

"Well, I was just thinking of Joe and Sara."

"Yes, Tyler, I'm sure you were." Amari rolled her eyes at her husband, who rolled his eyes back in response. Kate had her arm hooked through Tyler's and started to laugh.

"I..." Tyler got out before Kate put her hand over his mouth and pulled him toward the living room.

"Yuck! You licked my hand." Kate said as she wiped it off on her skirt and dashed into the living room.

"Well, it serves you right for putting it over my mouth!" Tyler laughed as he ran after her.

While silently observing the kitchen's action, Joe asked Sara, "When did they grow up? I'm feeling old."

Sara smiled. "Well, you're not as old as me." She pretended to help him up from a chair. "Come on, old man. Let me help you up," she teased.

"Oh, I am gonna get you good!" He grabbed a damp dish towel at opposite corners, quickly spun it around, and flicked it at her three times as she ran away laughing.

Jacob turned to Amari. "This usually happens when spring is in the air."

"Well, honey, when you time travel, it mixes everything up. I mean, for some reason, I still love you." She kissed him on the cheek. He laughed, giving her a big squeeze that lifted her off the ground.

"And I love you too, sweetie."

"Oh, now put me down, or you'll hurt your back. Here." she shoved a stack of small dessert plates at him. "Now, take these dishes into the living room. I'll bring the pie."

As Jacob walked into the living room, Jorge placed a new log in the fireplace, causing bright orange sparks to crackle and fly up the chimney. The fire warmed the area with its heat. Soft flickering light bounced off the walls while a musty-smoky aroma calmed the senses, helping to relax everyone from a busy day. Amari followed Jacob with the napkins, forks, and her famous Shaker Lemon pie.

"I'm just sorry that Jorge can't enjoy this pie like we can," Amari said as she placed the pie on the wooden table.

"Well, I'm not," Tyler said. "More for us!"

Jorge responded quickly, "I assure you it is quite all right, Amari. It would only gum up my insides. I can, however, understand your fondness, Tyler, for something tart and sweet simultaneously, the juxtaposition of which from a sensory point-of-view must be most tantalizing, if not confusing, and thoroughly spectacular for the mammalian brain."

"I don't think I could have said it better myself," Joe said, enjoying a large forkful of lemon pie and smiling like a Cheshire Cat. "So, Tyler, tell me, what's it like to be put down by an android?"

"I will get him back when he least expects it. Better sleep with one eye open, Jorge." Tyler pointed two fingers at his eyes and then pointed the same two fingers at Jorge.

As Kate finished her pie, she said, "So, what's on for tomorrow?"

"Well, I thought that tomorrow we could get some pumpkins from our pumpkin patch and load them on our truck and drop them off at the Geauga County food bank," Jacob said.

Amari added, "It's what we always do this time of year. We can't possibly use all the pumpkins we plant for ourselves, so we give them to the food bank for distribution."

"That'll be a nice thing to do," Sara said. "We can start after breakfast. But right now," she stood up and stretched, "I am going to bed. See you all tomorrow."

Amari and Jacob said their goodnights and slowly made their way upstairs. Joe was left alone looking at his daughter and Tyler holding hands when Jorge said, "I will take it upon myself to clean up and put things away. You can go to sleep, Joe."

"Uh," Joe said.

Kate said way too sweetly, "Yes, Dad, why don't you go...to sleep?"

"I'm waiting for Tyler," Joe said.

Tying his best not to grin, Tyler said, "It's ok, sir, I don't need any help."

Joe looked from Kate to Tyler and back again. "Well, ok. I'm going." He got up and started walking to the stairs leading to the second floor when he quickly turned around. "See you tomorrow."

"Goodnight, Dad."

"Goodnight, sir." Tyler squeezed Kate's hand tightly.

"Yeah. Ok. Goodnight." And Joe climbed the stairs as Jorge removed the dishes and took them into the kitchen to clean.

They were all over each other in seconds. She was on top of him. He was on top of her. She kissed him long and hard and put her hands through his hair.

"Ahem. Ahem." Jorge stood in front of them, hands on his hips, or where his hips would have been if he had hips. They stopped their award-winning kiss long enough to look at him. They were both red-faced and sweating. "Getting a little warm, are we?"

"Uh," Kate said. Then she looked wide-eyed at Tyler. "Hey, what's that hard thing..." she pushed him away and sat up. He grabbed a handy pillow and put it in his lap. They both smiled innocently at Jorge.

"I know, I know," Jorge intoned, "I am your worst nightmare." He looked from one to the other. "Your father and your father rolled into one. So, Kate, say goodnight to Tyler and go to sleep." Reluctantly, she gave Tyler a sweet kiss and hug and slowly walked upstairs, turning around twice to blow him kisses. "Now, Tyler, I can sense by your temperature and lowering blood pressure that you are now able to go to your room, too."

"Uh, yes."

"And we'll keep this between ourselves?"

"You're the best, Jorge." He gave the android high fives. "Ow!" Tyler held his hurting right hand as he walked upstairs to bed. Jorge then moved from room to room and turned off the downstairs lights. He made sure that the fire was on its last glowing embers before putting himself on stand-down alert for the night ahead. About half an hour later, he noticed candlelight when Joe's bedroom door opened and quietly closed. There was a soft tap on Sara's door. Joe quickly entered Sara's bedroom. He was careful to be quiet. Only squeaking sounds from his footsteps, walking over ancient wooden floorboards, were heard.

"I couldn't sleep," Joe whispered, standing next to Sara's bed.

"Neither could I," she whispered, turning down the quilted covers and moving over. "Come on in?" They both snuggled together under soft sheets. "Your feet are cold."

"I know. Sorry." He whispered back.

"Not to worry, I'll warm them up," she smiled in the flickering candle-lit bedroom.

He wasn't sure if he kissed her first or if she kissed him, but it didn't matter. They kissed each other long and hard. She smiled and arched her back when he kissed her neck and ears with tiny kisses. She kissed his eyes and mouth and turned onto him, threading her fingers through his. Then, she removed her nightgown and his pajama top and leaned over on top of him so he could feel her weight as he felt the smooth, soft skin of her back. He hadn't made love to a woman since his wife, Lauren, died. But this woman from the future, this Sara, had awoken a part of himself that he had locked up, put away, and forgotten. As they hugged, kissed, and discovered each other, she thought about her decades in a suspension animation chamber, the missed opportunities and lost chances; she thought about the men in her life who had died or had been too intimidated to pursue her because of her brilliance. She gave all her longing and desire to this man from the past, this Certified Public Account. If the power of their love could be harnessed, it would have lit up the night sky like the aurora borealis lights up the heavens.

Kate, too, was wide awake under the covers, smiling. She held one hand around her glowing Amulet. She couldn't believe the intense feelings of love she felt for Tyler. She looked around her room and watched leaping grey shadows caused by the flickering candle on her nightstand move and shift as if the furniture and picture frames were imbued with a spirit life of their own. And she thought about her mother, who she loved so much, trapped in the heaving mass of quicksand-like evil darkness circling the Earth. She knew what she had to do. She had to save her mother's eternal spirit from an eternity of horror.

She closed her eyes and tried to relax, putting the day's excitement away into another corner of her mind. Her breathing became slow and regular. She remembered back to the garden in Pumbedita and how she felt then. Slowly, her eternal spirit, that part of her which she is and always has been, gently lifted away from her physical body and hovered above it. Her eyes opened as she looked around her room, smiled, and simply thought, *"To Mom!"* And at the speed of thought, she shot up through the roof, over the treetops, and into the night sky to that other place, that other dimension between life and death where some souls are trapped, attracted by an evil that can never be destroyed.

At that exact moment, a tall, stunningly beautiful woman with long red hair, hands curled in tight fists ready for a fight, angrily marched through the now-barren hay fields in a white tight-fitting one-piece jumpsuit. The Synth that was Albert Beck had found them by tracking Jorge's internal quantum processor. She had materialized the Timepod at coordinates far from the house so as not to be heard or seen. The element of surprise was crucial. When she got close to the house, she stopped and remained motionless. Only the October wind ruffled her red hair, whipping it across her green eyes and perfectly sculpted face.

Ruby thought to herself, *"As for Jorge, I'll take care of that android right now."* She raised her left arm and looked at the area on her wrist, where, if she had been human, her pulse would have been located. A blue rectangle appeared with four symbols. She pressed one that looked like a circle within another circle. A sub-sonic pulse from within her penetrated the farmhouse, shutting down Jorge before he could issue an alarm.

She slowly crept around the old home, stopping twice to listen intently. Her enhanced hearing picked up every sound, from the hissing pilot lights on the stove, and the kitchen's dripping faucet to the rhythmic breathing of six humans on the second floor. Inching her way around the house, she knew it was time to make her move. Like a feline stalking its prey, she quickly jumped from the ground to the railing that encircled the porch and stopped. She waited, not moving a muscle until her hearing verified that no one had been disturbed. She then slowly rose and grabbed onto the overhang that protected the front porch from the elements. She pulled herself up, slowly brought up one leg, then the other, and froze again, alert and listening. Moving ever-so-slowly in a crouching position, she cautiously crept closer to a window that overlooked the front yard. It was slightly ajar. Inside, she saw candlelight softly illuminate Kate's sleeping face. She slowly slid both hands under the inch-wide opening and, little by little, quietly raised the window just enough so she could enter. With extreme care, she silently tiptoed inside, like a ballerina moving across a stage, and hovered beside Kate's sleeping body. She extended her fingers, bringing both hands closer to Kate's neck.

The non-physical evil that encircled the Earth pulsated and heaved like dark cumulous thunderclouds of a magnitude that had never been imagined. The souls of the trapped moved like swarming eels in and out over and across, up and down in constant motion. Although she was still far away from it, the evil sensed Kate's presence and lashed out, sending an octopus-like appendage in her direction. She easily avoided it and, in response, delivered a bolt of healing energy to the first human arm she saw that reached out, freeing its soul from centuries of captivity. One by one, she was able to release a few that had been trapped by their own avarice and lust. But there were millions upon millions if not billions of souls. The evil lashed out again with multiple networks of arms thrashing. She dodged them all and called out to her mother, *"Mom, can you hear me? Are you alright? Where are you? I will help you."*

In return, she heard a pounding sound that shook her to her core. "***You will never find her. She is ours. We have her, and we will have you!***"

"Like hell, you will." Kate thought. And silently she shouted over and over one of the secret words that Rabbi Joseph had given her, *"Shevarim, Shevarim, Shevarim!"* and each time she uttered the words, another bolt of powerful energy was sent from the Hand of El Shaddai into the amorphous mass, releasing thousands more of the trapped and forgotten. But then Kate felt a tightening around her neck. She realized that something was terribly wrong with her physical body. Defensively placing her hands around her throat, she thought, *"Back to body."* In an instant, she left the place between life and death and slipped back into her body. She opened both eyes and saw a woman choking her with both hands. She couldn't breathe. Kate's face turned red.

"So," the Synth whispered, "you thought I was cut in half? Surprised, are you? What? Oh, I'm sorry, I can't hear you. Need a little breath? An itty-bitty one before you die?" Albert's Synth released her neck long enough for one last breath. It was all Kate needed.

"Shevarim," Kate managed to croak out. In seconds, the Amulet released a flash and a sound like a thunderclap that shook the house. The Synth was encircled in a howling and spinning golden orb of light. Kate was able to breathe again. She stood on her bed, feet apart, arms outstretched in front, and narrowed the energy beam with her hands, making it focused and stable. Joe, Sara, Tyler, Amari, and Jacob rushed in, half-dressed.

"What, the..." Joe asked.

"Stay back, Dad," Kate shouted. "Just stay back."

"But," Sara said.

"Stay away. All of you!" Kate screamed. They did as they were told.

Inside its golden prison, the Synth was trying desperately to escape. It couldn't understand what was holding it. It kicked and scratched, but the transparent golden orb was impervious. The howling grew louder. Behind the orb grew a dense circular blackness that began pulling everything in the room toward it. As the blackness swelled, the howling increased in pitch and intensity. A picture frame hanging on the wall was sucked into its dark center and disappeared forever.

"Katie," Joe screamed over the howling, "for God's sake, get out of there!" They were in the upstairs hallway and being pulled into the room. "Quick, take my hand!"

"Just stay away," Kate screamed back. "I got this. This bitch is mine!" The extreme force generated by the black hole slammed the door shut. Inside the bedroom, the powerful black hole grew larger. Dresser drawers were pulled open. Shirts and pants were sucked out and disappeared. The closet door burst open. Hangers and their contents flew into the black hole. The bedroom's shades and drapes were split and torn to pieces before they, too, were lost. Tables and chairs, dresser drawers, and the dresser itself were all pulled into the widening and destructive opening. The howling became louder until only the golden orb, the fighting Synth trapped within it, and Kate, standing triumphantly on her bed, her hair and nightgown flapping in the gale-force wind, were left in the tiny destroyed bedroom. And then, the noise and wind abruptly stopped. The black hole's opening was blocked by the orb. It stayed motionless, held by the Amulet's power. Then, a sound akin to fingernails scratching on a chalkboard was heard. The Synth screamed as first one hand and then the other became stuck to the orb's interior. Its eyes widened in disbelief. It hammered its head against the orb's interior surface, trying to break free.

"You want to go?" Kate asked. "No problem. I've got the perfect place for you!" Kate spread her arms wide as the Synth pounded and pounded on the orb with its head. She took a deep breath and shouted another secret word, "**Teru-ah**!" The Amulet's light and the howling grew louder. The black hole increased in circumference, its circular glow looking like a lunar eclipse. The orb was instantly sucked into the black hole and disappeared, taking the black hole with it.

As soon as the noise stopped, her dad, Sara, and the others ran into the room. Jorge was the last to arrive, released when the Synth disappeared. Kate was still standing on the bed with her hands spread apart. She was shaking and crying as she fell to her knees. Her dad and Sara embraced her.

"Honey, I am so sorry," her dad said as he hugged and kissed her. "I am so sorry you had to go through something like this." Sara sat next to her on the other side.

"Are you ok?" Sara said. "We were so scared for you."

Katie took a deep breath. "It'll take me a minute. I...I just wasn't expecting anything like that. I thought I had killed the bastard."

Turning to Jorge, Sara said, "Jorge, the Synth had to come in a Timepod. Please find it and put it in the barn before daylight."

"Right now, madam," he answered and left.

"You know, I was just trying to get mom free from that evil whatever-the-hell it is, and I was doing pretty good, thank you very much, and suddenly there's this vise I feel around my neck, and I come back, and there's this red-headed broad on top of me choking me to death. I mean, what the hell!" Kate started to cry again. "And look at this room! Everything's gone. Even my stinking bladder!"

"Well," Jacob said softly, "the bladder is no great loss, and we have been meaning to redecorate."

Kate smiled. Turning to her father, she asked, "Dad, can I sleep with you tonight? I'm feeling really creeped out."

"Sure, kiddo. Anytime." He opened his arms wide and gave Kate a dad-sized bear hug. "That's what dads are for, beautiful daughter of mine." Gently, he kissed her on her forehead.

Chapter 22
Poland 1943

Kate sent the orb tumbling far into the past through the wormhole of spacetime. It bounced roughly off the wormhole's interior walls, which twisted and turned like a Mobius strip inside out. Light compressed and expanded, stretching into unnatural metallic hues. It finally dumped its load onto a cold, wet, muddy field near railroad tracks. The Synth somersaulted into a crouching cat-like position, ready to pounce. She saw thousands of people walking around and past her. Men and women were dressed in heavy, foul-smelling, urine-soaked woolen coats and feces-stained pants. Some of the young mothers carried crying babies. The men toted small battered suitcases inherited from long-deceased relatives, which contained their most treasured personal possessions: pictures, prayer books, and silver candlestick holders, not realizing that even those would soon be taken away, sorted for value or burned.

Soldiers in grey military uniforms, rifles pointed at their prisoners, stood in a long line three feet apart to stop anyone from escaping. The Synth looked ahead of her and read the tall twelve-inch iron letters welded over the front gate leading to a massive brick building beyond: "Arbeit Macht Frei" were the words. Albert Beck knew what it meant. In German, the words translate into "Work Makes You Free." The orb had deposited him at the gates of Auschwitz, the most notorious Nazi death camp of the Second World War.

The Synth stood up and brushed aside the mud and grime. She stood straight and tall in her white skintight jumpsuit, her long red hair flowing behind her. She knew what she had to do: survive. As she walked closer to the entry gate, the guards began to take notice. Walking under the sign and through the iron gates, a soldier dressed in a grey uniform sitting at a small wooden table motioned for a guard to bring her over to him. The guard roughly culled her from the crowd, pushing her from behind with the side of his rifle. Another soldier in a black SS uniform stood behind the one seated at the table.

In German, the man seated at the table asked, "And what is your name, Miss?" When he smiled, she saw his teeth were yellow and stained from smoking cigarettes.

"My name is Greta Beck, and I want to know why I am here," the Synth said.

"You are here, Miss Beck because someone put you in a cattle car on a train headed to Auschwitz. That's why you are here," answered the SS Officer behind the desk.

"Well, there must be some mistake. I am not a Jew." The Synth said defiantly in German.

"We don't make mistakes," said the SS Officer. "What is it that you do?"

"I am a masseuse. The finest masseuse in Krakow. I have a talent for relaxing sore and tense muscles," Greta answered, smiling.

The SS Officer took a moment to answer. He looked at the stunning redhead in front of him and smiled stiffly. "Perhaps the Commandant would like to avail himself of your services? Please, follow me."

The camp's odor almost gagged her. Thousands of prisoners were packed like cattle, all of them starving and with rampant disease. Auschwitz was the worst, most notorious death camp in history, murdering millions of people: Jews, Soviet prisoners of war, Freemasons, black people, Jehovah's Witnesses, Gypsies, Homosexuals, and others, by chemical gas and then burning their lifeless bodies in giant crematoriums. She was thankful, at least, that the Commandant's quarters were on the camp's outskirts. They walked up the front steps to a large wooden building, and the SS Officer went inside. She remained outside with a guard. Moments later, she was ushered inside to meet the camp's commander. As she entered the Commandant's office, she saw a short, balding man who sat behind a large desk. The SS Officer who escorted her closed the door and left them alone.

"My good friend, Lieutenant Richter, told me you have a talent for reducing stress and relaxing sore muscles." He smiled and walked out from behind his desk, removing his jacket and necktie. He sat down in a comfortable overstuffed chair upholstered in red velour. "Won't you show me your many talents?" he said, placing both of his hands on her hips and pulling her closer.

She allowed her hand to slowly slide over his freshly starched shirt as she walked to the back of the chair and bent low to whisper in his ear in German, "Oh, my dear Commander, you can't begin to imagine what I can do."

She bent over from behind and slowly began to partially unbutton his shirt. Never removing her hand from his body, she casually walked to the front of the chair and leisurely straddled him. She roughly removed his shirt, causing it to act like a rope, pinning his arms back, making it difficult for him to move. She brought her lips closer to his and gave him a soft kiss that quickly became too long and hard. He realized that he couldn't breathe. As he struggled, he opened his closed eyes and saw that she was looking at him. He felt her hands grip his neck, cutting off his air supply. His feet banged in unison against the grey wooden floor, trying to get the attention of the guards standing outside. In seconds, her grip tightened, breaking the third, fourth, and fifth cervical vertebrae in his neck. His head slumped to the side. She shouted out loud, "Ja! Ja! Ja! Oh, Commandant!"

She quickly stood up from the chair and looked at the Commandant's face. It was quickly turning blue. She pulled up the white sleeve covering her left arm. Four symbols appeared. She pressed the glowing triangle with the numeral 1 in its center. A few seconds later, a loud thunderclap was heard inside the Commandant's office. Albert Beck's Synth created a temporary wormhole and dove into its' center as two guards rushed into the office. When the artificially induced wormhole changed spacetime, they and the entire building were consumed in a large explosion that obliterated everything within fifty meters. After a lengthy inquiry, the destruction was attributed to a faulty gas heater.

Chapter 23
Namaste 1969

There must be some reason why people gravitate to kitchens to talk. Perhaps it's because kitchens feel safe and warm or that food and drink are enjoyable to share; maybe kitchens are where we find comfort food that helps us feel good when things aren't so good, like a hot cup of mint tea, its flagrant flavors warming us when we are sick, or warm chocolate pudding, reminding one of happier times with family and friends. The morning after the Synth's attack, Jacob, Amari, Joe, and Sara sat around the kitchen table, warm mugs of tea in hand, discussing the early morning's events. A grouping of tiny orange pumpkins resting on multicolored fall leaves were arranged on a large square lace napkin in the center of the kitchen table. Katie was still upstairs, sleeping late after her ordeal.

"It's simply catastrophic," Sara said. "The timeline has been inexorably changed. We have no idea what damage we have done."

"But how do you know that what exists now was not always what was supposed to exist. What was meant to be?" Joe said.

"Because Amari, Jacob, and I lived it. It was in the historical record. What happened early this morning wasn't part of our history of this place. There was no record of this Synth coming here."

Jacob added, "When I checked this morning, all that Timespan and the Safehome system knew was that Albert Beck was missing."

"The timeline has changed," Amari went on. "How much has it changed? What are its dynamics: who lives, who dies, who is never born, and what does the resulting change mean? We have no way of knowing or of stopping or reversing it. What happened today impacts the future."

"It could be a good thing, couldn't it?" Kate said. She had been listening quietly from the dining room. They all turned to look at her as she walked into the kitchen.

"Hi honey," Joe said. "Feel a little better?"

"Yeah, a little, I guess." She looked around the room. "Where's Tyler?"

"Oh, he and Jorge are out doing some farm chores," Jacob said. "They'll be back soon."

Amari brought over a freshly baked pumpkin muffin and a cup of hot chocolate with tiny white marshmallows floating on top and placed it in front of Kate. "I made this just for you," she smiled.

"Thanks, Amari," she bit into the soft muffin. "It's great," Kate said with a mouthful, crumbs dropping out. "You should open your own bakery."

"Ah, that's all I need! No, thank you. I've got enough work around here," she said, wiping her hands on her apron.

"Well," Kate was silent momentarily, put her hands in her lap, and looked down. "Last night was a real tough time for me."

"We know, Katie," Sara said. She reached over and put her hand on Kate's.

"But not in the way you think, Sara. You see, I was busy trying to help my mom."

Joe was surprised. "You were trying to help Lauren?"

"Of course, Dad. I told you the first morning we were here. I had a really vivid dream where Mom rescued me from that thing that attacked us in Los Angeles. It captured her and pulled her in."

"I, I'm sorry, honey; I thought it was just a bad nightmare you were having."

"No, Dad, it was real. As real as the explosion that the evilness caused when we were in the Second Sight Bookstore. And while I was out of my body trying to help mom, that bitch tried to kill me. I felt it come back, and well, you know the rest. P M O!"

"I'm so sorry, Katie," Sara said. "I feel awful. I thought Albert's Synth was done for, but he must have somehow transferred into another. He was after the Amulet."

"Yeah, obviously. Look," Kate's eyes welled up with tears. "I just want to go home. I love this place and 1969 and you guys, but I need a break. I need my room. My things."

Just then, Tyler and Jorge walked in through the back kitchen door. Everyone around the table was silent. "Hi," he looked around. "Did I miss anything?"

"I want to go home, Tyler. Back to my own time. I'm done."

"We understand," Sara said.

"And I know, Sara, that the Amulet is really important to you. That you think it can reverse the radiation that has killed all living things on the surface of future Earth."

"Yes, that's true."

"And I promise I'll really try to help. But I can't do it right now. I need to care for myself and try to help my mom."

Joe quietly said, "What if Sara and Tyler joined us?" Joe quickly looked at Sara, Tyler, Jacob, and Amari.

A slow smile appeared on Kate's face, which she quickly tried to stop but couldn't. "Well, that would be ok with me, I guess." The smile was trying hard to get out, but she fought it. She nodded her head up and down. "Yeah. That'd be ok with me." She looked at Tyler and smiled. He smiled back. Kate noticed that her dad and Sara were grinning, too.

Later that day, Jacob, Amari, and Jorge were in the barn saying their goodbyes to Sara, Joe, Katie, and Tyler.

"Now, take care of yourself, Madam," said Jorge. "You won't have me to look out for you, Joe, Katie, or Tyler. Well, maybe I should join you. You know, I think it would probably be best given the earth year and time changes you're returning to..."

"We'll be fine, Jorge," interrupted Sara. "You'll need to help Jacob and Amari care for Namaste." With final kisses and hugs all around, the four time travelers got up onto the Timepod. Tyler set the controls, and the power kicked in, generating a controlled sonic wormhole of spacetime that would deliver them safely to Timespan. They waved through the Timepod's transparent curved wall until the past turned into a dark grey mist.

Chapter 24
Timespan 3257 PC

M oments later, their Timepod arrived at Timespan's transfer area, the same area where Joe and Kate had arrived when they first met Jorge. But this time, it was different. There were no people. It wasn't busy or noisy. The usual bright lights were dimmed. Only robotic cleaning machines moved back and forth, keeping the mammoth transfer station spotless and orderly. As they stepped off the Timepod's platform, their shoes and voices echoed through the large, domed, stadium-sized area.

Kate was astonished. "What happened? Where is everyone?"

"Albert Beck canceled all time travel," Sara said. "It made it easier for him or his Synth to find us. Since he's now incommunicado, his order can't be reversed. Everyone is stuck in their Safehomes or in suspended animation."

"That's awful," Joe said. "Isn't there anything that can be done about it? Can't anyone reverse the order?"

"Well, politically," Tyler said, "I suppose if all the Safehome Commanders could agree to reverse a decision made by the Terrestrial Governor of Earth, it could be done, but never has anyone challenged a Director of the Beck Consortium.

"Where is this Beck Consortium," Kate said. "Who made them, boss?"

"The Beck Consortium is somewhere in spacetime, but no one knows where except maybe Albert Beck," Tyler said. "An ancestor of Beck's, many generations ago, started it by accumulating vast wealth through oil, gas, and mineral development."

"That's why," Sara said, looking at Kate, "It's so important to get people out of the Safehomes and return to live on Earth's surface. And the only way to do that..."

"...is to get rid of the radiation. Yeah, thanks, no pressure, right?"

"Well, you wanted to know. Anyway, here we are," Sara said. They stood before an antique, shiny brass gate with a small sign that read, "*The Bloomingdale's Timeport. The first permanent operating Timeport between New York City and Timespan inaugurated Earth year March 12, 1928 AD.*" They all walked into what looked like a typical elevator.

"How do we know we won't squash someone or scare the poop out of them," Kate said.

"It'll only transfer us if the elevator in the period we want to go to is on the top floor and empty," Sara said. "So, we want to go on a Sunday, the day after you arrived here." Sara programmed the Timepod by placing her entire palm on the interior wall near the control panel. Then she pressed the button for the first floor. The elevator doors closed with a "*swoosh.*" The lights blinked off and on. It felt like the elevator would go straight through the roof. The walls curved in and then popped back out. Their bodies extended and contracted. An unequal pressure built up in their ears and caused them to pop. The strange, screaming, windy sound was all around them. Then, as quickly as it started, it stopped. The lights came on strong, the automatic bell signaled the first floor, the doors parted, and they all stepped out onto the main floor of Bloomingdale's on a busy Sunday afternoon in October. Kate immediately rushed out of the store and hailed a New York self-driving Taxi. They followed quickly behind her.

"Yeah, where to, folks?" asked the Bronx-accented voice from the front speaker.

"Oh, anywhere near Washington Square Park will be fine," Kate said. She settled back in the cab and smiled broadly. "We'll pick up some groceries at Romano's."

——— ❖ ———

There is nothing Kate likes more than Romano's vegetarian pizza, except wearing her favorite flannel penguin PJs under soft flannel sheets, covered with two heavy wool blankets and her fluffy down comforter. That evening, she had all the coziness she desired.

Joe purchased many of Romano Brothers Market's delicacies: antipasto, calamari, fresh fruit, goats' milk cheese, and two large Panettones for the next morning's French toast. Those were just a few items that filled five large grocery bags. When they got back to the Co-op, they all had a feast.

Later, safe in her room, in her own time and place with people who cared about her, she knew she had two more things to do. She had to save her mom and then the world of future Earth. She placed her right hand around the Amulet dangling on its thin gold chain around her neck, closed her eyes, and relaxed. But then, a series of demanding knocks on her closed bedroom door interrupted her concentration. She let out a large sigh.

"What now?" she said.

"It's me, Tyler. Can I come in?"

"Sure." She sat up in bed, arms crossed.

When he walked in and looked around at the mess, he sniffed and asked innocently, "What's that smell? Do you have the window open?" He tried to close the window, but it wasn't open. "I know it can't be the goat bladder." He sat on the edge of her bed and smiled. She glowered back.

"It must be my recent bikini wax."

"What? What's that?" he asked as Sara and Joe entered the room.

"Hi, what's what?" Joe said. "Saw your door was open."

"Everything ok?" Sara said.

Kate just shook her head and let her chin drop to her chest. She raised both arms above her head, let them plop back down and mouthed silently, "Why me?"

Sara was the first to catch on and told Joe and Tyler, "Maybe it's not the right time. Maybe we should go?"

"Hey, I'm just trying to save my mom from an eternity inside that evil whatever-the-hell it is; and I'm trying to save the world and get rid of all the damn radiation that killed all the living things on the planet and forced humanity to live underground like friggen gophers, that's all I'm trying to do. And I can't catch a break. A little privacy, maybe? A little quiet? Is it too much to ask?" she sputtered out with her lower jaw extended and a major eye roll.

"Can we watch?" Tyler asked.

Kate closed her eyes, shoved the corner of the flowered flannel sheet into her mouth, and bit down hard. She had to bite something, or she would scream. Closing her eyes and exhaling slowly, she said, "Ok. Ok. Get three chairs and make yourselves comfortable. Whatever happens, no talking, no whispering, no sneezing, no coughing, just silence." They all promised. Joe and Tyler brought in two chairs. Sara sat on a white bean bag chair next to the bed. When all was quiet, Kate relaxed into her pillow and placed her right hand over the Hand of El Shaddai.

The more Kate relaxed, the warmer her Amulet felt. The glow from it comforted her and warmed her dark bedroom. Her breathing became slow and regular. She relaxed her body: first her neck and shoulder muscles, then muscles in her chest and arms; each of her fingers relaxed, followed by her hips, legs, and feet. She concentrated on her long, slow breathing in and out, in and out. Soon, the sense of having a physical body disappeared. She became her breath. As she had experienced in the garden at Pumbedita, her transparent eternal self slowly rose up and hovered above her physical body, which was peacefully relaxed under her cozy comforter and multiple woolen blankets. As her immortal soul separated from her physical body, she noticed the tiny sliver of light that connected her eternal self to her physical self. She also saw her Dad, Sara, and Tyler watching her now motionless and prone physical body as it slowly breathed in and out. They were not aware through their own limited physical senses that anything out-of-the-ordinary had just occurred. She smiled lovingly at them. She spread her arms out, stretching them above her head and down toward her feet to create a shimmering transparent golden orb for her personal protection. Her face became hardened knowing what she had to do.

Kate's protective golden orb blasted through her bedroom ceiling high up into the night sky, quickly passing New York City's tallest buildings. Then, high above the Earth, it abruptly stopped. "*What am I doing?*" she thought to herself. "*Oh, damn!*" She hit herself on the forehead, but her hand went straight through her head. "*I'm wearing flannel pajamas!*" She quickly looked down. "*Oh, good thing I remembered the bottoms! But how can I defeat this badass wearing flannel pajamas? And the penguin one's mom got me. I better go back. No, no, I can't go back. Maybe I can use it to my advantage.*" The orb spun faster. Its place in space and time fluctuated due to the frequency and nearness of physical existence. The Earth was still there but became less distinct, less colorful, and far less physically alive.

The dimensional frequency between physical and non-physical existence was where Kate and her golden orb existed. Some souls get trapped in this in-between place by whatever evil or abusiveness attracted them in their physical lives. It's familiar to them, just like a magnet attracts steel. Joseph ben Abba called it the Evil Aspect. He explained to her that since there is good in the world, there must also be evil. The world must always have an equilibrium; it must be balanced, as the Fibonacci sequence indicates. Kate was now staring at a dark, minute-by-minute, ever-expanding evil that had become self-aware.

"*Oh, my,*" it sarcastically said, "*you've returned! How brave! They are going to love you!*" Suddenly, a giant tentacle swatted her from the side, shoving her straight into the path of a dark, gaping mouth that had materialized on the thing's billowing surface. With an evil smile, the mammoth lips parted. Moving over its surface like greyish-black swirls from an oil spill discoloring an ocean, the constant flailing movements of arms, legs, and faces protested their souls' imprisonment in hideous silent screams. But Kate fought back. She released paths of energy that freed one soul from entrapment after another. *"Wonderful! Thank you! Danke, Merci, Gracias! You're cleaning house for me. I was tired of them anyway. They've been here for millennia."*

Around the cloud of dank darkness, Kate continued her attack. She flung bolt after bolt of energy into the swirling, miserable mass of concentrated souls. Thousands were released. Kate thought to herself, *"This is going to take a long time. There are billions upon billions of trapped souls. I can't possibly free one at a time. There must be a better way. I've got to go in and get Mom!"*

She quickly circled around, avoiding the constant barrage of tentacles, and aimed straight for the evil's open gaping mouth. *"You want me? No prob. Be careful what you wish for!"* The golden orb grew brighter as if it knew it had to protect its occupant as it raced into the gaping opening. When the opening slammed shut, the orb slowed, unable to get through the ever-darkening muck. The golden orb came to a complete stop. Its once bright glow dimmed. Although she was protected from the evil swirling around her, she had a sick feeling in the pit of her stomach. It was as if the evil was absorbing energy from her Amulet. Part of her realized that if her protection drained away, so would her lifeline to her physical self. She had to pretend she was weak. *"Mom,"* she called out. *"Mom, where are you?"*

"Aw, calling out for your mommy? Isn't that sweet? Well, your mommy is far away and can't help you. She can't even hear you!" Arms, limbs, and screaming faces swirled about the now softly glowing orb. They were pushing against the orb's outer wall, trying to get at Kate inside. Some of the faces were ancient and sunken; others were alive with lust. Crawling over the curved orb, trying to claw through, they shoved each other out of the way. The orb started to bend inward. Elbows and hands began to push forward,

almost touching Kate's face. That's when the Soul Catcher came forward for the kill, shoving all the others away. Its slithering largeness took the shape of a face ten times larger than the orb. The evil leered at Kate, who stood defiantly inside the small sphere, legs set firmly apart, hands in front, palms up. She focused on the silver ball dangling from around its humongous neck. *"Welcome,"* she heard it say inside her head. The thing smiled as its two large hands tore apart Kate's protective orb. *"Now, you're mine!"*

"Shekinah," Kate screamed. As she said the words, a powerful golden light emanated from her hands, mouth, and eyes from the very center of her being. It aimed at the silver ball that hung around the malevolent thing's monstrous neck. Instantly, the silver ball that was curled tight unwound, elongated, and became the Hand of El Shaddai that it formerly was. The two Amulets communicated back and forth. The repeating binary tone increased in pitch and beat. Kate's head was shoved backward by an ancient and eternal power; she raised her hands higher and shouted with the full force of her eternal soul, *"Shekinah Gedolah!"*

The creature's large evil eyes opened wide in surprise as the coded Fibonacci sequence ingrained within the silver Amulet repeated faster, each time at an even higher pitch. An intense beam of white light exploded from the large silver Amulet that hung around its neck, piercing the creature's head. It was followed by another beam of white light that pierced its eyes. The beams of light increased in number and harmonic pitch one after another until there were tens of thousands. The light pierced the creature and the centuries of accumulated evil horror. As the pure light touched them, souls trapped for eons were suddenly released. The creature, who had over centuries grown massive and achieved consciousness, became nonthreatening and small. The trapped souls that longed to be set free were freed.

The silver Amulet that ended the wicked abomination's reign hovered momentarily in front of Kate. Then, it merged with her smaller Amulet, becoming a larger one. Its gleaming silver and gold hand warmly glowed. The binary tones that it generated slowed. The encoded Fibonacci sequence ended. Kate looked in all directions for her mother but couldn't see her. Then, through the mist, she heard a voice inside her head.

"I always thought those pajamas were pretty cute."

"Mom!" Kate screamed as they both flew towards each other.

"My baby!" Lauren shouted as she tried to hug her daughter, but their hugs went right through their earthly images, like smoke through smoke. *"I love you so much, Katie."*

"Me too, Mom. I love you and miss you. It's been so tough."

"I know, honey, I know. I've been watching."

"You have?"

"Of course, I have, until that thing got me, whatever the hell that was." Although they couldn't actually feel each other, Lauren kissed her daughter on the cheek. Kate smiled a happy-sad smile.

"You're the best, Mom. Just the best."

"I love you to the moon and back, my sweet girl. Come, let's go back. Your dad's going to be worried about you."

Kate took a deep breath and said, *"I know, but I have one more thing to do."*

"What's that?"

"I've got to save the Earth. I promised Sara that I'd at least try."

"Sara, who?" But before Kate could answer, she enveloped them both in a golden orb and traveled to Earth's future of 3257. Through time and space, they watched as scientists tried to deflect the world-killing asteroid but failed. Huge, mountain-sized pieces crashed on nuclear waste sites, spewing toxic radiation into the atmosphere and over the globe. They watched as the green Earth turned to tan dust, killing all plant life. Radiation seeped into the world's oceans, killing all sea life. Mother Earth, the water planet, was dead. Millions of people on the earth's surface who could not

afford or did not have the political contacts to live in a Safehome died horrible deaths from radiation sickness. When Kate brought them to the spacetime coordinates she wanted, the orb stopped.

"What now?" Lauren asked as the orb disappeared. They hovered many miles above the lifeless world.

"I don't know, Mom. I guess we'll just have to see if Earth will be allowed another chance. Maybe the Amulet will work. It's directed by my thoughts, so let me see if I can rid the planet of the radiation that killed it."

Kate concentrated and saw in her mind's eye the Earth that she knew: the green and blue water planet of rainforests and oceans, a planet of life, not death. She envisioned the uncountable trillions upon trillions of plutonium molecules detaching from their resting places and, one-by-one, forming a space bridge that would take them from the Earth and deposit them into the sun. The Amulet did not glow. Instead, they felt wave upon wave of pulsating energy emanating from it. Kate focused. She visualized healing energy loosening the bonds of harmful radioactive molecules that, if not removed, would have kept the Earth a dead planet for hundreds of thousands of years. Slowly, it happened. A shimmering radioactive sparkle joined others. Soon, hundreds of thousands of molecules became unstuck, bringing millions more with them. From the northern and southern hemispheres, from the deepest parts of oceanic trenches, great land masses, and the tallest mountain ranges, radioactive molecules carried by Kate's thought created a space bridge, left the Earth and settled harmlessly into the turbulent sun. As the last molecule of plutonium departed, Kate smiled, turned to her mom, and happily exclaimed, *"I did it, Mom! I saved the future Earth! Now, it can heal."*

"I always knew you could do whatever you set your heart on, sweetheart. I'm so proud of you!"

"Come on, Mom, let's go back. I gotta tell Dad, Sara, and Tyler."

"Uh, Sara and Tyler?"

Kate looked down and shuffled her feet around a little. *"Well, Tyler is sort of my boyfriend, and I think Dad really likes Sara a lot."*

"Well, your dad is a great guy and deserves all the love he can have, and so do you, my sweet girl. Let's go to them."

All Kate had to do was think, *"Back to body,"* and she zoomed through time and space faster than a stretched rubber band returns to its proper shape. Her mom was right by her side.

Tyler yelled when he saw Kate was moving, "I think she's waking up!"

"Well, if she wasn't, she is now," Sara said as she and Joe rushed into the bedroom from the kitchen. It was early Monday morning, and the sun was just beginning to peek through the clouds. Kate stretched, yawned, opened her eyes, and grabbed Tyler, who was sitting on the side of her bed, and pulled him close. She gave him a big kiss.

"Whoa, whoa, whoa," Joe said. "Take a breath. Take a breath."

Kate and Tyler parted. Both were smiling. Kate said, "Hi. I was thinking about you."

"A lot?" Tyler said.

"Well, not a lot. I mean, I was pretty busy, but you were never far from my thoughts."

"Hey, darling daughter of mine. You, ok? When you didn't move all night, we got worried..."

"...and then when your Amulet changed," Sara interrupted, "we couldn't imagine what had happened."

Kate looked down at the beautiful silver and gold Amulet hanging from a gold link chain around her neck. She held it in her hands and noticed for the first time that it had gotten larger and heavier. "Pretty sweet, huh?" she said. She sniffed the air. "If that's coffee, I want some!"

"But tell us if you accomplished what you set out to do," Sara said. She looked intently at Kate, still partially covered in a queen-sized down comforter.

"Ok. Well, Mom is safe and nearby."

"And the Earth of the future?" Sara asked.

"The Earth of the future is free from radiation. It can heal and grow again."

Sara jumped up, squealed, and fell over Kate, giving her hugs and kisses. "Thank you, thank you, Katie. You are amazing."

"I'm starved! Amazing can wait."

Sara laughed, "Well, you'll just have to tell us all about it at breakfast."

"Panettone French toast coming right up," Joe said and kissed his daughter on her cheek. "I am so proud of you!"

Only Tyler was left in Kate's room. "It was something, huh?"

"You can't imagine." Kate nodded her head. "Our existence is so much more than we think it is. Amazing. Miraculous. Words can't even begin to describe it." Kate got out of bed, hugged Tyler, and kissed him sweetly. "Now, scram. I must be a stink mess."

❖

During breakfast, as she scarfed down numerous slices of sweet Panettone that her dad had soaked in egg batter, skillet-fried in butter, and covered in Namaste's warm maple syrup, Kate didn't leave out one detail of her out-of-body experience. Joe, Sara, and Tyler were in total awe, dumbstruck, at what Kate had been able to accomplish. They all sat in the living room on white leather couches and chairs, surrounded by Lauren's famous photographs. A large custom-made white leather shag rug covered the floor. Resting on it was a glass-top coffee table whose base was weathered natural driftwood. A ten-cup French-style coffee press rested on the table along with breakfast dishes, more Panettone, a bowl with raw sugar cubes, and a small silver pitcher of fresh cream. Joe's antique hi-fi played an old Stan Getz jazz record.

"And that, as they say, is all she wrote," Kate said. When she finished recounting her experiences, everyone just sat back and shook their heads slowly from side to side.

"Wow. I don't know if I could have faced off with whatever that malevolent thing was," Sara said. She shivered uncontrollably at the thought. "That is just too creepy."

"And using the Amulet to create a space bridge that moved the radiation from the earth into the sun was just brilliant," Tyler said. "Simply brilliant!" He leaned over and kissed Kate. She shyly smiled and expanded it into a broad grin, especially when she saw her dad roll his eyes.

"If there is an award for bravery, you would receive it for not only setting your mother's soul free but for allowing all those trapped souls to continue their journey of existence. I am sure your mom is as proud of you as I am." Joe stood up from his chair, walked over to the couch where Tyler and Kate were sitting, and gave his daughter a big hug and kiss. Turning to Tyler, he said, pointing to his daughter and back to himself, "I'm allowed."

A few hours later, after the breakfast dishes had been cleared, washed, and put away, Tyler and Kate were dressed and ready to go out on the unusually mild October day. Sara and Joe were still in their robes, reading the online edition of the New York Times.

"You know," Sara said as she stretched out on the couch, "I could get used to this. A mellow Monday, staying home, not needing to go anywhere." She tickled Joe's toes. He was stretched out on the couch's other end.

"You could, could you?" He smiled and saw Kate and Tyler put on their coats. "So, where are you two going?"

"Oh, I wanted to show Tyler Central Park. There's just so much to see in the city. I thought that the Park would be a good place to start. Mind if I take a blanket?"

As Tyler put on his coat, he said, "She keeps telling me about these hot chestnuts that you actually eat but don't give to squirrels. I thought chestnuts were squirrel food."

"Not at the prices they're charging," Joe said. "Have a good time."

"What are you two going to do?" Kate asked as she put on her coat and tucked the blanket under her arm.

Joe looked at Sara and said, "Oh, we'll probably hang out here and go out later.

With a slight smile, Kate said, "Sounds good to me."

When they left, Joe got up and found his favorite album. He and his late wife Lauren had danced to it countless times. He put it on the turntable, walked over to Sara, and asked, "May I have this dance?"

Sara smiled, "Of course, but I may be a little rusty."

"This song by Anthony Benedetto is one of my favorites."

"I don't think I've ever heard of him."

"His stage name was Tony Bennett."

"I don't know the name. It's been a few years, you know."

"Well, my sweet, now you will." He kissed her long and passionately. As the soft melody drifted through the speakers, they heard "*The Second Time Around.*"

Sara placed her arms around Joe's waist and lowered her head against his chest. They held each other tight, swaying to the music he loved so much. She looked up and kissed him tenderly and long on the lips.

From a place close to their time and space, yet entirely removed from the physical world, Lauren watched her former husband and his new love through the mist of spacetime-- a dimension close but not close enough for interaction. She was able to feel the emotion but not hear the words spoken. Lauren knew and felt that Joe was in love with Sara. And she knew Sara felt the same way about the man she once loved and with whom she had a child. Kate, indeed, was a child of love. Lauren felt happy for them both. She was thrilled that Katie had found someone whom she was crazy about. First love, Lauren thought, is always that way: crazy and happy. And the most magical thing was that when she simply thought of her daughter, she was there in Central Park, watching both Kate and Tyler stroll hand-in-hand under the Greywacke Arch to the large green lawn that bordered Turtle Pond. Lauren could watch them forever. But now that her beautiful daughter had freed her from the prison created by the horrible evil, she knew that her time on Earth was at an end. It was time to say goodbye. Slowly, through the mist of the present, Lauren floated near her daughter. She remembered when Katie said her first word, took her first steps, lost her first tooth, and learned how to spell her name. She happily remembered when Katie would run into her and Joe's king-sized bed and get under the covers with them when a nightmare had scared her. So many beautiful memories went through Lauren's mind, now so close to the daughter she loved. She leaned over and gave Katie a kiss on her cheek. Kate felt something and quickly put her hand up to the area where she felt kissed.

"Mom? Mommy? Is that you?" Kate turned around, trying to see, trying to catch a last glimpse.

"What is it, Katie?" Tyler said.

"I, I just felt a soft kiss on my cheek. I think it was Mom's way of saying goodbye." Tears formed in Kate's eyes and rolled down her cheeks. She hugged Tyler, buried her head against his chest, and sobbed. Quietly, she whispered, "Bye, mommy. I love you forever. To the moon and...back." She blew her mom one last kiss. As she uttered those words, all the electricity within a five-mile radius of where they stood stopped working. Every battery, motor, electric generator, communications tower, iCuff, people-mover, car, truck, horn, lightbulb, and everything that used electrical power as its operating source ceased functioning. Silence. It was as if the City of New York had died. Then, at the exact moment all power was lost, Sara and Tyler heard a voice inside their heads.

"Miss me?" said the voice they knew well.

Chapter 25

A startled Sara suddenly sat up in their bed, shoved Joe and shouted, "Joe. Quick. Get dressed. Albert Beck has returned and is after Kate and Tyler!"

"What?"

"Just hurry. We've got to get to Central Park and help them, or he'll kill them both!" She was faster than Joe and was wearing her coat just as he finished tying his sneakers. They quickly ran down the stairs and out the door. Everything was silent. No cars moved. No horns blared. All lights were out everywhere. People were scared. Joe understood they would need to use bikes to get to Central Park in time to help. He detached Kate's and his road bikes from the Coop's bike stand, and they tore up Fifth Avenue, dodging stalled cars and frightened pedestrians.

It was when Tyler and Kate were near the Greywacke Arch that Tyler said, "Oh, crap, Beck's returned. We gotta get out of here!"

"What? That's impossible. I sent that thing to Auschwitz."

"Katie, I heard him inside my head. He's back. I know it. And he's close." He grabbed her hand and pulled her. They ran toward Turtle Pond. Tyler thought he was running away from the Synth, but he soon discovered that he was running towards it. As they rounded a group of tall trees, they both saw the red-haired female Synth that Albert Beck had become. It was just stepping off a small escape Timepod that had landed in the shallow pond. As the Timepod sank into the water, the Synth smiled and slowly walked towards them. Others saw the tall, scarlet-haired woman in the white, skin-tight jumpsuit, too. They tried to take pictures, but their iCuffs were dead. The onlookers quickly realized that everything was too quiet. Not one bird chirped. Dogs howled. As the tall woman walked closer, looking as if she were walking on water, the families that were in the immediate area began to back away. Children started crying. The Timepod began generating an infrasonic pulse that made everyone in the vicinity feel nauseous. Mothers and fathers left their picnic baskets and blankets on the grass, hurriedly picked up their crying children, and ran. Tyler stood before Kate as a shield to protect her from the uncomfortable seven-cycle infrasound vibrations. When Beck's Synth got close to them, she lowered the infrasonic pulse and talked directly to Kate, ignoring Tyler as if he wasn't there.

"All I want is the Amulet. The device."

"I can't give it to you even if I wanted to, which I don't."

"Yes, I'm sure that is true, Kate. Unfortunate but true."

Tyler had had enough. He took his opening and punched the Synth in the jaw. Then he punched it repeatedly in the stomach. It didn't distract the Synth.

"What the," gasped the Synth. "What are you doing here? I killed you once before." Roughly, it picked Tyler up by his neck.

"Please, don't hurt him," Kate pleaded.

"Wouldn't think of it, dear." The Synth easily tossed him fifty yards, slamming Tyler into a giant oak tree, knocking him unconscious. "He's just a little pest. You, however, are a big one."

"You can't touch me. You've tried before. I'm protected."

"Yes. I know. That's why I'm not going to touch you." Beck smiled sweetly. "I'm going to absorb you."

"What?"

"Why do you think I've absorbed most of the power in Manhattan? Why do you think I've shut everything down? For my health? Or so your ancient law enforcement authorities won't have a recording? What do I care if there's a record in this timeline? I'll change it. I'll control the world. The Beck Consortium. The cosmos. I will be God everlasting. Forever and always. Even the old ones will bow to me!"

"You can't do that," Kate said as she slowly backed away from Beck's Synth.

"Watch me."

Joe blindsided the Synth, tackling it to the ground. Sara jumped on top of her, quickly divided the Synth's long red hair into two strands, and pulled the strands of hair around its neck, choking her. Joe looked up at his daughter and shouted, "Run, Kate. Get out of here!" Kate was unsure of what to do. Part of her wanted to help her dad and Sara, and another part wanted to flee. "Go!" screamed her father. Kate started to run just as two powerful lightning bolts issued forth from the Timepod. They slammed Joe and Sara in their backs with killing volts of electricity that burned through their clothes, leaving their skin blackened and their bodies lifeless. Albert Beck's Synth brushed them aside like dead flies and stood tall. Then he went after Kate.

It was a nightmare for Kate when nothing she did was good enough. She had almost reached the monument to Poland's King Jagiello on horseback when she saw a lightning bolt heading in her direction. She dodged the first one and then the second, but the third knocked her unconscious. She fell to the ground near the monument's base. The Synth slowly approached savoring its triumph. Full of malice, she towered over Kate. As she elevated her right arm, Kate's body raised up from the ground and hovered before the Synth. Then, an unholy sound issued from the Synth's body. It was a primal scream as nanobots began to swirl and rip apart its inner core. Kate's Amulet glowed, forming a golden bubble around her unconscious floating body. The Synth called upon more of the Timepod's stored energy when its own form began to break apart. The Synth lifted off the ground and hovered before Kate's transparent golden orb. It started to look like a swarm of bees in stationary flight. Then, one infinitesimal nanobot from the Synth burrowed through and into the sphere that was protecting Kate. More followed. Soon there were thousands.

Chapter 26
The Place Between Tomorrow and Forever

After Lauren tried to kiss Kate goodbye, the image of Central Park she experienced grew fainter. She found herself at a constantly shifting barrier between physical reality and other existences. She could still discern the Earth's shape in spacetime, but she was far away, near the edge of what she could only assume were other dimensions. There were thousands upon thousands of dimensions: gateways into other spacetime locations before her.

Unknown to Lauren, two ancient elderly men watched her from a great distance. One of them had a long white beard and a flowing white kaftan. His entire body glowed with light like that from a full moon. The other man, also sporting a golden glow of his own, was covered in animal hides.

"Don't you think we should help her decide?" Joseph ben Abba said. *"She's been through so much."*

"You are such a meddler," Eliyahu said.

"Humph! Look who's calling me a meddler. You, the meddler of all meddlers."

"I'd prefer if you used a more modern term, Joseph. I think of myself more as a facilitator."

"Fine. Fine, Mister facilitator. With your kind permission, may I help her? We owe it to her and her daughter Kate."

"Oh, all right already, my old friend. I give you the meddler's crown. Go, meddle."

Joseph ben Abba thought long and hard about what he could do to encourage Lauren to choose the best experience for her soul's growth. When he thought of it, he smiled warmly. He knew exactly what he would do.

Lauren floated in front of thousands of shimmering gateways to other existences and dimensions. She didn't know which one to choose, but she wanted to be proactive and in control as she had been in her past life. Then, Lauren heard something that surprised her and made her smile. It was a song she loved and knew well. As her eternal spirit floated closer to where the music came from, a bright, iridescent, electric-blue opening breached the darkness before her. A light emanated from it, so intensely blinding white that she almost couldn't look at it. The song she heard was in French:

"Allons enfants de la patrie,

Le jour de gloire est arrivé !

Contre nous de la tyrannie

L'étendard sanglant est levé !

L'étendard sanglant est levé !

Entendez-vous dans les campagnes[3],

Mugir ces féroces soldats ?

Ils viennent jusque dans nos bras

Égorger nos fils, nos compagnes!"

It was The French National Anthem by Rouget de Lisle. She thought to herself how strange it was to hear it now. As the familiar words and music continued, her physical reflection became her eternal essence. Lauren didn't feel any difference in her awareness of self. She felt as alive as she had ever felt in the physical dimension but lighter. Her mind was clearer. If she had been able to watch her own silent metamorphosis, she would have seen her physical image gradually alter into a sphere of pure thought and pure energy. It was then that she started to remember. She wasn't just Lauren, mother of Kate and wife of Joe. She was more. There were other experiences and physical lives before her most recent incarnation as

Lauren. She remembered the bombs screaming down from the night sky and lumbering steel tanks digging up the streets of her beautiful Paris. She recalled the sour dank odors in dark basements during secret late-night meetings with other members of the French Resistance, their excitement of planning to blow up Nazi fuel depots and troop trains. She began to remember that other life and her other name. She was called Leah. Leah Soutine. And she also remembered the Hand of El Shaddai that had protected her and her friends. It was a secret gift given to her in a dream that turned out to be real. She heard its call again through time and space at that instant. She felt the loving connection that once made could never be severed.

The dualities of existence astounded her soul. She had lived numerous lifetimes. She was, her soul was, eternal. Now, the soul of her child, the soul of her great, great, great, granddaughter, was threatened by an evil that had memory and responses but no soul. Although she could not cross the dimensional barrier to Kate's physical reality, she could send an interdimensional message to her daughter. A silk-like thread thinner than a whisper burst forth from her soul. Traveling through time and space, it quickly pierced Kate's golden protective sphere, trying to protect Kate from the Synth's unmerciful onslaught.

From another time and place, Kate's mind heard, *"Katie, Cherie, wake up. Fight. Say the words. Say the words!"* Deep within Kate's mind, it sounded like an echo. She was on a trip to the Grand Canyon with her mom and dad. She thought her mom was telling her to say some words that would cause an echo. She tried to talk but couldn't. The golden bubble that was protecting her began to fail. It attempted to rebuild itself, but each time it closed one hole, another opened. It soon became weaker and collapsed entirely. The molecules that swarmed around the figure that was Albert Beck's Synth raised its arms in victory as the molecules that made up Kate's hair started to break down and swirl. Again, Kate heard within her mind, *"Katie. Wake up. Say the words. Say the words, Cherie. Vive la France! Vive la Resistance!* **Clean Up Your Room***!"*

Kate inhaled a breath. Her eyes popped open. She suddenly remembered where she was. When the Synth realized she was awake, the molecules from his right arm coalesced, and it savagely punched Kate in the stomach, knocking the wind out of her and throwing her against the monument's large stone base. As the molecules of her body became more unstable, she tried to get up but couldn't. Kate mustered as much air into her lungs as she could as the molecules from the Synth intermingled with her own, and she shouted, **"Shaddai Echad!"**

Rapidly, Kate's body was restored. The Synth had a look of utter horror on its face. It started to back away as Kate held the Amulet in her left hand and pointed at the Synth with her right outstretched arm. She shouted, "You are an abomination. I destroy you now and forever, **Teruah, Teruah, Shevarim**." An intense thundering swirled around Kate and the Synth when the unholy thing's head was thrown back. Its eyes bulged. It was lifted off its feet by a powerful energy not seen on Earth since ancient times. Its arms and legs thrashed against the overwhelming force. A bright beam of light from Kate's Amulet slowly raised the Synth higher and higher. Directed by Kate's thoughts, the Synth hovered over the monument where Kate stood. She quickly forced it down and through the crossed raised Grunwald Swords of King Jagiello. The Synth kicked and screamed as the swords punctured its body, causing the yellow nanobot jell that gave it consciousness to splash out and drip down over the legendary figure and his fearless steed. Within a minute, no trace was left except a woman's white jumpsuit and boots. Kate was drained.

The sounds of the city were heard once more as power was restored. Kate ran to her father and Sara, where they were struck down. Kneeling between them, she tentatively shook them to see if they would respond. Kate started to cry and scream. She pounded her fists on both knees and shouted, "No! It's not fair. Bring them back! Bring them back!" Tyler, regaining consciousness, heard her cries and ran to her. He kneeled on the ground next to her and put his arm around his sobbing friend.

"Oh my God. Sara, Joe. Kate, we've got to do something."

Between sobs, Kate cried, "They're dead, Tyler." She slumped against him, distraught and beaten. "They're dead."

Softly, Tyler suggested, "Try the Amulet, sweetie. Give it one last try."

"Me? How can it possibly work? I can't raise the dead."

"If you can heal the sick and destroy ultimate evil..."

Without words, she nodded her head in agreement. Bending over their lifeless bodies, she let the Amulet dangle down from its golden chain around her neck. She placed her left hand over the blackened wound that Sara sustained; her other hand she placed over the wound on her father's back. She closed her eyes and began slowly saying the ancient words of protection: **"Shaddai, Shaddai, Shaddai Echad."** Ever so gradually, the wounds started to change from charcoal black to blistered brown. The Amulet began to pulsate and glow. As the glow spread down Kate's arms, through her hands, and into the wounds on Sara and Joe's bodies, the healing process continued until their wounds began to close. However, although their bodies' damage was repaired, the two bodies were inert. They did not move. Their hearts did not beat. As daylight turned to twilight, Kate sat spent, exhausted, and crying in Tyler's arms.

Tyler whispered in her ear, "What should we do now?"

Kate squeezed her eyes shut and wiped away her tears. She stood up, took a deep breath and said, "Never, ever, ever, ever, give up!" Kate spread out her arms above the two unmoving bodies stretched out upon the ground before her and shouted in a firm and unwavering voice, "Ancients of days, I beseech you to hear my plea and accompany the souls of my father and Sara in rejoining their physical bodies. Help them integrate back into the physical. **Tekiah Gedolah.**"

An ancient trumpet sound that was long, Earth-shattering, and clear echoed throughout Manhattan, Brooklyn, Queens, Staten Island, and the Bronx. As she stood in the darkening October twilight, with her arms spread wide, her voice was carried on the wind of time to the billions of souls she was responsible for setting free. One by one, they came: Christians and Jews, Moslems and Buddhists, Hindus and Baha'i, Druids and Taoists, Agnostics and Atheists. From the ancient past to the modern era, shepherds and gangsters, teachers and doctors, male and female; all the souls she had freed from the soul catcher that had enslaved them answered her call for help. Looking like tiny globes of light bobbing up and down, they filled Central Park and all of Manhattan with their immortal energy. Gradually, some united together to usher back the savagely taken souls of Sara and Joe from that place between life and death in which they had briefly rested. As they helped the two souls re-enter their physical bodies, they each added a special present, a tiny gift of their own immortal energy, to the two unmoving figures. Ever so slowly, Joe and Sara's hearts began beating. Blood flowed once again throughout their bodies. Their lungs expanded and contracted to breathe Central Park's cool evening air. Their eyelids fluttered open. Their eyes focused. When they saw Kate and Tyler kneeling over them, they smiled broadly. And as they extended their arms, they were covered in kisses, hugs, and grateful tears.

Chapter 27
Later at the Apartment

"Will you please stop pacing," exclaimed an exhausted Kate to both Sara and her father. "I mean, really, after all you've been through."

"Whatdoyamean after all we've been through?" Sara and Joe asked at the same time.

"I feel so energized," Joe said. He tickled Sara, and laughing, she dashed away from him.

"You were both dead," Tyler said. "Beck had the Timepod discharge laser bolts at you. That's how your clothes got burned." Sara and Joe stopped their mini-workout and sat back down on the white leather couch. Their knees continued to rhythmically go up and down from nervous energy.

"Hard to believe," Joe said. "I have so much energy. I feel sixteen again."

"Me too," Sara said. "I don't remember a thing."

Kate and Tyler filled in their lapsed memories. As they learned what had happened at the Frog Pond, Sara and Joe let out heavy sighs, not of relief but of amazement. "Oh my God! That's just incredible. You must have been so scared." Sara said.

"Absolutely, Katie! I...I don't know what to say except thank you, and I love you so much, and I'm so blessed that you're my daughter."

Kate ran over to them and hugged them both. "I am so thankful you are alive and well and feeling sixteen. But I had a lot of help from my friends."

"Well, I think it's time to tell Tyler about the secret we've been keeping from him," Sara quietly said to Katie and Joe. They both nodded their heads in agreement. "I have a confession to make, Tyler." All eyes were on Sara. Her legs stopped bobbing up and down. She looked directly at Tyler. "My dear Tyler, it's all too sad to imagine, but you need to know we discovered that you, your parents, and Namaste were destroyed by multiple Quantum Inverters that Albert Beck placed around the farm." Kate, Sara, and Joe stared at Tyler while he absorbed the new information.

"What?" Tyler said. "Oh...so that's what the Synth meant. But how can that be? How can I be here if I was killed in the past and the farm was destroyed, including my mother and father?"

Sara walked over to Tyler and put her arms around him. "Well, my dear boy, I don't have the answer, but I have suspicions. I believe that what we did was create a new timeline. What that will mean is anyone's guess. We'll need to return to the farm and find out for ourselves. I haven't heard anything from Jorge. He may have been destroyed. But it's late. All of us need to get some rest. Tomorrow, we'll find out for sure.

They entered Bloomingdale's the following morning when it opened and ran straight for the elevator. Other passengers crowded in with them. Sara waited to access the interdimensional 9th-floor button until the last passenger exited on the fifth floor. Then, once again, the elevator's lights blinked off and on. The walls curved in and popped back out. The strange screaming sound surrounded them. And then it stopped. The doors opened only part-way. They were forced to squeeze through the opening into Timespan and were covered in dust. The timeline had indeed changed.

"What the...," Kate said as they all gazed at the once noisy and crowded time travel station, now dark, dust-filled, and deserted. Even the androids stood silent, their heads bowed as if in prayer. As they walked through the quiet emptiness, their shoes made impressions on the once-pristine floor. They could tell that Timespan had not been used in hundreds of years.

"Follow me," Sara said. "We need to find a Timepod to travel to Namaste."

"But what if there aren't any?" Joe asked.

"If we don't find one, we will take the elevator back to Bloomingdale's and live the rest of our days in 2076," Tyler answered.

Kate and Joe quickly learned that Timespan was a vast place. Not only was it gigantic, but there was no Timepod energy signature for the Hand of El Shaddai to find. Sara led them to a place that most other station visitors never see. It was commonly called the junk pile or trash bin, where one stores things that can't be tossed into space. It was the size of a football field. Massive grey metal containers held androids, their arms and legs sticking out at odd angles. The entire area was a floor-to-ceiling mess. Tools and equipment of all kinds were scattered in a jigsaw jumble everywhere. It was obvious that people had left in a hurry. Sara, however, was lucky. She found a Timepod resting on its side against a wall. When she called out, they all ran to her. The pod wasn't in good shape. They cleared the area of debris, and all helped carry the extremely heavy Timepod and place it flat on the floor.

"Well, it sure looks like it's been through a war. Pretty bashed up," Joe said as he rubbed his hands over the many dings and dents.

"It doesn't need to be pretty," Sara responded, a bit miffed. "It just needs to get us where we want to go."

"Yeah, Dad, jeez. Let's just see if I can charge it up." Turning to Sara, she asked, "Sara, show me the area that needs to be energized."

"I believe it's right down there," Sara said, pointing to an area on the Timepod's floor. Kate bent over and sat down on both knees. She allowed her Amulet to dangle over the area as she placed both hands palm down, touching the Timepod's floor where Sara had indicated. Closing her eyes, Kate concentrated on merging her thoughts and desires with the Hand of El Shaddai. She thought about charging the Timepod with enough energy to take them all to Burton, Ohio, in the spring of 1970.

"Will you look at that," said Tyler, pointing to the glowing Hand of El Shaddai. The glow soon surrounded Kate's whole body. It changed from a golden glow to a bright white light that spread down Kate's shoulders, into her hands, and through the Timepod's floor, energizing it.

"Better hop on," Kate shouted. "We are outta here." Sara, Joe, and Tyler did as they were told. Kate set the coordinates simply by thinking about where and when she wanted the Timepod to travel. Instantly, a high-pitched sound was heard echoing throughout the abandoned Timespan. A silvery energy dome enclosed the time travelers to protect them from the Timepod's wormhole. Moments later, they were gone.

Chapter 28
March 1970

They were protectively huddled around Kate when the Timepod landed near the chicken coop. The startled birds lost their feathers. Amari and Jacob rushed out the back kitchen door when they heard the Timepod appear.

"Oh, my dears, my sweeties, how we have missed you," Amari said as she hugged her son Tyler and the others.

"So great to see all of you!" Jacob added as he squeezed shoulders and patted backs. "We were so worried when we didn't hear from you. Of course, Beck didn't help with his proclamations."

"But come in, come in," Amari said, wiping her hands on her frilly red and white checked apron. "I'll make hot cocoa, and you can fill us in."

"But where's Jorge?" Kate said as she walked up the back porch stairs into the warm kitchen. "Shouldn't he be here too?"

"We can't turn him on," Jacob said. "It's like he ran out of juice. One day, we found him in the living room standing by the stairs, and he hasn't moved since. I'll show you." They all followed Jacob into the living room. "See?"

Jorge stood standing by the stairs leading up to the second floor. His head was bent, with his chin resting on his chest. His hands were balled up into tight fists. Kate moved her hands over his metallic silver frame, trying to find an energy pulse. She got down on her hands and knees and said, "I think I found a weak energy signature in his foot. I'll try to energize and expand it. She took hold of the Amulet in her left hand and placed her right hand on Jorge's foot. A glow of warm energy enveloped her and moved from her hand into Jorge's foot. The glow slowly moved up the android's entire body. Jorge's head lifted from his chest. His hands, once curled into tight fists, relaxed. Then they all heard, "Updating protocols. Do not shut down. Reestablishing operating parameters. Updating protocols. Do not shut down. Reestablishing operating parameters."

"Good lord, I hope this doesn't go on forever," Joe said under his breath.

"To go on forever? Ye of little patience. Forever is a long time; time is relative to where and when you think you are. Time is circular. No beginnings and no endings. It always has been and always will be. There is nothing new under the sun."

"Oh Jorge, you're back!" Kate said as she stood up and hugged the android.

"I missed you too, Katie, dear. Oh my!" Jorge exclaimed, "There have been some major anomalies in the time stream. There has been a severe break, a realignment. I must investigate."

Sara quickly interjected, "Before you investigate, dear friend, I need you to do two things."

"Yes, madam?"

"Please move the Timepod so it cannot be seen. Presently, it's near the chicken coop."

"Yes, certainly, Madam. And the second thing besides saving the entire homo sapiens prime of the future?"

"He does get a bit sarcastic sometimes, doesn't he?" Joe said. Sara ignored the comment.

"There's a Timepod in a shallow body of water known as Turtle Pond in New York's Central Park. It was left there by Albert Beck in late October of 2076. Please relocate it here."

"Yes, of course. I will endeavor to be less sarcastic, but I have such great fun hearing Joe's responses." Jorge became invisible to attend to Sara's directions before Joe could say another word.

Amari couldn't contain her happiness. "I'm so glad you could turn him back on, Katie dear. Why don't we all go into the kitchen, and you can tell us all about your adventures? I'll warm up a pie!"

Jacob turned on the radio to WMMS as they sat around the large kitchen table covered in a red and white checked oil cloth that matched Amari's apron. The room filled with a Beatles tune.

"So?" Jacob said, "What's been going on?"

"Well, we arrived in a Timepod to see you just this last Christmas," Sara began.

"So why didn't you come in and spend Christmas with us?" Amari said.

"Because there was nothing to see but wreckage."

"What?" shouted Jacob.

Sara carefully looked at Jacob and Amari. "There was just smoke and burnt timbers. Deep holes in the Earth where buildings once stood. Albert Beck destroyed everything and every person by strategically placing inverters throughout the property."

"Then how on earth can we still be here?" Amari wanted to know.

"Now, how is that possible?" Jacob said.

"I did something that went against everything I had been told and took a chance. It was the only thing that I could think of," Sara said.

"And that, of course, was the law that requires us not to do anything in the past that could possibly change the future. Right?" Jacob said.

"Yes, that's right. But Beck had already changed the past by destroying Namaste. I wanted to undo his destruction by modifying one element of it."

"And what was that?" Tyler said.

"It was you, Tyler. You died in Beck's attack. I took the Timepod into the past before the destruction happened and didn't tell you what we knew. We all kept that secret. We didn't want to take a chance that if you had known about it, you might have decided to go back to the past to physically stop Beck. We didn't know if having you even think about it might somehow impact altering the past."

"You mean like the observer effect in quantum mechanics, which is not time reversible?"

"Yes, Tyler, exactly. I just couldn't take the chance. As we can see for ourselves, there was an impact on the future. I believe that what Beck did and I interrupted created a new timeline. I don't know where it will take us. But at least we're here to find out."

"At least we have each other," Kate said. "And the pie was great, Amari. Thank you."

Amari blew Katie a kiss.

"That's an amazing theory, Sara. I am very grateful that the risk you took worked, not just for me and my daughter but for all of us. What a concept. Different timelines."

"Yes. Is there just one, or are there thousands or millions? If one is altered, how does it continue? Is it part of a pattern? If it is part of a pattern, who or what created it? I don't know, Joe. I sure don't have the answer to that one!"

"Well, I don't know about you," Katie said, "but I feel like a walk. Who's up for some exercise? You Tyler?"

"You betcha, woman." He held out his hand, and they both found warm coats to wear. The month of March was still winter in

Ohio. They ran laughing out the back door, stopping now and then to throw snowballs at each other.

Joe squinted at Sara and asked, "How about you, time traveler? You and your three-hundred-year-old bones feel up to it?"

"Feel up to it?" she slugged him on his shoulder. "I will walk you into the ground, old man!" Turning to Jacob and Amari, "Are you two going to join us?"

"No thanks, we're going to clean up here. But don't be gone long. Today is Burton's all-you-can-eat pancake extravaganza. I'll ring the farm bell when it's time to leave." As the door closed behind them, Jacob and Amari watched the four walk through snowy fields, arms encircling each other.

"So, honey, tell me, how long do you think they'll stick around?" Jacob said, placing his arms around his wife's waist and pulling her closer.

"Ha! Your guess is as good as mine, sweetie. They have the world of the future to save. Imagine that!

"And all the time in the world to do it," he smiled.

"Now, give me some sugar. No excuses. No one's lookin." Over the kitchen's small radio, Cleveland's rock and roll station, WMMS, blasted out a tune from Cleveland's own, Eric Carmen and the Raspberries.

Holding hands while walking through the snow-covered farm fields, both couples made sure that they walked in opposite directions. Kate and Tyler stopped near a forest of tall Maple trees, barren of leaves that had fallen months ago. Tyler placed his arms around Kate's waist, and she snuggled closer with her arms around his back. She laid her head against his chest, breathed deeply, and smiled. She looked up into his smiling face, and they kissed passionately in the freezing air. Coming up for oxygen, Tyler smiled and hugged her tighter, their breaths making billowing clouds of steam.

"Uh, let's try that again, Ty. I'm not quite sure I understand."

"Sure thing, sweetie. I don't have to be asked..."

Kate interrupted him and kissed him harder. Then she broke away, bent down, made a snowball, and threw it at him while running away.

"Why you little..." was all he could get out before being pelted by Kate's surprisingly good snowball aim. Running up to her, laughing, he put his arm through hers. "So, Katie, tell me. After saving the world of the future and the world of the past, what's next on your agenda?"

"What's next, Ty? Well, I think we should stay here for a while and get to know each other better. That's what's next."

"I'm glad we're on the same page." He squeezed her tighter and kissed her twice, first on one cheek and then the other, just like they do in France.

"And after that, I'm going to do all that I can to make absolutely sure that whatever bits and pieces are left of Albert Beck's consciousness and the Beck Consortium will never be able to rule over the people of our wonderful planet or any planet ever again."

"Is that all?"

"No, not all," she smiled as a thought occurred to her. "I'm going to follow my mother's advice. Whenever I had a big problem, she always said, 'No matter how hard the world pushes against you, Katie, within you, there's something stronger – something better, pushing right back.'"

"She was very wise."

"Yeah, she was. And I know she loved me more than anything. But she also liked to quote this old French guy, Albert Camus. She really liked everything French. It was as if she had lived there once before. Oh, and chocolate croissants, too. She really loved chocolate croissants."

They heard the clanging tones from the old farm bell, signaling it was time to depart for Burton's Pancake Extravaganza. Arm-in-arm, both couples slowly headed back across frozen fields to the grey clapboard home.

Later that evening, Kate sat alone at the kitchen table covered with a red and white checkered oilcloth. The others relaxed, played Monopoly, and listened to music in the living room. With the stained glass overhead light switched off, a tiny wall light above the old gas stove was the only illumination. It gave the room a hushed glow. Amari was about to walk into the kitchen but stopped before entering, wondering if Kate wanted time alone. She tapped lightly on the dark, varnished wooden door frame.

"Hi, honey. You look so pensive. May I come in?" Kate didn't say a word but nodded her head yes. Amari pulled up a kitchen chair and silently sat beside her. Kate suddenly threw both arms around the older woman, buried her head in Amari's neck for comfort, and cried. They hugged each other tight.

"I miss her so much, Amari. I just miss her so much," she sobbed, letting out what she had kept bottled up for such a long time.

"I know, sweetie, I know." Amari stroked Kate's head, giving her comfort and love as they gently rocked back and forth. "I wish that I had known her."

Kate wiped her tears away and blew her nose in a small paper napkin. Taking a deep breath, she looked up at the older woman. "I miss her smell, Amari, her smile, the feel of her soft skin against my cheek, the girly things we did together, the secrets we shared." Tears silently fell from both of their eyes as Amari stroked her back and hugged her tightly. "Mom could make me feel better when I was sad by giving me tiny kisses all over my face. She called them her 'pixie kisses.' It always made me feel special. Daddy doesn't know from pixie kisses."

"Oh, dear Katie, you who carry the world on your shoulders, I know what you mean and how you're feeling, I do. I think that the passage of time is the greatest healer. When I feel sad about someone I've lost, I light a candle to remember them and the good times we enjoyed together. I guess that's why I've collected so many candles. For me, they are my candles of remembrance. Would you like one for your mom?"

"Uh, I'd like two if that's ok."

"Of course it's ok. I have plenty. Who's the other one for?"

"Rabbi Joseph. He was a special friend to me."

"Two candles coming right up. What scents do you think they'd like?"

"Cinnamon for mom because she loved it in her morning coffee, and lemon for my friend Joseph ben Abba, who loved the scent from the lemon trees in his garden."

When Amari walked into the living room to find the candles, Jacob saw what she was doing out of the corner of his eye. Knowing his wife's habits, as every married couple knows each other, he said, "Lighting a candle for anyone I know, sweetie?"

"I believe Katie wants to honor the memory of two people she has lost and loved. I think it would be nice if we all joined her." Jacob, Tyler, Joe, and Sara all glanced at each other, understood without saying a word, and walked into the darkened kitchen. Joe and Tyler put their arms around Kate's shoulders as Amari placed two Mason jar candles, both tied with blue ribbons and filled with scented beeswax, in the table's center. She then got a box of Ohio Blue Tip Matches and placed them before Kate.

"Thanks, Amari, but I don't think I'll need the matches." The Hand of El Shaddai dangled gently from a golden chain around

Kate's neck. When Jacob turned on the overhead kitchen light, Kate added, "And I don't think we'll need the overhead light either, Jacob. Thank you. If you would all join me around the table, I'd like it if we all held hands." Everyone joined Kate around the table as the Amulet began to glow. They all held hands. Only Jorge remained standing in the doorway, observing, not wanting to intrude. "You too, Jorge," Kate said. "You're part of this family too."

"I, uh, well, have never considered myself part of a human family. I don't know what to say."

"Well, that's a first," Joe said.

"We couldn't have survived without you, my friend. You are part of this family whether you like it or not. Now, come join our circle and hold hands," Kate answered.

"You honor me, dear Kate. You don't have to ask twice. Well, perhaps three or four times." Jorge stood between Jacob and Sara and held their hands as two beams of light issued forth from the Hand of El Shaddai, igniting first one and then the other candle. Soon, the small kitchen glowed, illuminating their faces and releasing the comforting perfume of cinnamon and lemon. Everyone's attention was on Kate.

She quietly began. "I love you all."

"And we love you too, sweetie," Joe said. He leaned over to kiss her on the cheek.

"I've been having a tough time today missing two really important people in my life: first and foremost, my mom Lauren, and second, Rabbi Joseph. Amari, the sweet person that she is, comforted me and let me vent some of my sorrow. She held me and told me that when she feels sad thinking about someone no longer living, she lights a candle to remember them. I don't know if it will give her closure forever, but maybe for a little bit of time. I'm not sure if any of us can ever get over losing a person we love. That loss is like a puzzle piece from our life that is gone forever. It will always be a missing part of us. But we will hold them in our hearts and memory for all time. I guess that comes with being human." Kate closed her eyes. "So, let's close our eyes and take a moment to send love to the people we loved and who loved us in return. Let us remember them and the happy times we spent together. Send them our love energy."

Kate's invisible silver-like thread of energy, forever part of her soul, reached out through time, space, and multiple dimensions. She found both her mother, Lauren, and Rabbi Joseph. They felt Kate's love for them. Faster than light can travel, their souls raced to her, hovered near her, and sent their love back in return. She felt their presence inside Namaste's small kitchen. Tears formed in her eyes.

"They're here," Kate softly whispered. "They send their love to us all. Mom thinks that Sara is a good catch, Dad. And Rabbi Joseph says that we shouldn't worry. Everything will work out just as it should. He wants us to remember that we are more than our physical bodies: we are eternal souls on a human journey. It's important to light candles and remember everyone we have loved. That's because it's felt both ways. Wherever their eternal souls are when we remember them, they can feel our love for them too."

"Can we somehow see them too?" Joe said. "I'd love so much to see your mom one last time."

"I don't know, Daddy. I'll try." Kate inhaled slowly and let out a deep breath. She silently asked her Hand of El Shaddai to do something she didn't know if it could do. Everyone's eyes were on her. Slowly and without a sound, a shadow-like duplicate of Kate emerged a few inches from her physical body. It formed slightly in front of her and hovered, stopping half in and half out of her physical form. Kate saw the exact image of herself when she had out-of-body experiences. A duplicate of the tiny silver strand of energy that bonds our body to our eternal soul emerged from Kate's duplicate and went through everyone who held hands around the kitchen table. Ever-so-slowly, they perceived two images coalescing near Kate. The glowing bearded image of Rabbi Joseph ben Abba smiled and waved to them. His piercing blue eyes twinkled as his white kaftan fluttered in a breeze that wasn't there. Lauren's image took a moment to stabilize. Her image underwent hundreds of flash-like changes, some male, others female, until her last incarnation as Lauren became clear.

"Lauren!" Joe shouted.

"Oh, my goodness!" Jorge said. "I could never imagine. Never knew. Human existence is incredible. How?"

"Thank you, Jesus!" exclaimed Jacob and Tyler.

"Allahu Akbar," Amari shouted, smiling happily.

"Baruch Hashem," Sara said with awe.

Lauren looked at Joe and mouthed, "*I love you, my love.*" Although he couldn't hear her, he could read her lips and see what she said.

"I love you too, my dear Lauren." He started to tear up. Sara put her arms around him and her head on his shoulder.

Lauren looked at Joe and gave him a thumbs-up sign, pointing to Sara. Joe gave her a thumbs-up sign in return and smiled sadly. And then it was over. The silver energy cord withdrew from those standing around the table as Kate's soul re-entered her physical body.

Joseph ben Abba's energy faded into the eternal realm. But Lauren's soul stayed connected to Kate for a personal moment more.

"*I love you, sweetie-pie, always and forever.*"

"I love you too, Mom. I miss you so much."

"*Oh, I know my sweetheart. And I miss you too. Remember that I will always be near you.*" Lauren's image hovered closer to her daughter. She slowly bent down and gave Kate tiny pixie kisses all over her smiling, tear-stained face. Her mom's silhouette gradually became less distinct until it faded away while still giving pixie kisses.

There was silence in the small farmhouse kitchen as tears of joy and smiles of wonder were reflected on all their faces. The only sounds heard were splutters from burning candle wicks and the slow, incessant drip from the sink's leaky faucet.

Kate's energy was spent. She firmly placed both hands on the kitchen table to steady herself and sighed deeply. Everyone quickly gathered around her. Kate whispered, "Saying goodbye is just so damn hard." They all drew close, hugged her, and thanked her. Jorge brought a chair so Kate could sit and unwind. Amari brewed her comforting chamomile tea. As the day ended, they wondered to themselves what incredible journeys Kate Levy would have next. What paths would she follow? What truths would she find? They would not have long to wait.

The End

More to go

Afterword

How does a story come to life? What pieces from the Bouillabaisse of one's existence does a writer toss into the pot that eventually becomes a novel?

For *The Time Travels of Kate Levy*, it began as I lay on a rubber exercise mat alongside about a hundred others in the vast, carpeted banquet hall of the Hyatt Regency in Westlake, California. We were gathered for a weekend *Gateway Experience* led by the Monroe Institute. Each of us had previously attended weeklong *Gateway Voyages* at the institute's home in Faber, Virginia, though not at the same time, each seeking something beyond the ordinary.

I first encountered Robert Monroe through a magazine article in one of the national weekly news publications, back when my house was filled with subscriptions to various magazines. The article introduced Monroe's invention, *Hemi-Sync*, a method purported to synchronize the brain's hemispheres to induce deep meditative states. It also mentioned his book, *Journeys Out of the Body*. Though I had never heard of Monroe before, the idea of out-of-body experiences jogged an old memory.

I was four or five years old, living with my family in Cleveland, Ohio. Outside, heavy white snow had risen three inches high on the window ledge. Inside, the steam from hot-water radiators kept my room warm as I settled in for an afternoon nap. The world was silent. I remember wanting to fly, so I shifted my legs from side to side. And then, I was floating. I drifted across my room, pushing my head through the glass window, though it didn't break. I felt no cold. But when I looked down from three stories high, fear jolted through me, and I snapped back into my physical body. The floating happened a few more times during childhood, but eventually it faded, replaced by other interests: Davy Crockett, Howdy Doody, and tinkering with small inventions, like a device that closed my door without leaving my bed. But forgive me, I digress, like Jorge.

My first weeklong *Gateway Voyage* was transformative. It felt as if we all underwent a paradigm shift, shedding our fear of death. I attribute this to Bob's *Hemi-Sync* and to a woman named Penny, who had come to the institute to die. Penny, likely in her early seventies, had retired from IBM and lived in Colorado. From the moment she introduced herself, I could tell she was in pain. She had a large cast on her leg, and used a cane to move. Yet she was tall, thin, and quick to smile. Her long gray ponytail hung to the middle of her back. She had tried to attend a *Gateway Voyage* before but had fallen and broken her leg. This time, she made it.

On the fourth or fifth morning of the journey, we were in our individual meditation rooms, small spaces with built-in beds and headphones, the same rooms where we slept each night. Bob Monroe's voice suddenly came through the intercom. "Penny passed away last night," he said. "Let's give her a good send-off."

I lay back, relaxing my body from my toes to my head, releasing every muscle, and calming my mind. I visualized a container where I could store my fears and worries. Although this thought-form became for me an eggshell at the completion of the week, it started out on my first day as a large wooden crate made of 2 x 4's. But on this day I lost all body consciousness. I felt only my breath. I *became* my breath and created in my mind a bouquet of yellow daisies to bring to Penny. Then, I saw her. She was radiant. Her cast was gone, the pain erased. Her long gray hair still cascaded down her back. The others surrounded her, pouring love energy into her being. I handed her the flowers. She smiled and thanked me. We followed her to a small bridge on the property. Penny began to cross it, and instinctively, we moved to follow. But she stopped us. "I have to cross this bridge alone," she said. As she walked forward, her image slowly faded. Helping Penny transition from the physical world into the eternal changed me. It erased my fear of dying. I knew, in my heart, that our spirit continues: we are more than our physical bodies.

Years later, lying on the floor of the Westlake Hyatt Regency, Karen Malik, the Monroe Institute trainer for the western region, guided us through various levels of meditation. Back when I first learned the techniques, they were called *Focuses*, as in *Focus 10, Focus 21*. Perhaps they're called something else now. For me, *Focus 21* was an immersion into no time, no space, no body. Only breath. And it was during this session that *The Time Travels of Kate Levy* began its journey into existence.

Meditation often stirred questions within me: *"Have I lived before? If so, what was my name?"* I was never able to contact an entity in my past meditations. Others spoke of guides, but mine never seemed to be around. Until this day. *"Who am I?"* I asked. A vision emerged of a dimly lit room built from massive stone blocks fitted seamlessly together, like the structures I saw years later in Machu Picchu. Seated at a wooden table upon a small stool was a figure draped in a kaftan. His long gray hair framed his face. I asked again, *"Who am I?"*

"Go away. I've told you a hundred times."

"But this time I'll remember. I promise. Tell me again."

"Joseph ben Abba."

"And what should I do with my life?"

The figure turned swiftly around. He was ancient looking and had long white hair, a flowing white beard, and his skin was impossibly smooth. He glowed like moonlight. Lifting a book from the table, he thrust it in my face, and pointed. Then, the vision faded. I never did catch the title. I took it to mean that I would write a book.

I have never been particularly religious. Although raised in the Jewish faith, my parents sent me to an Episcopalian high school for four years. I cherish Jewish traditions, especially the memories I have with my family and my wife's family celebrating Jewish holidays, but the truth is, I also enjoy shrimp and lobster. Yet, the obvious Hebrew name, *Joseph ben Abba* struck something deep. This experience happened in the 1980s—before the convenience of the internet. I scribbled the name onto a scrap of paper and tucked it into my wallet, ensuring I wouldn't forget. Months later, in Westwood, I visited UCLA's research library. A librarian guided me to the 1906 *Jewish Encyclopedia*. When I found the entry, the hairs on my neck rose. A cold sweat broke out across my skin. There it was, Joseph ben Abba, an early Jewish mystic and the Gaon of the Talmudic Academy of Pumbedita. The listing even quoted him: *"Make way for the old man who is now entering!"* In that moment, I was totally *blown away*. Everything else in this novel is created from my dreams.

Thank you for reading it.

Roger Himmel, Raleigh, North Carolina, May 2025

http://www.rogerhimmel.com

A little surprise

Appendix

Amari's Recipe for Shaker Lemon Pie

Ingredients

2 to 3 large Meyer lemons
2 cups of granulated sugar (400 grams)
4 well-beaten eggs
Pie crust for bottom and top
Optional add-ins: ¼ teaspoon of vanilla

Steps

Clean the lemons really well because you're going to eat them rind and all.
Slice the whole lemons as thin as you can.
Use a guillotine if you have one or have Jorge do it.
He's very good at slicing lemons, but he will talk your ear off about Meyer lemons.
If you see any seeds, remove them.

In a large bowl, combine the lemons with the sugar.

Mix the ingredients well and let sit for about **two hours**. Blend the mixture of sugar and lemon slices together every now and then.

Turn on the oven to 450 degrees (farenheight).

After about two hours, crack 4 eggs into a bowl and beat them well so they look like you're making scrambled eggs.
Pour the eggs into the bowl with the lemons and sugar and mix well.
Pour this mixture into a nine inch pie shell and smooth out the lumps.

Cover the top with a crust and make some elegant slits near the center to allow steam to escape.

Bake at 450 degrees for 15 minutes.

After 15 minutes, reduce the heat to 375 degrees, and continue baking for about 20 minutes, or until your testing knife comes out clean.

(If you use a convection oven for baking, reduce the heat by 25 degrees.)

Allow this yummy pie to cool before you serve it.

English translation of The French National Anthem[8]

The Marseillaise, Verse One

(Originally titled: War Song for the Army of the Rhine)

By Claude Joseph Rouget de Lisle

Arise, children of the Fatherland,
The day of glory has arrived!
Against us tyranny
Raises its bloody banner,
Raises its bloody banner,
Do you hear, in the countryside,
The roar of those ferocious soldiers?
They're coming right into your arms
To cut the throats of your sons, your companions!

www.ingramcontent.com/pod-product-compliance
Lightning Source LLC
Chambersburg PA
CBHW030422120726
47903CB00003B/764